T0064448

The *Flesh*
and the *Soil*

The *Flesh* and the *Soil*

LOVE FOR THE FLESH
AND LOVE FOR THE GOOD EARTH

Emil Murad

PARTRIDGE
A Penguin Random House Company

To order additional copies of this book, contact
Toll Free 800 101 2657 (Singapore)
Toll Free 1 800 81 7340 (Malaysia)
orders.singapore@partridgepublishing.com

www.partridgepublishing.com/singapore

A WORD TO
THE CANDID READER

From the author: EMIL MURAD

Thank you for picking this book, thank you for deciding to read it and I hope you will live through its pages. It is not a normal book, not an ordinary one. Every sentence of it was typewritten in different hours of the day, on different days of the month, of the year. It is the fruits of the whim of a young man, lonely and alone, with a friend that can neither hear nor speak: an old typewriter!

Parts of this book were written when I was 19, in 1950, on my arrival to Israel, as a volunteer at Kibbutz Kfar Menachem (agricultural communal settlement), on a typewriter which the Kibbutz secretariat granted me upon my request for my hard word at the Kibbutz. Other parts were typewritten when I was a soldier, about six years later, others on the same typewriter, while I served as liaison officer with the United Nations in Sinai Peninsula. Some years later I put in more chapters and pages. The typewriter never got tired, nor did I.
Computers didn't exist then.

I wasn't sure it is going to be a book. I was never sure, after having published several other books in the "computer age", and being chosen as Poet of the Month in New York for my book "ROSE PETALS DOWN THE STREAM", or acquiring Honorary Doctor title for my recent book "THE QUAGMIRE", I could relax and savor the idea that one day I will be able to see my "baby" THE FLESH AND THE SOIL, see the light of day!

Dr. Yigal Har-Zahav, once a valiant, zestful fighter and an active member at an agricultural communal settlement in the North of Israel, had lost all that was so dear to him, his wife and son. Yet, there was one more dear "momento" that he kept so close to his heart, that became part of his very being.

He came to me one day, handed it over to me, "Here, Emil, take it. Write a book!" he managed to say between sobs and sighs. I was flabbergasted!

This book, dear reader, that you hold in your hands was typewritten over a period of almost four decades of the history of a new nation!

When the computers largely supplanted typewriters, no publisher wooed me, or expressed the wish to see 500 typewritten pages! the manuscript was left unattended to in an old attic.

Until the time has come for it to see the light of day!

Sometimes things do come, and NOT too late, even when you are in your late eighties!!!

We are all Pilgrims on the Road of Life. We come, and we must go! None of us is great, but there is some greatness in each and every one of us. Let us realize it while we are living: Believe in your greatness!!

When I finished writing this book I asked myself: Who is my favourite character, Danny, Esther or Yigal. To my surprise I found out that all three of them. I am all they, and they are all me, all three parts of my body and soul.

EMIL MURAD - JUNE 2015

The story in this novel, according to the book you hold in your hands, begins in 1948 and ends in 1981. But, for those who read between the lines, those who love not only the fruit but also the tree, not only the tree but also the roots; for them, this story dates back to the birth of mankind, to Adam and Eve, and lives forever with the eternal dawn .....

I love both the flesh and the soil, for the one begets the other .... and they make a full circle ....

EMIL MURAD

I dedicate this book to my closest contacts,
my two sons, Moshe and Ilan, with all my love.

PROLOGUE

...

SPRING 1982.... HOW IT ALL BEGAN.. THE END
THAT'S THE BEGINNING

PART ONE

I stood and watched him as he moved from one tombstone to another. He kicked some leaves on the road, and he looked as though he were studying each and every tombstone. I knew it was he, Dr. Yigal Har-Zahav. His gait was so familiar to me. All the members of the Kibbutz had already returned a few hours before; only he was missing. We were worried about him, but I knew where to find him. I thought I'd drive back to the cemetery and fetch him.

There were many names on the tombstones, names of our beloved boys engraved so deep in the stone. Yoav, Gad, Dan, Yoram, Danny, Esther, and many others. They grew up together, they played and laughed, they kissed, joked, studied, graduated, joined the army. United they lived. Then wars came. United they fought. United they died, but divided they lay there row by row..

The man looked again and again at that small piece of soil. Yoav.. It read. Tears welled from his eyes. This holds everything you treasured in life, he reminded himself, and choked back his tears. He put the flowers on his son's grave, sat and thought and wept. Then got up and walked along the long rows of graves, remembering in deep sorrow, whispering half to himself: The return of the flesh to the soil!

Back home memories would begin to hurt again. Those thousands of memories that refused to recede and scorned burial. It was only yesterday, or so it seemed to be. Yoav had answered the call at the door. 'Tis for me, he had said, then took a few things and departed. It was only yesterday. The young, innocent and boyish smile was still fresh in the old man's memory. Every time he looked in the mirror there were those wrinkles, those sad eyes, those hairs that grew grey before it was time. Only a year had gone by, and now he looked years older: falling shoulders, bent back, sad and weary looks that came from drooping wrinkled eyes, popping out of a weary, heavy forehead, propped by veiny, bony temples. Sometimes he could hardly recognize his own image in the mirror. He was well aware that life had to go on, but with little meaning. Everything around him had long become colorless, pale and meaningless.

Yigal, the man, felt guilty, guilty because he has loved and lived his full life, and his son's ended before it had really begun: guilty, because he survived all the wars, while his son fell just like a fly; guilty, because he was not at his son's side in his last moments, when he might have needed him most. He could imagine those horrible moments of the crash, that cruel airplane crash which took away many dear lives, and his son's as well. It was only yesterday when he would come up to his bed in his room and pull the bed sheets over him to keep him warm and comfortable. He used to tuck him to his bed, kiss him goodnight and wish him happy dreams. But, no, that was many, many years ago! The old man was beginning to lose trace of time. The years ran faster than he could think. Everything was different now. He would whisper "happy dreams" and go out of the room for fear he might wake up, then he would whisper to himself, "God bless him!" Now, it was all over. God had blessed him with everything except years of living. Now he slept there for good, to wake up no more!

All those years when he was a schoolboy, Yoav was not just a dear son to Yigal. They were friends. Yoav's mother, Ruth, had died when he was very young, and the diligent medic had to look after his only son. All through the years he had showered upon him all his love, and he even succeeded to save the boy's life on the surgery table, back in the October 1973 war!!

Dr. Yigal stood by the tombstone and heard the image that rose before his eyes, saying, "Daddy, it is me." But to the old man's dismay, the young innocent image would disappear soon, and his outstretched arms to embrace the beloved son would fall back dead and powerless. Since that fatal airplane crash the smiling face of Yoav was everywhere in the house, in the bathroom, the living room, just everywhere in the world. His room was still there, but actually there was nothing except the empty sleeves of the cadet officer's coat, the pictures that he had collected over the years, the stamp albums, the coins and other collections, his mother's photograph, and other childhood collections. There was a moment during which everything was blurred, and he began to hear voices, murmuring and whispering from the graves:

> "What death takes away, no man can restore,
> What Heaven has blessed, no man can punish'
> What love has joined, no man can divide'
> What Eternity has willed, no man can alter …"

By night, Dr. Yigal waited for the lovely image to rise again before him, by day he would go to the graveyard and be connected spiritually to his beloved son. Entering the holy place, he had always been overwhelmed by the intensity of its color. Here in Kibbutz Deganya, it looked like a big flower garden, like a huge rainbow after a cloud-burst. Many a time he would stop and look and let his eyes wander over the marble and the abundance of blossoms. The rows of tombstones. They ran in straight, orderly ranks like a vast military paprade. Yoav had always loved military parades. Every stone had a laconic inscription, similar to that of his own son: Born... Rank...Fell in.... Stone after stone, representing the hopes and future of the nation. Lives cut short before they could blossom. Esther.. Danny, Yoav.... the names made history! Yoav was his son. Esther and Danny had died long before, but that was another story. The lump in his throat choked him, and he wiped off a man's tear.

That evening the kibbutz members watched him as he stood helpless, and lighted a memorial candle. His hands trembled, and would not even allow him to light one candle. The breeze swept across the cemetery and blew out that candle several times; but he finally succeeded and put the candle into the holder, as if it were a shrine. He looked into the holder and the little flame danced in front of his eyes, throwing shapes into his mind. Tears rolled down his face, fell on the grave and were soaked up by the dry ground. Next to Yoav's grave there was a twin grave. Brothers. Ben and Adam. How could fate be so cruel? We, at the Kibbutz, know of all the love, anxiety and toil it takes to raise children, and of the one bullet that puts an end to all those dreams. Dr. Yigal stood and watched the twin graves. He tried to multiply his own ordeal and pain by two, and he could not grasp the result, for his own pain was deeply set, and no other pain could be stronger or deeper.

He was murmuring half to himself

Just like the hordes that graze off leftovers on terraces
I crave to cling to a distant past, dead but not forgotten
Am biding my time to catch a glimpse of the have-beens,
But returning to the Past would be a daredevil challenge.

As I sit and watch the pictures file by in my memory,
Merging with others from the forced-upon-me present
And the beyond-the-veil, unknown future
I hear the hiss of the snakehead, soft and seductive
Perfectly pitched to the ear of the wanton, young me
Who dreamt of castles in a air and a better destiny.

A bumpy road it was, experience scarred my soul,
And thus the predator has become the prey.
We learn the value of a thing when we have lost it.

This is God's punishment for those who bite off
More than they can chew, who wriggle out of speaking.

Alas, all those naked bones. Whom do they belong to?
King or soldier? Rich or poor? master or slave?
I feel fobbed off with promises that were not kept
Words that never turned into actions, nor been intended to.
And war against the tide I made. Sometimes won,
At others lost. Sometimes by deception
For by deception thou shalt make war!
Now, am on my way up to Heaven or perhaps Hell
I succumb to an insurmountable daymare
It has been a nice trip on Earth, though at times
I felt like sailing from tedium to apathy with a wide trip to
torpor.

With all these million pictures that keep recurring
Like an incessant dream. Not dream-immutable facts!
Couldn't face life with a more pugilistic approach
Yes, I've learnt my lessons too late, I submit with deference!

I've learnt that laws are like-spider webs:
If some poor creature comes up against them
It is caught, but a bigger one can break through
And get away. Also, learnt that love is a crime
That needs an accomplice. Also learnt that we are all one
Yet we do everything with an eye to something else,
And deep within us we are always happy to believe "I won!"

And now I smile at the world I'm leaving behind
I bid you all farewell without a valedictory speech
That has an elegiac quality since words don't count anymore
With tears of sorrow and joy, doubt gnaws away at my conscience
I cast glances to every direction, and know it was a wonderful
world,
With all its drudgery and broken dreams, it was great:
But, Almighty God, if ever I shall return to Earth, I beg You
No more man's propensity for lying, no more cheating or wars!

I stood there beside him and could see his lips quivering, shivering, as though murmuring to himself the awful words: "This piece of soil holds everything you treasured in life!" He was scrutinizing the words engraved on the tombstone. "Are you all right, doc?" I asked as I approached him. My tone was solemn, and I took every care not to startle him.

"Ah.. yes..." he said without even lifting his eyes from the grave "Ah..yes," he repeated. "It is you, Emil," he said without lifting his eyes. "I'm O.K." he uttered the words indifferently, and as if a gentle voice was coming from the silent graves and whispering to him in his ears the words: "He will not come back!" he turned to me and repeated, "I am all right, Emil. Let's go!" I took his hands in mine. "Came to fetch you, doc. The whole settlement is worried about you."

"Are they?" he asked, as he raised his weary eyes to me, then up to the sky above. There was a tear in his eyes. He managed to say a few more words: "He will not come back!" as if reminding himself.

Dr. Yigal stepped forward and took the hand I offered him as I led him to the command-car parked just outside the entrance to the settlement cemetery where each and every tombstone hid a treasure of stories and memories.

I looked at the man beside me. Dr. Yigal was not that old, only in his fifties, but looked years older. A well-known personality and a respected member in both settlements, Deganya and Tel Katzir, Dr. Yigal had built a shrine for himself, had made a name, and many stories are told about young Yigal of Tel Katzir or the healer from Deganya, the surgeon Dr. Yigal Har-Zahav. This book will tell everything. But the name Yigal goes with Esther, and if you mention Esther the name of Danny follows, for on the bark of many a tree in Deganya the words Danny..Esther..ever..are engraved with a heart cut asunder by the arrow of Cupid. But why jump ahead when first things should come first, and I better tell how I myself came to know Dr. Yigal Har-Zahav...

It was from that horrible experience of the October 1973 Yom-Kippur War. Not many years ago. All the picture came to me as I led the man into the command-car and drove with him back to the settlement, through the orchards, lanes and to the central dining-hall in the last rays of the setting sun.

The tenth of October, 1973... Israel had been deep in war with the Egyptians in the south and the Syrians in the north. After sixty hours of fierce battles on both fronts the Israeli forces overcame one of the greatest blows inflicted on them in that surprise attack the enemy had waged. The fight against two strong Arab nations simultaneously was in full swing, and defeating them was an exceptionally hard and hazardous task. However, this was finally achieved but not without heavy losses, and not with only moderate casualties. Many a dear life was lost, and the loss of each individual soldier was an agony to his family and a blow to the small nation.

I, too, was drafted to serve my country. I was a reporter, journalist, but I served more as an attendant at a military field hospital somewhere in the north, not far from the settlements of Tel Katzir, Deganya and the vicinity. The space was overcrowded. All the beds were occupied and the corridors and halls turned overnight into operation rooms and first-aid stations. There was no room, and surgeons, physicians, nurses and attendants worked in shifts round the clock. The whole "camp" buzzed with life, but the face of "death" could be seen moving around. The sirens of ambulances kept whining throughout the night. Each and every "case" was urgent as the wounded and the injured kept flowing in. Dr. Yigal Har-Zahav, an old member of the settlement, Kibbutz Deganya, was a high-rank officer, a surgeon in charge of critical emergency cases. He headed the medical team to which I belonged. The "doc" who was in his mid-fifties, loved his humanitarian work beyond words; and most of the times, especially then when he was badly needed and when his only son Yoav, a twenty-year-old cadet officer, had been flying and bombing the Syrian

Front in the north, Dr. Yigal worked twenty-two hours a day without a break, except for a brief meal which he snatched hastily between operations. Dr. Yigal was a widower, having lost his wife, Ruth, six years before in June 1967.

It was just like any other day, with a dawn and a beautiful morning, except that most of the grow-ups and the older people had already been, long before dawn had broken, in the synagogue holding their ritual prayers, chanting, all clothed in white, skull-caps and prayer shawls, the teffelin,(prayer shawl) a rabbi reciting prayers at the podium, while others at home were just dressing up at their ease getting ready to join the worshippers at the synagogue or just to go outside to meet friends, neighbors, acquaintances and thus celebrate another Holy Day, for it was YOM KIPPUR (the Day of Atonement - the holiest day in the Jewish calendar) in an autumn day on the 6th of October in a never-forgotten year, 1973.

I was 42 years old. I woke up early to take my usual morning walk and then after an hour or so be prepared to go to pray at the communal, neighborhood synagogue for an hour or so until my wife and sons would join us, and mix and mingle with people as any other Yom Kippur tradition, the ages-long tradition passed to me by my father, and to him by his father, while the children and the youngsters rode their bicycles freely on the streets, not minding the traffic lights since traffic was suspended altogether on that very Holy Day. Again, the ages-long tradition for the children and youngsters who had been waiting for this day for the last couple of months before its arrival, as well as for the elders who ritually fast over 25 hours, from the eve of Yom Kippur to the end of the Holy Day when the Shofar announces the termination of fast, and hold prayers at synagogues or at their own homes, to atone for their sins and trespasses.

Already dressed decently and properly to fulfill my obligations at the synagogue, I started out with the Holy Books tucked under my arm, but being an avid consumer of all nature stories, and a great nature –lover I had the desire to enjoy a short walk through the orchard and the alleys and the lanes flanked by the evergreen trees, before going into the synagogue.

How I love the early days of autumn. I was in good spirits and chose my way through the nearby orchard enjoying the early morning breeze! Thoughts began to file by in my head. It was only yesterday, In my thoughts I saw the day I had graduated from school, weaved so many dreams and aspirations, got married, my elder son was born, then five years later another son.

I am still that young boy, just embarking upon the years, standing by a stream, wishing I could be like a tree beside the running waters with my roots running deep, existing but not seen. I watch the rose petals that I disperse as they float over the clear waters. They look so much like our young lives going with the current, over the ever-flowing stream of life, going, all and each, one by one to a known destination. I know there are broken dreams and drudgeries, but in spite of all that it is a beautiful world. Live for today, and you are not alone on this Road, a Pilgrim as you are, till you reach your destination, where you will be no more! Too sad!

I listen to the silence of Nature, God by my side, and I sing all to myself to the birds of the air, the rustling water, the whisper of the trees, and like the hordes that graze off leftovers on terraces, I crave to cling to a distant past, dead but not forgotten, biding my time to catch a glimpse of the have-beens though it seems a daredevil challenge.

Take a deep breath, sit and watch the pictures file by in your memory, see them as they mix and mingle with the reality of the present, close your eyes for a second and see with your mind's eye what the future has in stores for you, and believe that one day, after you are gone, another one will be sitting there watching different pictures as a new day will dawn.

You dreamt of castles you built in air, you heard the hiss of the snakehead, soft and seductive, perfectly pitched to the ear of a wanton, young boy. Now you compose your own prayers, in the company of God. You enjoy talking to Him. His are the only attentive Ears, He will listen and keep silent, for His Silence speaks louder than any speech.

I checked my time, doubled my steps and started back to the synagogue to join the other praying people, unobserved lest they would note that I was late for prayer, though I was and had never been an ardent religious citizen who observed meticulously the prayers hours. Yet, Yom Kippur was a special day that needed to be observed accordingly - Yes, a special day, but that Yom Kippur was different.

Different, I said? I was hardly out in the open over an hour when.....

Suddenly a siren was heard, and another, then another. People stared at one another not knowing what was going wrong...The stunned worshippers held their breath to grasp what was going on that special Day.. Aghast, confounded, the holy books in their hands remained open. The siren went on and on. Megaphones announced the horrible news that Israel was attacked.... It took less than an hour and trucks were in the streets to call the young people to arms! Israeli soldiers were away from their posts observing Yom Kippur, and the entire army was caught unprepared...

Knowing my duty I hurried back home...In ten minutes I found myself all dressed up in my military uniform, the truck outside honked for the second time, and all I managed to say to my family was: "There is war. I am going....." And so I did.

We headed south.....Other trucks were heading north...... We learnt that coalition of Arab States led by Egypt and Syria had launched early that very day a joint surprise attack on Israel....

I am not going to tell you about the war that began with a massive successful Egyptian crossing of the Suez Canal in the south, coordinated with a Syrian attack on the Golan heights in the north. The Egyptian troops swept deep into the Sinai Peninsula, and this offensive that coincided with the Syrian attack made threatening gains into Israel-held territory.

I was deeply enveloped with my thoughts about that morning walk with God, and I began to ask Him questions as the truck drove on and on to the front. Do I have to see flowers flicker and die? Do I have to hear people whine and cry? Children play with toy guns, and when they grow the guns become real, and the dead lie row by row. Turning swords into plowshares, is that possible in this ugly world?? I wanted to peacefully worship the earth, and live anywhere, in a tree house or in the middle of the ocean, or up above the crest of a mountain. Why don't babies pronounce the word "love" when they first see-the daylight of this world? The truck crammed with so many soldiers drove on through the desert while I kept asking who will return alive and who will die there. I asked God, the Almighty Creator of this Universe why He can't make people avoid wars with one magic touch of His.

I thought of an autumn day in October when leaves begin to fall, the trees shiver and sadly wear a frown, each tree like a body stripped of soul, each like a king without a crown. When the morning of October 7th dawned, I lifted my eyes to the pacing dawn as darkness began to break apart. Like the trees I felt naked and shorn, but within my chest was beating a heart. Like the dead strolling among the graves or like feathers in a wild wind my thoughts ran over the waves of time and all I remembered was that winter was close at hand, and that the rains of December will soon wash away the memories each and every soldier reluctantly had left on the summer sand, or they will wash away the blood stains, like poppies, on the battlefield.

Here comes the dawn, I said to myself, it plants a foot over the trees, the tops of mountains. Is there hope coming riding over the balmy breeze?. I had to return alive to my family, I wanted so much to embrace the whole world with my short arms, I missed my long walks with God .....God, are you there? I asked.

War taught me so many lessons. Millions of pictures kept recurring like an incessant dream. How could I approach life with a more pugilistic approach? I wasn't master of myself. I had to submit with deference. A world without laws, a world without the right to live freely and in love and peace, a world where laws are like spider webs when if some poor creature comes up against them, it is caught; but a bigger one can break through and get away. I was a suppliant, a worshipper with love and peace can exist only in his imagination. The lessons we learnt from war cost too much blood shed....

October 25th....ceasefire....Ten days later I was sitting in my living room with my family, watching TV solemnly. So many canons, many dead soldiers, so many coffins, so many salutes to the dead, to the young soldiers who weren't lucky to return alive like me, so many bereaved families, so many young dreams nipped in the bud...so many tears shed....there was a lump choking me in the throat.. The only words I could utter as I lifted my eyes to the sky was: "God, why????" Silence..... I heard Him whispering in my ears: "I was with you all these horrible days, we were out there. One day we shall again take a walk together, hand in Hand, and...."

Yes..."and what? another war?" I thought to myself.

The night of the tenth of October was exceptionally long. The Israeli forces were already cutting through inside the territory of the enemy. We at the hospital cared very little for the news. There was no real victory for us, only when we saved somebody's life. It was difficult to cope with the situation, but we had to fight our own battle, and between operations I had to find the time to cover some stories, and report. Time pressed, the efficiency and deftness of the medical staff proved valuable, and the hours slipped by. The clock on the wall struck one. The "next" wounded was wheeled into the operation room. All covered with a white linen revealing only the right thigh which had been almost entirely smashed, with a deep open wound apparently caused by a bullet which had penetrated down to the muscles and hit the bone. It looked badly hurt. The soldier was unconscious, and every moment was valuable for his life. Anesthesiologist Alex at the patient's head started oxygen respiration while Dr. Yigal stepped to the table and extended his gloved hands. The operation began. My eyes caught the first digits of the soldier's number ... 238..., tied to his neck. The white linen covered all the upper part of his body and his face. The only sounds heard were the clicking of the surgical clamps and the clink of the discarded instruments. Through the deft fingers of the nurse forceps, clamps, sponge and strands of surgical sutures flew back and forth to the surgeon's hands. Next to Dr. Yigal, on a low stool sat anesthesiologist Alex at the patient's head keeping a second-to-second watch on his respiration. The bullet was removed and the wound was partly sewn but the patient was not out of danger. Dr. Alex reported that breathing was not satisfactory.

"Blood!" Dr. Yigal responded without even raising his weary eyes from the wound he was operating on. There was horror in his trembling voice as he repeated the order: "More blood!"

"Doc, we're short of his type of blood. No more bottles in the blood bank.." That was naturally B RH plus.

"More blood," the doctor's words cut like his knife as his hands worked deftly on the wound. "Check recent donations!" His orders were brief.

"None." Nurse Lora's feeble voice cut back through the silence. A brief moment passed before I suddenly could hear my own voice this time: "B RH plus is my type. I donate." Soon I began to roll my sleeves, and in a few minutes my own blood was running in the transparent tubes feeding the wounded soldier's veins. Late that night, or early in the next morning, the patient was wheeled out of the room with the infusion set and the stands that carried the bottles of blood and plasma. The masked face of Dr. Yigal revealed only a couple of weary eyes that met mine. The door behind the nurses wheeling out the patient swang back.

There was another operation early that morning. The minutes slipped into hours. On high, behind and through the cloud shreds the crescent moon hurried on. The stars were already beginning to fade. Above the tree-crests beyond the hills the new day planted a foot. The other team was already coming down the corridor to relieve us when suddenly the emergency loudspeakers blurted out: "Emergency! Dr. Yigal .. Room 54 calling .. Dr. Yigal, emergency!" Now all the team were racing down the corridor to room 54, and as I entered I saw the two internes already handling the emergency. Dr. Yoram was putting his mouth directly down to the patient's mouth and blowing in air, while Dr. Sol was assisting him. Just as Dr. Yigal set foot into the room, he hastened to massage the patient's heart. He placed his hands on the heart bone and leaned. Practicing every care possible not to cause injury to the delicate freshly operated-on thigh, which he had sewn only a couple of hours earlier, he continued his massage, depressed the bone and squeezed the breast against the spine. It was a tough work, and I could almost feel the pressure as he pushed on. I stood close to Dr. Yigal, ready to take orders. The patient in whose veins my own blood was running looked pale and closer to death than to life. Dr. Yigal's eyes were wet now. Beads of perspiration covered his forehead and were gathering in the corners of his eyes and made them look like tears. At a closer look I judged that there really were tears in his eyes, while the perspiration trickled from his forehead and cheeks. "Let me wipe off the perspiration," I was going to say. I didn't say that, for the doctor was aware that I had been watching him, and I might have noticed some tears in his eyes. I had never before seen him cry. He managed to bury his head between his two arms as he resumed his tough movements of massaging frantically, thus making it difficult for me to check and make sure that perspiration and tears really intermingled there and then. He was choking back his tears, I could bet, as he struggled with death over that soldier's body. Dr. Sol was now checking the neck pulse, Dr. Yigal repeating his massage sixty times a minute, and a nurse pushing the electro-cardiograph on wheels to the patient's side. Now it was already five minutes after the emergency bell had rung. The crucial struggle was to get the patient's heart going again. All pairs of eyes watched the telltale wiggle line the patient's heart wrote on the long graph spewing from the ECG apparatus. The heart was racing now so fast it could not pump blood. Dr. Yigal was now trying to shock it back into action. Would he succeed? Silence was cruel. Ilana, the young trainee nurse, was biting her lips. Dr. Yigal and Dr. Yoram resumed their massaging and respiration. Suddenly to our relief, there was a brief smile peeping through the corners of Dr. Yigal's eyes. I could read the message it carried. The patient was out of danger. The ECG showed fine results now. I hastily prepared an injection of sodium bicarbonate and handed it over to Dr. Yoram.

"Well done." Dr. Yigal murmured half to himself.

"He is alive," Dr. Sol put in. A sigh of relief came from the Ward Chief Nurse. Dr. Yigal continued his tough work fighting to get the heart to work regularly. The ECG showed that the heart quiverings were irregular but strong enough to pump blood. The muscles in Dr. Yigal's face relaxed. His looks lingered speculatively on the young soldier's face that lay pale before him. Color was beginning to come up, and his breath was regular now. The doctor's eyes remained fixed on the young face.

Pairs of eager eyes kept watching the surgeon as he stood in utter silence staring at the young soldier's face and his steady breathing. Everybody was beginning to go except nurse Ilana who stood by the patient's bed and took instructions from Dr. Yoram. Suddenly I was aware that Dr. Yigal had left the room without being noticed. I hurried out down the corridor trying to catch him up. I felt I wanted to congratulate him for the fine job he had done.

I passed by the dining hall. They were already serving coffee and breakfast. I was dead hungry. I cast a quick look inside, but Dr. Yigal wasn't there. I went out and raced down the corridor to the doctors' quarter. I was short of breath when I stopped at one of the doors and knocked. "Sorry to disturb you, Dr. Yigal. Are you there?" I gathered the courage to speak. "This is Emil. Can I get you some coffee?" At last I found the words to excuse my intrusion. A moment of silence.

"Come in, Emil." Dr. Yigal's voice was low. I pushed the door open. He was lying on a sofa. "Sit down," he said.

A large photograph of a young cadet officer that hang on the wall attracted my attention. "Thanks for thinking of me, Emil," Dr. Yigal said as my looks lingered speculatively at the photograph.

"Sit down, we both need some rest," he said pensively. "I have a good reason to thank you personally. Your donation of this rare type of blood saved...."

"O, the soldier," I interrupted. "This is the proper thing to do, doctor." The face in the photograph on the wall was smiling boyishly.

"That soldier, Emil, is my son Yoav," Dr. Yigal's voice was trembling and his eyes blurred. He didn't look at me. He just stared in the air. Whose eyes blurred? Mine or his? To this day I cannot tell.

A soft music came over the balmy breeze of an early morning. It was the tune of "Jerusalem, the Golden" the hit of the Six-Day War some six years before. There were more tears in the doctor's eyes, but he managed to say choking his tears back, "Six years ago I lost his mother... I was aware of your looks at me while I was massaging his heart into action. I was crying, Emil.. We all have our weak moments. I broke, because I wanted him to live."

...

Yes. That was several years ago. Now everything is over, and death has caught his only son round another corner. This time the cadet officer had no chance to escape death.

Since then both Dr. Yigal and I became good friends. He knew everything about me, about my flair for writing, and I confided in him and consulted him. To me he was a dear father, an intimate friend and an esteemed tutor. He talked me into joining the kibbutz. I loved the idea, and when the war was over I and my typewriter remained in the kibbutz. Little by little I came to know more about Dr. Yigal. He had been only 24 years old when his son Yoav was born. Danny was in his age when he died, and Esther was in Yoav's age, too, when she died leaving young Yigal her diary. Oh, but that was about three decades before. Now Yoav, too, had gone down the Trail of the Lost Others. An airplane crash took away the lives of three of our dear boys. One of them was Yoav.

Knowing that I had a flair for writing, Dr. Yigal approached me one day, a couple of months before the airplane crash, with a bundle of papers. "This belongs to Esther. Her diary. Almost thirty years have gone by. I kept these papers for thirty good years. Everybody knows everybody here in this settlement in the Galilee. They all know everything. Now I give you this diary. Emil, write a book about Esther and Danny..."

That evening I drove Dr. Yigal back to his home, and was going to bid him goodnight when he stopped at the doorstep saying, "Emil, thank you for giving me a lift. It is a long way from the cemetery. Anyway, I was too tired to make it on foot. Emil, you still have that diary. You will write everything," he insisted. Now the picture is clear and the circle is full. You have everything. I lost everything in life: my wife, Ruth, my son, Yoav, and over thirty years ago my first real love, Esther. I feel there is nothing better than writing a book that will perpetuate the names of the dead. It is a sacred and an esteemed way to remember them all. They are always living in its pages, between its lines, and they live till the end of days. Dr. Yigal was so serious that he made me feel his words deep into my heart.

Back in the kibbutz Dr. Yigal Har-Zahav is enveloped in his thoughts and memories, while I sit down to write the story of Danny, Esther, ever!!, the story of young Yigal of Tel Katzir, his love for the "flesh" and for the "soil", the story of Dr. Yigal who had just come back from the cemetery where he was a witness to the return of the flesh to the soil. Since I began writing I have been stricken several times by the writers' cramp, and I decided to drop the pencil. One night Dr. Yigal came to me in my dream urging, "Emil, you'll have to continue. Write down the story!"

Writing the story means writing everything about Esther, about Danny, the birth of a new nation, the story of Yigal and those he lived among. "Danny doesn't belong here anymore, he is dead," I said.

"Don't say a word more. Write it. Write everything as it came to pass," the metallic voice in the dream urged.

I sternly refused to question him further about his whereabouts, and his objectives for the future. I shut myself up in myself in my cloudy solitude with the Diary and the Letter in my hand. I couldn't pluck up courage to ask more. I had a mission now. I looked up to the sky. Twilight time. The days were lengthening and growing warmer It was no longer cold. How I loved those beautiful, starry evenings! I remembered that Dr. Yigal, whom I loved like a dear brother, a comarade in arms, had entrusted me with what was so dear to him, the diary that he had kept for years, mostly in his heart, I had a mission. I felt in a cage, like a canary that may love its cage more than its freedom. It was a MUST. I had to write this book for him, for me, for my characters in the story!

...

Right now as I write these words reports pour in from the Israeli-Syrian borders or the Israeli-Lebanese borders about terrorists organizing sabotage. Tension is still there, escalating now and then. No final solution has been reached in the Middle East, and "peace" is still a dreamt-of aim. The Fatah organizations are working out new destructive plans to plant bombs in Israeli buses, public houses, bus stations and their aim is damage and sabotage.

Here from my room I can see the Sea of Galilee. Situated at the entrance of the lower Jordan Valley and at the place where the river emerges from the Lake is Kibbutz Deganya. By the gate of Deganya stands a trophy of the war in the form of a Renault Tank belonging to the Arab assailants, which was halted at the entrance to the village by a "molotov bottle", the only defensive arm which the villagers possessed in 1948. The members of the Kibbutz today pass by the tank, ponder a little and step onward with their work tools. There is a memory attached to this trophy. Many tourists come to the oldest kibbutz in Israel to see the tank as it stands today. Not far from here is the cemetery of the settlement, the opening scene of this novel.

Here is the book! Here's the "Pandora Box" of Dr. Yigal. It contains almost everything Dr. Yigal Har-zahav treasures. It is Israel, its soil and flesh!

Have you ever loved someone? Have you ever felt a special affection towards a son, a friend, a little girl, a woman, a young boy, a brother, a piece of soil, a land, someone, anything? Have you?

You will see that this book is like a big, big box, which I tried to fill with wonderful things such as love and beauty; also, with hatred and war, ups and downs of life and vicissitudes of time, but it is still empty, or it looks so. I give it to you, dear friend, try to fill it yourself with your own feelings of love and affection. If you believe that "Omnia vincit amor - love conquers all, you will see the resemblance between love and this book, for "many waters cannot quench love, neither can the floods drown it".....

EMIL MURAD -   1984   Alfe Menashe, Israel

....

All the characters of the novel, THE FLESH AND THE SOIL, with their names and traits are complete fictional inventions. Unintentional duplication of actual names of people, kibbutz members or places may have occurred, but any resemblance to actual people or events, in names, traits, or physical description, is coincidental.

Most of the events in THE FLESH AND THE SOIL are matters of history, and are on public record. Some of the scenes were created around historical incidents for the purpose of fictions. Real names of places and correct dates have occasionally been used where invented names would have sounded forced, but beyond that, all the characters are the creation of the author, and entirely fictional.

EMIL MURAD.   Alfe Menashe, Israel.

PART TWO

"How beautiful upon the mountains are the feet of Him that bringeth good tidings..." Isa. 52:7

...

The Lake of Tiberias, or Kinnereth, lies seven hundred feet below sea level between Israel and Syria, entirely surrounded by the hills which seem to isolate it from the outside world, and fed by the river Jordan which rushes down from Upper Galilee. The highlands of Golan border it to the northeast, whilst the mountains of Gilead close up to the south. All these mountains, dwarfed by the enormous snow-crowned massif of Mount Hermon, are bare and parched, except during the all too short weeks of spring. Yet, except for the north-eastern quadrant, where Syria reaches the shore, the Sea of Galilee is surrounded by a border of perennial green, an emerald setting for the enormous sapphire which is the beautiful lake. This mountain-encircled sea, which forms the central link in the chain of the Jordan lakes is of a peculiar beauty. The shores, strewn in places with basaltic shingles, are fairly narrow where the Jordan hills rise sheer from the water leaving only a narrow strip of land at the northern end. The lake is subject to sudden and violent gales, especially in the late afternoon and fishermen refrain whenever possible from crossing it at this time. The best fishing grounds are along the northern shore where there are a number of creeks formed by rivulets, the favorite haunt of fish. Along the shores of the Sea of Galilee lies the town of Tiberias. Near the bridge over the river Jordan, which emerges from the lake, there lies the Canaanite city of Beit Yerach. Here are remarkable ruins. On the right at a road junction is Kinnereth, a settlement close to the Jordan clan and bridges and near the lake. Here in a tiny cemetery under a clump of date palms is the grave of Rachel Blaustein, the poetess, whose love poems are recited and sung by all the young people of Israel. Near the Kinnereth Kibbutz is a Moshav of the same name with a cultural centre, educational seminary and the Ohalo Museum. On the right, after crossing a bridge over the Jordan, lies Kibbutz Deganya, situated at the entrance of the lower Jordan valley and at the place where the river emerges from the lake to wind its way through the valley into the Dead Sea.

Dagan means corn. Deganya was founded in 1909 by Russian immigrants. The area was swampy and desolate, and the first settlers in that tropical climate, exposed to the attacks of looting Beduins, and with no previous knowledge of work or experience in agriculture, needed the utmost determination to persevere. The first years saw many unsuccessful experiments, but slowly by painful trial and error, the methods of farming best suited to local conditions were evolved. Deganya served as an example and as a training school for hundreds of young pioneers who came with the dream of reclaiming soil neglected for centuries. So rapid was the growth of the settlement that a second village was founded a kilometer away from its boundaries, called Deganya Beth, where activities such as intensive fruit and vegetable growing, dairy farming, poultry, and carp breeding the cultivation of olive groves and production of cereals, were developed. Today, the village, set amid gardens, eucalyptus groves and orchards forms part of the flourishing settlements of the Jordan valley.

Deganya has a cultural institute, concert and lecture halls, reading rooms, library and central school of agriculture for all the community farms of the valley. The regional Natural

History Museum, built in 1941, known as Beit Gordon, is a model of its kind. It was erected in memory of A.D. Gordon, who lived at Deganya until his death at the age of 74, and wielded the pick right up to the end of his life. His philosophical work, which deals with the liberation of mankind through the return to nature and the tilling of the soil, has had a profound effect on the Israeli pioneers. His will contained the following words: Love one another in your common toil. The job of tilling the soil is a lasting boon. Gordon rests under the eucalyptus trees of the little village cemetery, and his tombstone is inscribed with a quotation from one of his best-known works: A Servitor of Man and Nature.

By day the view is spectacular: green stretches of land sweeping down to the Sea of Galilee. Further north one can see the misty, purple hills of Gilead and the gigantic, fertile Jordan Valley. By night it is even more beautiful and romantic, especially now on the night of May 14th, 1948. A night of joy and celebration. The British Mandate over Palestine expired and the Declaration of Independence was promulgated. With it a Jewish Homeland was born: a nation dedicated to freedom was released from the grips of imperialism and persecution which lasted over two thousand years. That was a cause for celebration. The big yard opposite the dining hall was decorated with Israeli flags, and inside the communal dining-hall music played. The walls were hung with garlands, the laden tables beautifully decorated. Wine flowed, and above the sound of music the voices of the happy people intermingled with the rhythmic noise of hundreds of dancing feet. There was a medley of songs in Russian, Yiddish, English, French, Polish, Arabic, Yemenite, Hungarian and above all: Hebrew. Country songs and army songs, palmach (volunteers) songs and the Brigade songs, love songs and madrigals, all rendered by a variety of happy voices, sweet and hoarse, bass and soprano, voices that knew no fatigue nor limit. The young and the old joined hands and danced in one sweeping hora after another.

Their beaming faces bore witness to their happiness, and their voices vibrated through the air, were carried far away to the neighboring settlements on the waves of the Sea of Galilee. A light spring breeze stirred the branches of the trees, bright with strings of colored lights, and the night sky was suddenly alive with fireworks, soaring and bursting in showers of rainbow sparks, to the "oohs" and "aahs" of the watching people. The kibbutz had received many guests that evening. They had come to rejoice over the news with their friends and relatives, and now many of them streamed from all the corners of the settlement and crowded in front of the social dining hall to join the group of dancers in their swift, sweeping horas. They were all united in shaking off a heavy load they had been carrying for so many years, and in tapping fresh streams of energy and joy for the future. One hora after another! Here Benny and Martha performed the hora of the peasant, there Ephi and Dora danced the country lovers while Laxie, the faithful setter, trotted among them all, wagging its tail all the time.

The attention of the onlookers was attracted to a swift hora performed by twenty-four young dancers, boys and girls with Laxie in the centre. The dog has always kept the company of Esther and Danny. Friendly as she was she could not bear to be stroked - a thing people were always wanting to do. Her ears pointed, and she managed to hold them constantly erect, as though they were starched. She loved to join them on their walks, and always wagged her tail when they were happy, and lowered her head and muzzle when she sensed something wrong. Now she was wagging her tail, turning around herself joyously. Esther had just turned eighteen, and Danny three years her senior. They led the "circle" to another swift hora, and when her fingers tightened on his, he gave her a quick squeeze in response and their eyes met. Shmuel and Rina hopped in to pull them apart in order to join the "circle", but Esther and Danny didn't give way so the newcomers had to break elsewhere and enter. More fireworks crackled in the sky.

Esther's eyes roved as the "circle" rotated. There were Tiqva and David, Rina and Shmuel, Martha and Benny, Ephi and Dora, and others. For a moment her eyes rested on Ephraim. Once he had shaken hands with her. He had hard and strong fists. Now he was staring at her, perhaps admiring her agility and quick steps. Esther was light as a dove when she danced the hora.

"I'm exhausted!" Esther gasped breathlessly after a long and strenuous dance. "Let's get away and have some rest.." Much of what she said was lost because of the noise but Danny was able to interpret her expression and nodded with a smile drawing her gently out of the circle, and they made their way through the throng leaving the merrymakers behind.

"Ah, that's better!" she drew a deep breath of relief. "Come on," Danny led her by the hand down the hill. They passed through a belt of trees and into a dark lane that led to the poultry quarter. Wet grass brushed their ankles as they followed the lane that turned and widened, finally getting them out on a deserted open lawn. They danced for a minute alone on the grass, humming a sentimental tune, then laughing and giggling they threw themselves down on the grass beneath a spreading cedar tree.

Suddenly there came the explosion of a great rocket which left the earth with a great gush of force and shot to a surprising height. A fountain of fire burst on the climax of the arc. The spray bloomed white, faded into scarlet, lazily fell, and by its light Danny watched Esther's face lovingly. When the rocket had vanished they lay back full length on the grass, pleasantly tired and glad to be quiet and away from the crowd and the noise. She lay motionless, her eyes fixed on a twinkling star in the sky. A large comet rose above the horizon, its broad, flaming train streaming out behind it like a blazing banner. The comet was headed in a burst of its own iridescent glory towards the evening star.

"Make a wish," Danny said softly. "Before it disappears!"

Esther ..Danny, ever.." she murmured half to herself as she watched the comet before it was disappearing. He was like a big brother, a loyal friend, like a mentor. They were just friends

To know more about Danny and Esther in order to write this book, the writer had to have a long talk with their training counselor, Zvi, who was in charge of a group of 40 boys and girls. The duty roster Zvi had to prepare every evening, usually put Danny and Esther in the tomato fields. They made a good team with several others. After work, the members and their children got together. There was hora-dancing almost every evening, and there and then Danny and Esther used to meet again. Youngsters loved hora-dancing, lining-up with their hands on the next person's shoulder, all the while jumping up and down in a straight line, holding their bodies rigid and using their feet as springs. Almost like the Kurdish folk-dances and the debka dance of the Druze tribes. Naturally, Danny and Esther became friends. They took long walks through the orchards or to the brook, the fish pond, the bridge that crossed the parks, or just wherever their feet led them. Their talk was mostly about the plants, the birds of the air, they picked flowers here and there, and Esther loved to arrange them in artistic bouquets after returning to her room, which she shared with other girls her age.

In the beginning Danny was just one of the boys, then a friend, a close friend. They didn't even touch hands, he respected her, but he didn't have the temerity to say that he liked or loved her, or had any special feelings for her.

She was too reserved, she dared not even steal glances at him or look deep into his eyes, though she had felt that that special boy had made her think too long and too deep about him all the time, even before she closed her eyes to sleep at night she had him on her mind. She composed her personal prayer, which included Danny to be always by her side, before she closed her eyes to sleep. She had known instinctively that his coming into her life had been providential - a part of her destiny. Hitherto she had so heeded her mother's warnings that she had made out her own rules about necking and kissing, and clung to them closely. She had known well within herself that boys were not to be trusted, and the teachings of her mother, who had died a few years before, had had a deep and lasting effect on her. Esther knew that boys would try any smart trick with a girl if they thought they could get away with it. Her studies in hygiene and biology had taught her everything about sex, and she knew the whole business like a doctor, tubes and eggs and male sperm and fertilization, etc.. When she passed the age of sixteen she was as physically well developed and as sensible as an eighteen year- old and had a keen mind. Esther was very attractive but her instinct, backed by what remained in her memory of her mother's vague but horrid warnings, made her firmly reject boys' advances. But that night the stars were telling her that Danny was different from all the boys. He was totally different. All boys were bores, and dates were mostly disappointing. The rules she had made about not kissing and petting didn't work with Danny, for she loved him and she couldn't resist him. At the age of sixteen and half she had surrendered herself to the pleasant process of kissing him without fear. That was the limit, her mother had taught her from a very early age. That was in the spring of 1945 and from that day onwards all the bright arguments she had put forward against marriage or against boys as nasty louts collapsed completely.

Lying so close to Danny, Esther's thoughts were becoming like a film, projected on her mind, running faster and faster and she imagined Benny and Martha making love the way Martha had described it to her. She had even told her that she could seduce Danny if she wanted to, and Esther had almost gone mad with jealousy.

How could she use such an obscene language after all she had known about her and Danny? That Martha and her gestures, sexy and suggestive as they were! She hated her.!

Martha's quirks and aberrations must have been caused by some emotional conflict. Whatever the reason, she was the biggest liar since the snake fooled Eve, but would she succeed to fool her Danny? There was always a sort of running antagonism between Martha and Benny, which sometimes resulted in slaps and insults. The poor girl never knew when she was in love, or when she was out of it. The very thought of Danny and Martha hurt Esther, and her thoughts roamed on dreamily. Then Ephi's picture came to her head and she wondered why he had been watching her dancing. Ephi was a handsome guy, but she would never consider any boy-friend other than Danny.

Some months later, after work Danny and Esther were enjoying a starry evening

"What secrets are the stars revealing to you?" Danny's voice cut her thoughts abruptly, as he drew her close to him, his arms touching and his eyes glittering in the moonlight with an angry expression. Love was a tiring experience for Esther. It made her blood either boil or freeze, and made her heart swell like a balloon, and her nerves taut as bowstrings. Was love really like those fruits that tasted sweet at the first mouthful and sour at the last, as she had once been told?

"Danny," at last she found the words to speak up. "Sorry for the way I feel, but when I think of all this love and kissing and petting, it all seems ridiculous and a waste of time."

"Esther, what're you driving at?" he propped himself angrily.

"I mean.." she was going to say something about faithfulness, fidelity, Martha, and the sex urge, specially a boy's sex urge. She felt the blood throbbing in her veins as she lay there close to him while his eyes moved over her face almost as though to kill her or worship her. His body almost touching hers he scanned her from head to toe, while her eyes remained steadily on his. She wanted him to speak, to defend himself, but he preferred being silent. There are some people who appear at their best in moonlight. In the glamour of the moon-rays, such people, romantic, self-conscious as they are, find for themselves a pleasant environment, making use of the dramatic instinct latent in their natures. Danny was such a person. He was intensely aware of the moonlight all around them, wrapping their whole world in the enchanted mantle of glory and beauty, covering them with its silver radiance. He looked deep into her eyes feeling himself a king chosen by fate for power and glory making love to his queen, chosen by fate for the completion and perfection of his manhood.

For a moment Esther saw him not as a man only, but as a frail symbol of powers on whose surface his life was tossed. She felt compassionate and asking for compassion, his refuge and the living being whose only refuge was in him. A flame passed through her as he drew her closer. His body became a single pulse, leaping from strength to strength; and suddenly, lifting her hand that lay motionless on the grass, he pressed it to his lips. He felt her fingers move upon his hair and raising his head he gazed long and silently into her face with growing comprehension of the change in her, in himself, in the destiny and significance of their love. He sprang to his feet drawing her towards him with both hands, and so easily did she follow that her hair was lifted from her shoulders by the swiftness of her movement.

"Esther, what do you see in the future?" his breath was warm.

"Danny.." There was a great lump in her throat that choked her, and she burst into tears. If only he could understand the language of tears.

"I love you, Esther." He understood. "It has all been like a dream; this summer, the last one and the one before. Thank you for making me understand the magic that is in love. The only thing I'm afraid of is that I shall wake up and not find you close to me. Don't cry, Esther." His tender, constraining hand on her waist tightened trying to draw her closer still, but she didn't give way. She sighed and sobbed as though on the point of making a very serious decision of which she was not sure.

"You know that I love you, that I intend to marry you.." Again she heard that unique pity and affection in his voice, but again Martha's face and sexy body preening before the mirror, rose before her eyes. Martha used to tell the girls about how she drifted from the embrace of one boy to another and how the boys liked to make love to her. Now Esther felt Danny's arm around her waist, and the face of their youth leader and that of her dead mother would rise horrified at her shocking conduct. What if Roni, the youth leader, knew! She tried to pull herself away, but Danny would not let her go.

"Close your eyes, Esther. You'll feel better. You always said it helps." Danny whispered in her ears. "What's wrong? Are you afraid?" Why should she be afraid? Only two months before she had crossed the age of 18, living up to the promises she had made to her mother.

In no mood to confess, Esther refused to speak. Then in order to shake off his insistence and the sound of the distant music she closed her eyes, and at once a warm sensation ran like electricity from her head to her toes. She was tightly embraced as Danny's mouth was upon hers, full, sensual and loving, and she felt his jaw slacken and the tip of his tongue slide over her lips. His body arched into hers, and for an endless moment their hearts beat together. She was breathing deep and fast, with the urgent tempo of sensuality, but she held back with that measured strength of a thoughtful, desirable yet very strong, young woman. His lips caressed her cheeks, her eyes, her ears, the corners of her mouth; avid little kisses that sent ripples of pleasure through her whole body.

"This flower-like mouth of yours against which I press my own, feeds me with honey and the elixir of youth!" Danny's passion gradually stirred, and then inflamed her flesh. She clung to him, and while he kissed her warm throat she let out little, cooing gasps of protest and delight. In her bliss it seemed to her as if her senses had been narrowed to their two selves. The moonlight that bathed them made them feel shame. She could see the stars above, hear their heart beats above the faint sound of music, singing and dancing that became fainter and fainter, far away from the ecstasy she and Danny were sharing there and then.

She couldn't contain her heart's turbulent happiness, and began singing with all the voice she could find in her chest

"O, Danny, I love you so much!" she managed to utter the words at long last. Bathed in the soft, white radiance of the moonlight they lay together in their love-bed, on the grass, unaware. "You will marry me, Esther, my love. Won't you?" his fingers were now unbuttoning Esther's shirt. His breath was warmer than before and the touch of his fingers on her breasts made her lustful and desirous. There was something peculiarly pleasant in the comfort and nearness of being undressed; it was not so much exciting as cozy and intimate. It was tender and nice. Then everything suddenly changed. It became rough and strange. She lay powerless, willing and loving. It became rougher and rougher, and more awkward - and horrible! There were shocks, ecstasy, ugly uncoverings, pain, joy, again pain, joy and pleasure, incredible humiliation, shock, shock, shock...!! The two of them lay naked on the grass, two bodies in one.. Nobody knew their secret, only the soft grass and the sweet-smelling cedar tree... and these wouldn't tell..

Esther clung to him wordlessly. How marvelous, how exciting was the touch of a young man's flowering nakedness to the naked body of his beloved!

At last she had known the meaning of love, and tasted its pleasure. She had tasted the apple of Eden. She was a woman, eighteen years plus two months and six days old on that night of May 14th. Esther ceased to be a virgin. "I feel grateful, but I don't know whom to thank", she thought. She was of age, but there was remorse, there were bad feelings towards her own self! How could she make up for it?

...

That night Esther was exhausted. The diary she had received on her eighteenth birthday lay open on her desk. She had not written a single word before. Now she took her pen and wrote:

"It is from this night that I choose to begin my diary. Not from the moment the anguished cries of my mother were heard, nor from the moment I was being slapped into my first wail and properly washed marking my advent in the world, but from this night of May 14th, 1948. I have always wanted to keep a diary, and sketch in broad strokes the picture of my childhood, youth and the picture of our love. I cherish thoughts and nurse memories that refuse to recede and scorn burial. Moreover, I've always wanted to draw a picture of our home, Deganya, landscapes, hills, green fields and all the hiding places that know so many secrets about boys and girls, about stolen apples and the history of the pioneers. I know the place like the palm of my hand, for here, where our love was born, I can follow in my mind's eye each and every memory. Of all these pictures, some vague, some clear, the one depicting this night of May 14th is the clearest.

Danny, I don't know what happened to me after I had closed my eyes and surrendered to you, my soul and my body. A small part of my mind stood apart and watched curiously as we kissed again and again, enjoying the discovery of pleasure. The rest of me was drowning in the sweetness of your lips on mine, and the sweetness of your throbbing blood that flooded my body with boundless pleasure. My innocence vanished, and in a moment, in a blink of an eye, the barrier was gone, and I was seeking the adult satisfaction of an adult desire. I write this poem in my diary.

IT TASTES SWEET LIKE A SIN ....

O, my God, I sinned
What shall I do with the sin

She came riding over the wind
Opened her doors and let me in

There was talk, a look, then desire
O, God, I couldn't help it
I am but a poor creature on fire
She opened her doors and let me in

I thought it was all but a dream
When I realized I was going to win
I said to myself, "Tis all but a whim
But God she opened her doors, let me in

O, my God I say I sinned
If love-making is a sin
It all came fast like the wind
She opened her doors and let me in

Help me, God, couldn't wait more
I made love to her from head to toe
She opened before me every door,
Am happy, yet ashamed, too!

I am so ashamed of it
It all began with fantasy.
But, Lord, I must admit
That it all turned into ecstasy

We both coo and feel in vain
She coos and utters voices
We do it over and over again
And the world outside is all noises

I say I want to hold her now
And I feel quite insane
I cry, I tremble and call "Wow!"
But, O, my God, I will do it again

I lost my senses and sobriety
She cooed and I felt so well
Both of us sank in ebriety
I knew not if it was Heaven or Hell

We were both carried away
In the heat of our bodies and the night
There was no pause all the day
Beneath the bed-sheets there was delight

Just imagine, all love and sex galore
As she lay upon me joyfully
I whispered in her ears "I adore"
And, O God, I entered her carefully!

She screamed and cooed all the time
I trembled and went crazy
O, my God, is this a crime
When all our senses become hazy??

We sank into a world of our own
And the world outside was far away
I cried, uttered voices of many a groan
And didn't know if it was night or day

Tossing in bed to the rhythm of night
In the heat of lust and desire,
Not knowing what's black, what's white
Like two hearts roasting on fire

I pray thee, God, let it not end
For no ecstasy surpasses that of love
All your blessings you will send
To lovers the world over, the peaceful dove.

God Gracious me!, we have sinned
If love-making is in Your Eyes a sin
Let it all go and fly with the wind

For Love will always survive and win!

Somewhere two lovers are locked together
Tossing and turning, come what may
You, God, created us, also birds of feather
Who cares if 'tis night or day

Locked into each other we remain
Until we both become one
Life without love is in vain
A lesson to teach every son of man!

I'm ashamed, but satisfied and happy for thinking of you.
Good-night, my beloved Danny!"

...

A beautiful morning dawned. The sun poured its golden rays from a cloudless blue sky, and every other minute a yellow thrush gave its three-note call, followed by a pause to let the whole of the fluting song sink and soak into the countryside. The noise awakened Esther. She stood by the window facing her reflection in the looking-glass that hung on the wall. A feeling of shame and guilt made her turn her face from the looking-glass. How beautiful and green was her village!

In the early dawn the trees before the houses looked like ghosts creeping from the mist. A sparrow careened joyously, a darting atom of happiness dancing some ritual cosmic dance in the blueness of the spring sky. Did sparrows fall in love? Did they forget their good resolutions and make fools of themselves?

The day after the celebration was a public holiday. Everyone one sleeping late. Esther stood at her window and thought of the night before. Two night-watchmen had just finished their duty, and were going back home. Pessah, short and compact of build, with a mobile face and a mellifluous voice, was a round-faced, pussycat-like man with glasses which he took off and polished as he fell into step with Mordechai. The latter was tall and thin. Black hair, parted exactly down the middle, was slicked flat to a long, narrow head. His sharp nose suggested a cutting instrument and his small, piercing black eyes, not quite in focus, peered through rimless spectacles. As the two men passed right underneath her window, Esther heard their conversation clearly:

"Pessah, what do you think of the situation? The British are leaving though, but what next?" The flashlight in Mordechai's hand looked long as a club.

"Well, peace of course! A Jewish Homeland!" Pessah put in.

"You think the Arabs will sit and watch?"

They went on talking about Safed falling in Jewish hands, the Arab retaliation, and perhaps an outbreak of enmity or the like. Their voices died away as they walked away from her window.

Then Mordechai, rifle slung on his back, went to the right, and Pessah taking off his glasses and wiping them with the tail of his battle-dress, took the left lane hunching his shoulders and walking with a stoop.

Esther remained at her window gazing thoughtfully across the parks and green fields, orchards and hills that stretched endlessly, across the fields of corn, already shimmering in the heat, and tears rose unbidden to her eyes. God... that was what she was thinking of. God, her mother had told her, isn't exactly a man. He is..well.. He is just God. He is a divine Being. He is greater than any human being.. God had always been the greatest puzzle of all to Esther, the child. She had begun to worry about Him before she was seven years old. In those days He was to her an ancient, white-bearded giant who lived up in Heaven, but had a sneaky way of being everywhere else at the same time. He could do anything He wanted, and just lurked about waiting for you to make a mistake - whereupon He would land on you and whop you good! And here she was now with her biggest mistake of all, her unpardonable sin, waiting for His punishment. If only she could cry!

Martha was still lying contentedly in her bed, her hair a disordered mass of brown curls, her shirt and skirt lay crumpled on a chair, her pink underwear thrown on top of them. Simha and Tiqva had just jumped out of their beds and were beginning to dress. They were saying something about a picnic or an excursion. Tiqva was lacing her shoes, Simha combing her hair, while Martha stretched and yawned lazily. She got out of bed and began rummaging in her drawers for fresh clothes. Esther cast a glance at her as she strolled around almost naked, picking up clothes, not at all troubled by the absences of blinds at the windows, her tanned flesh bulged like dough around the tight edges of her pink bras and girdle, and she undulated her plump buttocks as she walked around the room. Still in her undies, Martha began to plait her hair. Suddenly male voices were heard outside and she shrank behind the wardrobe.

"Ready, girls? A lovely day for a picnic. The trucks and tractors are already waiting by the dining-hall." That was Benny.

"Come on, girls!" Yoske added. A group of half a dozen boys walked past the window, and Simha let out an indignant shriek as she was just fixing her bras.

"How dare you, boys, come to the girls' camp? Suppose we invaded the boys' camp, what would you do?" she shouted angrily.

"Drag you into bed," Benny's prompt reply came, and the boys ran off laughing.

"Idiots, that's what they are!" Tiqva put in.

"Why? Have you never slept with a boy?" Martha eyed her slyly.

"Stop it. I'm sick of your stupid talk about boys."

"Why," Martha said again, round-eyed with mock surprise. "Don't you know what boys think about us girls? I heard them one day expressing their beastly desires. When the talk turns on girls, they behave like beasts."

"How do you know?" Tiqva asked.

"Benny told me. One boy says 'Think of her voluptuous body in bed." Another says: 'When I see her with those two soft-nosed fawns trembling under her blouse I melt like wax in a flame." A third one says: "I melt like ice. I lose my voice and utterance. I become inarticulate!" Martha's imitation and expressions were so comical that all the girls burst out laughing except Esther who stood and watched silently.

"They're all the same. Boys! And Danny is no exception.." Martha's knife cut deeper into Esther's wound. The latter eyed her with contempt. Martha leaned at the window. She read Esther's looks.

"What a gorgeous day for an outing! Aren't you coming, Esther? Don't stand there like a stuffed dummy." Esther kept silent.

"It must be love. O la la.." Martha went off into a peal of sarcastic laughter while Esther, hands clenched, longed to slap her jeering face and silence her forever."

"Danny is teaching you your first lessons in love! Or maybe you're pining for a lost lover! Come on, girl!" Martha went on. Esther's lips curled with anger, but did not speak.

"Believe me, Esther," Martha whispered in her ears. "All boys are the same. We all know where you disappeared last night. Don't pretend you are so poised and invulnerably pure like Bracha and many others. Such women are always volcanoes of passion when aroused. We know all that stuff. Your Danny whispers words that drip honey and sweetness in your ears, then he tells you that nakedness is the most mysterious clothing in the world. He'll sing you praises and cover with kisses, but after he's taken what he wants he'll cast you aside to drown in your own shame. Listen to me, young girl in love. Boys. They're all the same." Martha put her hand on Esther's shoulder in a maternal way.

"Don't touch me!" Esther jumped as if she had been stung.

"You need some rest," Simha approached the girls. "Esther, you look pale. You know Martha! Don't get cross." She pulled Martha aside and they left with the other girls leaving Esther in her room alone.

Martha cast a glance at her from the corner of her eyes and stalked angrily out of the room, her long and slender back and primly-held shoulders motionless. Martha had a cute, bouncy way of walking moving her shoulders with little thrusts and swaying her hips.

Esther's rage had evaporated, and she shrugged. She actually pitied that girl. She had once been told that her mother, a bony woman with warts in the recesses of her fleshy cheeks, and her father had both died in a mental hospital when the girl had only turned two. Perhaps the poor girl knew what she was saying. One should bare one's teeth and laugh like hell. Esther reached her comb. The picnickers were gathering just opposite the dining-hall. The first truckload of hand-clapping youngsters had already left. Joyous boys and girls were climbing on the other trucks and tractors. Their voices reached Esther's ears. She envied them their peace of mind. The trucks, buses and tractors made their way down the lane winding towards the hills and beyond the mountains. Esther sat down at the edge of her bed. Soon Danny would be coming to fetch her. The night before they had agreed to meet and join all the picnickers. She lay back, clasping her hands behind her head, gazing sightlessly up at the ceiling. The very thought of her mother seemed to magnify her sin. An idea struck her.

"Danny," she wrote on a piece of paper. "I've not the courage to face it. I had no experience with boys. It was you who taught me kisses and love play..." She held the pen in her hand. The noises of the outer world suddenly were muted into a distant hum, so unceasing that it seemed to belong to silence. "What made us do it?" she went on writing hastily. "Was it a celebration or an opportunity for us to make fools of ourselves only to repent it thereafter? It's true that we've always craved for the mere touch of each other. We've often been more hungry and dissatisfied after love play than before it; we could think of nothing except ourselves and our sexual desires. But was that a good reason to flout the laws laid down by God? I feel so ashamed of the wrong I've allowed you to commit, the wrong I perpetrated. If only my mother could forgive me!" She lay down the pen. The clock on her bedside table ticked eagerly, its pulse hurrying on like a child towards some imagined joy. Her mind wandered and abruptly there was a loud double knock on the door. Before she could even arrange her features into a false smile to meet the intruder, the door opened and there stood Danny, Laxie by his side. "Esther!" he exclaimed angrily, hurrying forward. "Are you O.K.?" Laxie wagged its tail, and Danny, flute tucked under his arm, approached her closer. "I was worried. Why didn't you come?" His mouth tightened and a frown creased his brow between the eyes. Esther was mute, frightened. Suddenly her strength failed her, and she sank down on the edge of the bed. She buried her face in the pillow and burst out crying like a child. The wet and warm tears moistened the linen cover beneath her cheek. He picked that written paper and began reading. Her face was still pressed against the pillow, but she could see him fishing a cigarette from his side pocket, lit it, inhaled the smoke, filled his lungs with it, then exhaled it through his nostrils. He must have had a bewildered expression on his features. Turning over on the bed she covered her face with her palms and kept on sobbing like a child in trouble, mistreated child. Through the film of tears that blurred her eyes she saw the smoke curling and wreathing blue about his head.

"I don't think we should meet again!" Esther couldn't believe herself. How did she manage to gather so much courage to say words that almost stunned him?

"Please don't misunderstand me. I didn't mean to harm you or take advantage of you. "His voice was hoarse with emotion, eyes calm but sorrowful. Well, then Martha had been right: boys do take advantage! "There's life in my dreams. I want to marry you. I shall be your loving husband..." His words beat against her head like a drum. "A kiss is the tenderest exchange in the world, silent and lovely as a flower. Long ago we agreed that..."

"Kissing was the limit we agreed upon the first time we kissed three years ago," she interrupted. "But last night it was different." Esther gathered more courage and went on, "And what is all this philosophy about a kiss being the tenderest exchange? It is all sugar to catch flies. You boys speak of love and think of the flesh, the bare skin of the body."

"A pair of lips..." Danny was going to say when Esther kept on shooting. "The skin of the lips is thin and tender, so tender that the blood is right behind it, and that's the reason for all this poetic talk about discovering a pair of lips. Suddenly Martha's image was feeding her with courage to go on. "What you have in mind, boys, is to be naked with girls, skin against skin, and teach us the absurd satisfaction that one miserable creature finds in savoring with lips and hands the body of another."

"What a theory!"

"Yes. And I cling to it." Esther felt her temples throbbing. She thought he would throw down his cigarette, grind it beneath his heel and fling angrily out of the room to see her no more. Instead, he drew closer to her, looked deep into her eyes, his hands were trembling, "Esther.. you are an enchanting girl, but your idea of love is extremely odd and almost comically distrustful. Do you think that love is only related to the secret behavior of nasty small boys and that it has nothing to do with the female sex? Do you believe that flirtations are begun exclusively by young boys for the purpose of enticing girls into unseemly behavior? Esther, you know well enough that my love to you is different from the one you describe. You suddenly find out that you were deceived. Is this what you're heading at?

Do you really believe what you're saying? You know what you mean to me, don't you?"

Suddenly Esther knew what he meant to her. There was a smile of relief on her face as her lips parted and planted a brief kiss on his forehead. "Let's go! A lovely day for a picnic!"

...

Some old coffee remained from the morning in the kibbutz kitchen. They gulped some, made a few sandwiches, and with Laxie at their heels, walked into the boulevard shaded by tall trees that led to the open garden down the hill. Suddenly they became aware of the beauty of nature and the loveliness of spring. In the centre a wide expanse of smooth green lawn was a sparkling fountain, twittering birds filled the place. "One is nearer to God's heart in a garden than anywhere else on earth.." Danny could hear himself saying.

A long, winding road lay between them and the distant shores of the lake. Around every curve in the road was a breathtaking view that was typical of Deganya, the home that they loved so much!

Beyond the curve of the road, where few people ever came, lay the shores of the Kinnereth, a serene, beautiful lake with a million shores and faces. They stepped out of their shoes and sat on the edge of the shore dabbling their feet in the water. The afternoon ebbed and flowed around them in waves of warmth and contentment, the murmur of the lake constant on the shores and among the rushes. They walked along the firm shingle towards the palm trees that lay beautifully on another shore. Frogs croaked from the shallows, the rushes swayed, the water-birds called plaintively.

"My hair is coming down." A balmy breeze was blowing. Esther plucked out a pin, let the whole left side of her hair fall around her face, put the pin in her mouth and started to wind the hair back up again. "Let it fall," Danny's voice was husky.

He was looking directly into her eyes. She slowly took the pin out of her mouth as he put his arms around her and touched her mouth with his. His lips were warm and alive. She slid her bare arms around his neck, pressing her slim young body close to him. They embraced. The little waves lisped against the shingle at their feet breaking into delicate, lace-like frills of foam.

The lake was like a sapphire touched with silver. In the distance the green summit of the hills rose against the blue of the sea and the unfathomable sky.

"There's not a single soul round here," Danny scooped up a few pebbles and dropped them one by one into the water. They dangled their legs in the cool clear water by the weed-covered breakwater. Laxie splashed through the shallows and plunged in for a swim. Esther watched absently, her thoughts busy with the whole span of years in which she and Danny had been friends. "Besides ourselves," she said completing Danny's sentence. Looking at him, she felt once more the stir of adult desire.

"Nobody ever comes down here. Could we?" he eyed her. "Could we perhaps have a dip?" Their eyes met. Esther was smiling mischievously. Their eyes fell on a nearby tree. She darted behind it. Danny followed. Each one stood on one side of the tree. Their eyes again met, and they quickly undressed.

"Have you ever tried it?" Danny felt happy.

"Tried what?" Esther was pulling down her underwear.

"Swimming naked in the lake?"

"Never!" Danny's hand touched hers, and they stepped out together to the bank. They glanced shyly at each other, then suddenly burst out laughing, ran splashing through the shallows and plunged into the clear blue water...

...

It was evening. The sun had become a blood-red globe hanging over the ancient hills beyond the lake. They were not ashamed of their nakedness as they strolled hand in hand on the share. The red disc of the sun was sinking slowly into the waters of the lake. They sat down close on the dry warm shingle, then they lay on their backs watching the last rays of sunset while the lake blushed in response to the deep pink afterglow.

Esther writes in her diary

AUTUMN TEARS

When Autumn comes and leaves begin to fall
The trees shiver, and sadly wear a frown.
Each, like a body stripped of soul
Each, like a king without a crown.

I lift my eyes towards the pacing dawn,
As darkness begins to break apart:
Like the trees I feel naked and shorn
Yet not unlike 'em, inside me beats a heart.

And like the dead strolling among the graves,
Or like feathers in a wild wind
My thoughts run over the waves of time,
And all of a sudden I remember
That Winter is close at hand,
And that the rains of December
Will soon wash away the memories
That I had reluctantly left on the summer sand!

A song is heard, then slowly dies, and again
Beyond the horizon a tune comes to my ears.
As dawn plants a foot over the trees
Come those first light, lively drops of rain
Along with fresh hopes of peace, love and life,
They come riding over the balmy breeze!

With my short arms I embrace the whole world.
Naked though, the trees and I feel warm,
With the fresh, wet smell of earth
Filling my nostrils they call me back home!!!!

...

There was a talk that evening in the dining-hall that the Arabs were preparing an attack on Israel. News was bad. War! After supper was over, the diners moved to the library hall and the educational centre to continue their arguments, discussion, comments propositions and speeches. There were suppositions and plans. Some of the elders, the "fathers" of the settlement such as Stern, Pessah, Mordechai, Motke, Ehud and many others were discussing the news with the help of a map on the white-washed wall.

"If the Arab Legion attacks," Stern was saying looking through his thick-lensed spectacles at the map, "The Egyptians will probably also strike up from the desert to the southern gate of the city of Jerusalem." The talk resumed throughout the night. Everything was discussed, the Hagana's marching and occupying Bevingard, the business centre which had been left by the British, and turning it into a fortified zone, etc...

"It seems that the whole of the modern city of Jerusalem is in Jewish hands, but nobody knows how the Arabs will respond now!"

...

The stars shone brightly outside Esther's room. The sinister word "war" echoed in her head as she lay down to sleep having said her customary compline. That night her prayer was longer than usual. The safety of Deganya, her unpardonable sin and her vow to Danny were only a few of the points that worried her. There was a smile on her face as she laid her head on the pillow, the smile faded and a variety of pictures began to file by. There was a vision of a speeding train. It was like a thunderbolt of driving rods, a hot hiss of steam, a blurred flash of coaches, a noise, a deafening shriek, and abruptly her eyes were filled with tears. She buried her head in the pillow as she sobbed, and there came pictures of people running to catch the train, excited, their movements feverish and abrupt. Some were weary, others exultant with the thrill of the voyage; some thrust and jostled, others stood quietly and waited. Again she seemed to hear the shriek of the train, the murmur of a distant sea, the sound of the laps and flow of water on a beach. Gradually her muffled sobs ceased and she fell asleep.

In the middle of the night she woke up. The room which seemed wrapped in majestic loveliness and great silence was bright with moonlight. The moon hung low in the sky, surrounded by a million twinkling stars. A thread of cloud floated across its face. A strange thought came to her head. Her wedding day! She saw herself in a flowing white dress, a white bouquet and the words: "...To have and to hold from this day forward for better, for worse, for richer, for poorer, in sickness and in health, to love and to cherish, till death do us part... With this ring I thee wed, with my body I thee worship, and with all my worldly goods I thee endow.. Bone of my bones, and flesh of my flesh..." Her eyes were moistened. There were tears... of joy ...or of fear of the morrow.

...

The next day was a regular work day. The girls got up as the alarm clock announced five-thirty. Martha yawned lazily, rubbed her eyes lazily and groaned, "Work! Always work. I could use another hour of good sleep."

"I had a terrible dream. Gunfire! War! "Tiqva put in as she buttoned her shirt.

"There's not going to be any war!" Martha jumped off her bed. The girls donned their shirts, shorts, socks, heavy boots, and snatching their head-cover, the Kova-Tembel,(field head-cover) they hastened to the dining-hall where Shmulik had already been waiting to drive them down to the vegetable fields, the orchards and the groves.

They ran the last few yards to join their comrades. The dining-hall was already buzzing with the young and the old getting their warm drink and hurrying to work. There was a rumour that shots had been heard before dawn. Coffee drunk, sandwiches being made for the morning break, the girls hurried to take their seats on the broad trailer of Shmulik's tractor that was going to drive them to work. Shmulik started the engine, and the air vibrated with its thunder. Esther's spirits began to rise. She had always loved to sit on the broad trailer behind the tractor and be driven down to the fields. She had been doing that for several years, and yet she loved the very monotony of it. Everybody there was brought up on A.D. Gordon's "Religion of Labor", and they loved the land and the work involved in its care.

Love made one's heart beat faster, senses sharper and it was a marvelous feeling, she thought as the tractor zigzagged its way down the hills.

There was another tractor on the other side of the road. "Hi, Esther!" Danny was calling. "Hi!" "See you!"

Esther was still waving her hand and smiling long after he disappeared behind the silo. The truck turned so that the sun was directly in her eyes, and she screwed them up, shading her brow as she took deep breaths of the pure morning air.

Shmulik's tractor was passing through the avenue of pungent-smelling eucalyptus trees, and was driving now to the vineyard. Esther looked dreamily at the site of the old well nearby, and thought that it must surely be dry by now. Danny had told her that many years ago the Bedouins had gathered round that very well to draw water for themselves and their thirsty flocks. She wondered at their indifference to the time and energy wasted by the crude methods they used to bring up the water from more than eighty feet down.

Using a battered, leaky oil drum at the end of a rope made of knotted pieces of old string, two of them would work with gently alternating rhythm, pulling up the rope overhand with a co-ordinated movement of the whole body until, nearly a hundred pulls later, a few capfuls of water were brought up at the end of this line. The tutor had explained one day that the Bedouins used to pour the few capfuls of water into clay jugs or black leather goatskins- the latter with the openings for the head, vent and three of the legs sewn up, the fourth acting as a pouring lip- for the womenfolk to carry away when they are filled, to water the flocks.

Now the tractor came to a halt, and Esther roused from her reverie. There was a lot to do in the fields!

Some time before noon Esther stood under a tree in the speckled shade to rest her aching back. The twin sisters approached her. She was taking off her head Kova-Tembel and mopping her wet face with it when Nira said, "Lucky it isn't hot today!" Her sister Nurit rubbed her back ruefully, "My poor back. It feels almost broken," she said.

Nira and Nurit had arrived at Degnaya several years before, having travelled from Poland on board an old ship. The kibbutz life appealed to them and they had decided to remain despite the repeated requests of their rich uncle, residing in Haifa, to join him. The twin sisters were orphans. Their parents had been exterminated in the concentration camps. Their uncle, who had managed to escape to America where he established himself as a wealthy Jew, arrived to Israel and bought a house in Haifa. The girls preferred to remain at the kibbutz. They looked so much alike, even their hair was worn in the same rather childish style, drawn back behind the ears. Esther had made friends with them since their arrival, and actually it was she who had suggested their Hebrew names. In Poland they were called Lilian and Julie.

"What do I hear?" Esther cocked her head on one side. They all listened attentively. There were shots! Three shots followed, and suddenly an airplane was seen in the sky over Semakh. Everybody stopped working. More shots. This time from the direction of Ein Gev, the settlement on the other side of the Lake, close to the Syrian border, at the foot of Mount Susita.

"It must be the Syrians," Nurit said. The girls resumed their work in the field, but the fear of war took away their high spirits. Esther thought longingly of Danny. The sun almost scorched her back. She had to discuss with him the meaning of the shots. He'd know. The heat made a little humming noise in her head.

"We're expecting a guest this evening," Nira said.

"Guess who?" Nurit added.

"Your uncle from Haifa." Esther replied indifferently.

"No. An old friend. You remember Yigal, don't you?"

"Of course, I do," Esther said. "What's he doing nowadays?"

Nurit shrugged, "He never says. Has no specific base. Since he left Deganya three years ago, he has been going from one place to another, doing odd jobs for the Haganah, the Palmach. He loves adventure, you see?"

"All I know is that he joined the Haganah at the time he left the kibbutz. I didn't know that he's still with them," Esther straightened her aching back.

"He volunteered. That's why he originally left the kibbutz," Nira said. "I can still remember that vow he had made on board the ship from Poland. He said he'd join the Hagana."

"Then why did he come to the kibbutz?" Esther showed some interest.

"Well, because he was so lonely. He was here a few months until he met some of the Haganah men and was able to fulfill his ambition," Nurit paused as she heard another burst of firing. The girls exchanged apprehensive looks.

The rest of the day dragged on just as any other day: Noon break, back to work; three o'clock break, four o'clock announced Shmulik's tractor; then back home to the showers, the giggling of the girls and shouts of the boys, Martha's obscene language and all the rest that hardly interested Esther, specially that day when fear of war was creeping inside her. She wished she could move to the twin sisters' room, but Tiqva and Simha wouldn't let her. They liked her.

Evening came. Danny's face bore a broad smile. His boyish looks reminded her tenderly of their sweet childhood for then when they were very young their relationship had been one of idyllic romance in which each pledged eternal devotion to the other. The years had not changed anything between them except that love had grown stronger and Ephraim, a boyhood friend of Danny's, had given up threatening to elope with Esther and carry her away to the jungles of Africa. He had transferred his affections to Dora long since, and they were soon to be married.

Hand in hand Esther and Danny stood by the dining-hall watching the bus coming along the winding road. Yoram used to drive the bus, the only transport from and to the city. Every evening at 7 o'clock the bus arrived with mail, passengers, newspapers, parcels and other surprises. That evening Yoram looked tired and worried. Esther had always liked his cheery smile, but that evening he handed the mail and the rolls of newspapers to Raphi without saying a word. "What's wrong, Yoram?" the old man asked.

"A big mess! Jerusalem is in great danger.." Yoram murmured half to himself.

Esther and Danny followed old Raphi to the dining-hall where he'd sort the mail in pigeon-holes in one corner. There was a piano at the far end, where Thelma was playing "Scheherazade" .. Children clustered around her admiring her diligent hands. Thelma had arrived from Romania a year before.

"There's no letter from Tammy, nor from Yehuda at Maale Hahamisha," Danny said. "Bracha and Yossi from Kiryat Anavim haven't written for over a month."

In the library hall everybody was listening to the news bulletin. Jerusalem was in great danger. Attack and invasion! They exchanged appalled glances. There had been over four months of continuous sniping, ambush and dynamiting, with steadily diminishing supplies of food within the boundaries of the city. The news bulletin went on to tell about the Syrians opening fire on Ein Gev, Massada and Shaar Hagolan. That was a blow to Deganya, only a few kilometers away!

"The oath of those who buried their dead at Kfar Etzion, the brave settlement in the south of Jerusalem, is our oath: Above their open grave we swear that we shall go forward!" a young man was saying. Danny turned his head to him and was surprised. "Look who is there!" The young man was talking to the twin sisters.

"Yigal, shalom!" Danny saluted warmly. "Shalom!" Yigal's voice was hoarse.

"Well! This is..." Danny turned to Esther.

"Of course! Esther! She's grown into a real beauty!" Yigal scanned her face with an admiring smile as he shook hands with her.

"Esther has always been a beautiful girl," Nira said generously, But Nurit's smile held a tinge of envy. Nurit had her hair bound up like a woman's, showing her long, white neck; her face, which was rather small, was deliberately serene, the chin held high, the rather full mouth primly closed. The very wide-apart green eyes, her most attractive feature, looked calmly at Yigal. She had put on a white, short-sleeved shirt and a blue skirt which set off her full breasts and slim waist while concealing rather broad hips. Her arms were long and angular like a child's.

"Nurit is jealous," Nira said.

"Why? No. Yigal is a friend, and I like him as such. Friends are not necessarily lovers!"

"But lovers are friends!" Esther said pressing Danny's hand in hers, and bestowing upon him a fond smile which he returned.

Yigal stood taller than everybody there. He led the group towards the dining-hall. "The situation is bad in Jerusalem.." he was saying. Esther studied the young man covertly and with interest. A tall fellow of twenty-three, massively built, big-boned, with long limbs and a magnificent breadth of chest. He was clean-shaven, his mouth was attractive and his face radiated Jewish light and warmth which you could also read in his eyes. He went on talking about Jerusalem before the British left, while she watched that inborn alertness about his face and posture. He wore a pair of tan shoes of the kind the Haganah (national defence forces – considered illegal and clandestine) used, hob-nailed and with half-circles of steel, like horseshoes, to protect the rims of the heels from wear. He also wore khaki trousers, a khaki shirt, the usual uniform of the Haganah. "Let's take our seats here," he said as he led the group into the dining-hall. Everybody was talking about war, shots, attack and whether war was inevitable. Esther was impressed by the way Yigal talked, self-confident, strong and self-assured. The twin sisters were asking him about his life with the Haganah, his obligations as a volunteer and his whereabouts. He spoke frankly and fearlessly. "That was a man who feared neither bombs nor fire." Esther thought without saying a word.

"Esther isn't saying a word," Yigal remarked with a smile. "She's too intent on her supper."

"O, no," she said. "There're some people who learn best by keeping silent." Danny laughed proudly.

The conversation returned to Yigal and his decision to remain with the Hagannah. "No, I shall not come back to Deganya. I have sworn to volunteer for the Palmach," he was saying. His eyes returned again and again to Esther until she became quite uncomfortable under his scrutiny. His mouth was moving in a slow pleasant smile as he talked, but his deep-set eyes were grave, and there was something almost possessive in his expressions. His speech drifted now to the mandatory power and how the Hagannah had been formed.

"The men were trained under cover of night. Girls, too. Anybody who could carry a gun." Yigal sipped his coffee. More youngsters stood by to listen to his moving and exciting stories about the siege of Jerusalem, the Hagannah tactics and the adventures that put many a life at stake. Yigal looked at his "class" with enthusiasm. He took out a cigarette from the pack he was holding in his hand, offered one to Danny and struck a match. "The girls don't smoke, I suppose." His eyes lingered speculatively on Esther as the cigarette smoke rose and made a thin curtain between them. Was she "all the girls" for him!

Yigal's stories were long and interesting. The group moved to the library hall where Yigal stood in the center and spoke eloquently about the situation before the British Mandate and after. He was aided by maps that hung on the walls and the youngsters listened with rapt attention.

"So this is what you've been doing over there!" Nira said.

"I've given my soul, my heart, my courage and valor for the Palmach. I'm happy I've done so. The journey is nowhere near its end yet. I must go back tomorrow morning. I'm needed there." Yigal surveyed the "class" solemnly. "The Hagannah are proud of their operations. They give code names to these operations," he explained.

"Israel is surrounded by enemies. The Galilee is in danger now. Deganya, too, is threatened." His words shocked the young people around him. "As an objective for the Arab forces, Deganya is an important one, being the gate to the Galilee," Danny put in. "It's our turn now to teach them a lesson," Ephi added.

There was a little ripple of laughter. "If we can!" Dora shouted.

"Either they march over us and take all the Galilee, or we stop them here. Right here, I say!" Yigal's grave voice had not altered. Esther remembered him as a young boy when he had arrived at Deganya a few years before with the twin sisters, and compared that boyish face with the brave man, his self-confidence and fearlessness.

...

That evening after leaving the twin sisters and their guest, Danny and Esther went for a walk through one of the settlement's many woodland areas. The strongest hindrance to many illicit love affairs is the fear of being found out. They, however, had no intention of keeping their passion a secret. "As soon as everything returns to normal I shall apply to Waadat Hashikun (housing committee) for a "family house"!" There were no words sweeter or more pleasant to Esther's ears.

On her bed that night she thought of Yigal. She was afraid of war. Yigal had known horrible days in Germany, but she hadn't, and she was frightened to death.

Just before she went to sleep she took out her diary and wrote:

> "Danny, I must tell you how very confused and afraid I am. It's all so sudden, this war! I have been thinking of Yigal. The very thought of him appeases me. He is not afraid of anything, anyone. He is ready to go to the front, and am sure that when he does he will still wear that smile on his lips. He has sold his soul to the Palmach. I think of him, and fear leaves me. How are we going to face war if it does come!? The thought terrifies me!
>
> I'm going to keep my diary with me always,
>
> Goodnight, my love."

...

YIGAL turned and tossed in bed that night. His limbs ached, and his brain was active, thoughts chasing round in his head like caged mice in a wheel. He had had a long and exhausting journey that day, almost five hours by bus, and now he was stuck here for who knows how long. Deganya was in real danger, and he wouldn't be able to leave, an invaluable member of the community as he was.

Sleep wouldn't come to his eyes. His story was different from Esther's or Danny's. The whole thing was coming back to him now before his mind's eyes as he lay on his bed. He tried to stifle it, to stop those memories of Germany, but they kept coming back, those bitter memories that refused to recede and scorned burial: It had all happened some ten years before: Germany.. 1937-38...Yigal was only twelve years old, a very happy child loved by his parents dearly. The best times at home for him were those nights when there were no visitors and the whole family would sit together round the fire. In 1938 many strange things began to happen that Yigal could not understand. People were afraid and spoke in whispers. There was wild talk, printed accusations and insinuations, boycotting Jewish businesses and public humiliations such as beating or beard pulling. The night terror of the Brown Shirts followed. Everyone was against the Jews. All the Jews had to wear a yellow armband wit the Star of David. In November 1938 Yigal was chanting from the Holy Book preparing himself for the Bar-mitzva.(ritual, celebration for a 13 year-old boy for becoming a man) Suddenly there was a knock on his door.

"Open the door. It is I, your father. Open quickly!"

"What's it, daddy? I locked myself in as you told me. No one can hear me."

"Come quickly. Your mother is already packing!"

"Packing? But, why?"

"You're leaving. Soon!"

"Where am I going?"

"Come here, boy. I've spoken to..." his father didn't know how to put it .."Well, Yigal, there's a secret society here which specializes in smuggling out German Jews. They call themselves Mosad Aliya (immigration institution) I've spoken to a Palestinian who is in charge of the escape. But I warn you, you must not breathe a word of this to anybody. Come with me. Your mother is packing your things." There was a tear in his father's eyes. "I'm going alone, daddy. What about Mommy and Grandma Rivka, and you?" Yigal choked back a tear as his father said, "There will be other nice children going along with you. Your mother and I will come later."

"I want to see Grandma Rivka first," the boy insisted.

"She's ill. She has to stay in bed."

"Daddy I must kiss her goodbye before I leave!"

"You can't see her. She had another heart attack last night, and the doctor..." Yigal burst into tears, and ignoring his parents' commands he ran upstairs to his grandma's room. "Your Yigal is here, grandma," he called and pushed the door open. There to his horror he saw the old woman lying dead in her bed, and flinging himself to his knees beside her bed he wailed aloud.

The train that took him to Berlin rumbled into motion. "Take this, your Bar Mitzva gift." His mother handed him a gold watch. There were anguished parents who called final farewells and departing children pressed against the windows shouting and blowing kisses and waving hands. Yigal wept bitterly as the train raced to Berlin. The figures of his parents grew smaller and smaller, till he could not see them any more among the crowd. The first few nights without them were terrible. He prayed fervently for them. So many tears he shed on that golden watch.

December 1939.. War in Europe. Poland crushed. Mosad Aliya had to speed up its operations concerning the children and refugees who had been smuggled from Germany. The Germans were already close to the borders, but somehow the children must be got to safety. March 1940.. Yigal and a handful of boys his age were smuggled from one place to another by train, by bus, by boat and on foot. April 1940.. The German army crossed the borders. Life was hard for the boys being shunted from one place to another, but it was much better than being in Denmark.

December, 1940.. A young Palestinian, a member of the Mosad, (office for private state security affairs –clandestine) approached Yigal with a written piece of paper. From his mother. She had been smuggled to Denmark. His father had to remain in Germany.

February 1941.. twenty boys and six girls, among them Yigal and the twin sisters, haggard and exhausted, hungry and weak, arrived at Haifa Port on an old ship loaded with cement. The waves that slapped against the shore were those of the Mediterranean Sea, and the high peak in the distance was that of Mount Carmel, they were told. Yigal and the girls were taken to Kibbutz Deganya. Yigal loved his new home. He learnt Hebrew, worked in the fields and in the kitchen. In the middle of 1941 all Denmark was occupied by the Germans, and during the ensuing months, which became years, he didn't hear a single word from his mother.

August 1943.. The Germans were furious with the Danes, and a fierce battle broke out.

October 1943..Sweden.. That was written on top of a letter, written by shaky hands and delivered to Yigal. She was safe, she wrote. It was cold, but she didn't mind. She missed him, but couldn't tell him anything about his father...

Yigal cried bitterly, and his friends, specially the twin sisters, Danny and Esther, were his only solace and comfort. Everybody wanted to make friends with Yigal.

May 1945.. The war was over.. Yigal wondered where his father could be? Was he still alive, or had he perished in the dreaded gas chamber. Or perhaps he had cheated the gas chamber by throwing himself on the quick mercy of electrified barbed wire. The boy imagined stacked-up emaciated corpses thrown into unmarked ditches, with logs placed between them and gasoline poured over them. He could imagine his poor father buried alive, or standing with other Jews in a row to be shot or strangled. He could see the Germans mutilating his body, boring holes in his head, pulling out his fingernails or gouging out his eyes, or swinging him naked on a pole. Yigal had many sleepless nights, and he discussed everything with Danny and Esther. They told him to forget, but would he?

Spring 1946.. An old ship zigzagged its way slowly, inching past treacherous reefs and shoals near the shores of Sdot Yam. On deck the refugees pressed themselves toward the rail chattering and pointing excitedly: They reached the Holy Land. Hundreds of Palmach soldiers waded out to meet the refugees, among them was Yigal's mother. The fishermen and the Palmachnicks worked quickly, taking some of the refugees into the village, and putting others into trucks which sped them inland.. Suddenly a piercing sound of sirens was heard, and the ear-splitting crackle of rifle fire. Many fled from the beach, but the soldiers worked faster than ever. It was the British, of course, and a fight started. Very few were hurt. Yigal's mother was slightly wounded. The next morning a message was delivered to him at the kibbutz that his mother was in the Holy Land at Atlit. That was in British hands. Later that night the Palmach staged a raid on the British camp, and many of the refugees escaped through a gaping hole blown in the barbed wire. There were casualties on both sides, and early the next morning the body of Yigal's mother was found among the corpses.

The few months he had spent at Deganya provided him with warmth and love which he had been denied since long. He made up his mind to volunteer for the Palmach, help defend and build the nation, join the clandestine army which was trained by stealth and in the dark. His love for Deganya hadn't killed his love for adventure. Eretz Israel was his family now. No, he couldn't forget his good friends, the twin sisters, Esther and Danny, and many others who loved to see him, talk to him and enquire about his whereabouts. There were times when he admired, liked, almost fell for and was really in love with Esther, but there was no way snatching her from her beloved Danny, or hurting his best friend's feelings.

...

DANNY tossed restlessly in his bed that night. He admired Yigal, and the way his character had developed through adventure, danger and sorrow, into one of total self-confidence and bravery. It was hard comparing those boyish, shy looks to the young man who had stood that evening and talked about the adventures of the secret army, the savior and main defense of Israel. His thoughts wandered to a distant day one early spring day some five years before. The tomatoes in the fields had begun to ripen. Yigal, the twin sisters, Danny and Esther were assigned to work in the vegetable plantations. The boys used to tease the girls, and when one of the girls bent over too far or wore her shorts too brief revealing a great deal of thigh, a boy would yell and pass it all over the field. One day Yigal introduced them to a new game. He called it "tomato slapping". One of the boys would slip up behind a girl and drop a small, juicy ripe tomato down the back of her shirt. When the tomato stopped, usually midway down her back, the boy slapped it good and hard, squashing the tomato and causing red juice to ooze through the cloth making a big, round stain. Nira got more tomato-slapping than any other girl, and she enjoyed it as long as it came from Yigal.

There was another memory. The girls had just finished picking a large quantity of tomatoes, and all they had to do then was to carry them in baskets to the packing shed. Danny and Esther started off side by side to the shed. It was hot and the slight breeze that had been blowing earlier had died.

Suddenly Yigal stole up behind them and dropped a juicy tomato down the back of Esther's shirt, and slapped it against her back. She screamed at the sudden shock, but then began to laugh. He, Danny, was furious. He could still remember why for a whole week afterwards he was not on speaking terms with Yigal. Yigal and Esther still thought it a great joke. They kept laughing about it, which made Danny more jealous than ever. How silly of him! That was no reason for jealousy then, was it? Did he have any reason to be jealous now, after so many years?

...

May, the seventeenth, brought bad news for the Arab Legion had gone into action against the villages of Sheikh Jarrach, and mounted an attack on Musrara. Worst of all was the news about Semakh, the town a mile or so east of Deganya on the southernmost tip of Lake Kinnereth. Intensive shelling forced the Jews to evacuate it and also give up two communal settlements to the south: Massade and Shaar Hagolan. The defence of the western shore of the lake and of the gates of the Galilee were hinged on the twin settlements of Deganya. Danger was creeping near and fast to the kibbutz. There was much work to do. The few rifles with armor-piercing bullets, and a number of various guns, were not enough for the settlers to defend themselves with. Home-made molotov bottles were being prepared, zigzag trenches were dug, bags of cement and leaves were placed in position to secure and camouflage them. Boys and girls, young and old, worked all throughout the night hand in hand. Yigal and Danny stayed up all night working with Uzi and under his instructions. There was no sleep, no rest, no time to think. All the boys were there, sleeves rolled up, foreheads beaded with perspiration, digging trenches or carrying sand bags.

Esther had a strange feeling. She was terrified. Apart from the physical danger she knew that war meant the end of her dreams about marriage and Danny. The number of patrolmen and watchmen had been increased and that meant that some kind of attack was certainly expected. Her heart almost stopped beating at the very thought of the next few days or hours!

Esther said her prayers that night, but sleep wouldn't come. She was satisfied that Yigal had stayed there. Anyway he had no way returning to his base in the South. The very thought of Yigal at home made her feel secure, yet desperately afraid of what might come.

...

News spread fast, but events even faster. Semakh fell. The Syrian attack was well coordinated and directed. There were commotion, worry, preparations, consultations and decisions to be made and taken. Degnaya had to act fast. As an objective for the Arab forces, the settlement was of great importance, for there was a bridge there spanning the river Jordan. If the Syrians could capture Deganya, the gate to Galilee, they would have a hold over the Jordan and the way would be open to Tiberias and Haifa, which is the heart of Israel. Not until the war began did the settlers of the Kibbutz really know exactly what it was all about.

During the previous couple of days Esther had only about ten minutes talk with Danny. She hadn't been able to write in her diary. The Syrians were advancing in force. Some settlers met them at a little distance from Deganya, but were beaten back to the village. In that engagement, which lasted an hour or so, Deganya lost sixty people. Among the dead were Benny, Martha's boy-friend and Shmulik, the tractor driver. Esther's grief knew no bounds as fear crept within her. When the Syrians stopped about two hundred yards from the settlement to rest and re-organize, the Deganyans hastily evacuated all the children and their mothers to Haifa. Yigal was a great help in that operation. Standing guard with his sten-gun over the departing women and children, he assisted the convoy to get through in spite of the shelling that was going on from the surrounding hills and the air raids. By some miracle he remained unharmed.

"You'll have to go with a delegation of elders to Tel Aviv to ask for help," Uzi said to Yigal.

That night there was no sleep for anyone. It was nearly dawn when the delegation came back from Tel Aviv. "The Government has no help to offer, "Abrashka, one of the elders, said.

"The people of Deganya must stand alone... fight for their lives," Yigal put it briefly and to the point.

May nineteenth... An unforgettable day. An assault on the twin Deganyas was begun, mainly by infantry supported by artillery. During the day, for the first time in the war, Israeli aircraft intervened in the battle, and by machine gunning and bombing managed to slow down the Syrian advance. The sweet smell of spring was drowned in the stench of war, of smoke, burning wood and high explosives. Reinforcements were scraped together and sent to the settlers of Deganya from Tiberias and Haifa, 65mm guns, Molotov cocktails, flame-throwers and guns.. Now it seemed doubtful whether the Syrians would resume their attack, but the whole of the settlement remained in readiness.

For the first time, since tension had begun, Esther met Danny in the Library Hall. Everybody there was close to exhaustion. The evacuation of the children and their mothers to Haifa, the preparations for self-defense, the digging of trenches and the fear of war, took their toll.

"Sarafand, which had been occupied by Iraqi irregulars after the British evacuated it, is now in Jewish hands," Yigal broke the good news. "A form of civic life is now returning to Jerusalem." Esther was jubilant with delight at the good news, and craved for more. "The newspapers say that street sweepers are about again, and postmen are delivering the mail there,"

Yigal's voice was warm and appeasing as ever. "Things seem to have calmed down in Jerusalem," he was adding. "I don't think the Syrians will attack us again!!" Everybody listened to Yigal as he spoke, and they clasped their hands happily.

Danny slipped an arm around Esther's waist and whispered, "If everything goes well, I shall speak to Dov about the "family house". By the palm trees, eh? You've always liked that spot!" She planted a loving kiss on his lips and they walked out of the library hall, down the lane to the dining room.

"I'm starving!" Danny kissed her and led her gently for supper. The dining-hall buzzed with life. Some were drinking for peace. A toast for the end of the war! Some were planning for the future, while others were busy with their supper. The battle must have aroused their hunger!

Danny was sipping his coffee when Yigal and Shmuel approached him. "Uzi wishes to speak to all three of us," Yigal excused himself. Danny gulped his coffee and cast a glance at Esther. "Right now!" Shmuel added.

Uzi Ben-Dor was considered one of the best-trained men of the Haganah. An officer in the party of the Haganna who had entered Syria in advance of the allied forces to gather information for the British during the World War 2, Uzi knew everything about arms illicitly required and clandestine training and war tactics. All those members who had served in the "fifth column" in those times became the nucleus of the Palmach, its "command arm". Uzi was such a one at Deganya, and Yigal went in his steps.

"Right now?" Danny asked. His heart sank, for he realized how serious the matter must have been.

"I'll be back. Stay here, Esther," he kissed her again. She tried to return the smile which he flashed, without much success.

Ten minutes later he returned to her, his face pale, eyes tired, mouth set in a grim line. Fear was clutching at her heart, and she was trying to utter a word.

"I'll be quite honest with you," he was saying as he took her hands and led her out of the dining-room. "The Syrians will attack again. Deganya is in great danger. If they win, we are finished.

"The whole Galilee is finished," she managed to say.

"But if we beat them, or trap them right here, they are finished!" Danny drew himself up to his full height and spoke with zest and self-confidence. Was he quoting Uzi or imitating Yigal!

"Will we?" she asked helplessly.

"We will!" his jaw tightened with resolve. "There will have to be more patrols, and our boys will have to take risky and adventurous steps within the enemy's territory, or close to the enemy's strongholds and posts.

"How?"

"Blessed be the God of Israel!" he said, and Esther murmured a fervent "Amen!"

...

There was no sleep that night in the settlement. Uzi was right. At half past three in the morning the Syrians attacked. This time with eight medium Renault tanks deployed across the fields facing the eastern fence of Daganya, and supported by some ten armed cars. The sten-guns which was the only weapon the twin Deganyas had were useful in street fighting and at short range, but of little use at distances over a hundred yards. Apart from these light arms, the settlers had nothing with which to defend themselves except their determination not to surrender.

Bullets sang through the trees like angry bees, lopping off small twigs and smacking into the bark. Heavy shelling began when Esther was on her way to the carpentry shed, with Laxie panting at her heels. A round shot crashed through nearby trees, a brutal chunk of steel smashing down branches in its passage. Suddenly she found herself full length on the ground, and as she lay there she heard a little fluttering sound, seemingly in the air overhead, but growing louder. It ended suddenly, and a hundred feet away in front of the gate the earth spurted up in a fountain, mixed with black smoke. Dirt rained all over the area. There was utter silence, then she picked herself up and ran quickly across the lawn opposite the "social hall". Near the fence she caught sight of Danny lying at the base of a tree with three others, David, Ephi and a third fellow. "Danny," she yelled. He turned his head, but before he could say a word, the fluttering, whining sound came again and again, and more shells fell in the field in front of them.

Any one of those shells, she thought, any one of those bullets might be for her, or for him. Shaking with terror, she flung herself down beside Danny.

"Send her away. It's dangerous here!!" Ephi cried.

"To the children's quarter. Hurry up. Make it, Esther!" Danny shouted. Clouds of dust almost concealed them from one another, and then came another shell, so near that it almost deafened her.

"Esther, you can't stay here," he said loudly.

"Find shelter somewhere. Quickly. Run. Now." Ephi urged.

"Esther, I love you." Danny's lips were caked with powder, his hands blackened and smeared with sweat and powder, his ears blocked with the whining noise of the shells.

"I want to stay with you." Esther clutched his arm.

"But..." There was another crash, and dust blew into Danny's face as a bullet thumped the ground in front of them.

"Esther, go away! Now!" his sudden fury brought tears to her eyes, but she had to obey. She walked quickly along the lane that led to the nursery and the children's houses, then she broke into a run. She heard a shot, and another. The noise was sharp and deafening. She began to tremble violently. Faint with terror, she took shelter behind an old shed. She was perspiring profusely, panting like a dog. Where was Laxie, she wondered. Suddenly she heard a noise behind her, quick gasping breaths.

"What're you doing here?" the voice startled her. She turned sharply, then went limp with relief as she saw the tall figure of Yigal, a molotov-bottle in his hand, and a sten-gun slung over his shoulder. "Why are you here?" he asked.

"I'm on my way to the children's quarter," she said.

"You should be taking shelter!" Yigal's face was grimy in the pink dawn light. What a lovely dawn it would be, without that ugly battle!

The Syrians were advancing in three columns, their planes screamed low over the roofs of the village. There was a sudden ear-splitting crackle of rifle fire. A plane was swooping over their heads. As Esther watched, rooted to the spot with fear, Yigal seized her hand and jumped with her into a nearby trench. They crouched deafened by the din of rifle and machine-gun fire. Then Yigal took his machine-gun and started shooting.

"You shouldn't be here, Esther," Yigal made use of the short lull.

"It's terribly dangerous!" His brow was beaded with sweat, his eyes red and tired. "Watch out!" he suddenly shouted, and pulled her violently lower into the trench. Then, when the firing ceased, they both climbed cautiously out and walked over to the fence.

They walked together. Near the outer fence of the settlement they heard a great rumbling and rattling.

"Syrian tanks!" Yigal warned. They crouched again. She crouched so close to him she could smell the sour sweat from his body.

The tanks were now only ten yards away from the fence nearest the lake, and the noise was terrifying. Suddenly he pushed her quickly behind him, and drawing back his arm, Yigal threw the molotov-bottle with all his strength.

There was an explosion, a burst of orange flame, and a rising column of smoke. Yigal blinked his eyes, threw up his arms with a yell of triumph. "I hit it!" he shouted frantically. "I hit the tank! The Syrians are retreating...."

Esther regarded him with tears of joy and pride. She remained in his arms for a while. There were tears of joy in her eyes.

The battle over Deganya ended there and then. The Syrians were pulling back.

That evening all the radios in the settlement blurted out the news! It was all because the Syrians had advanced in a hesitating, undecided sort of way. Animated discussions followed, and Uzi made his statement clearly and understandably, "Eight tanks arrived at the outer fence of the settlement. The first one, on the flank nearest the lake, was incapacitated by a molotov-bottle which hit its caterpillar chain. The third, which came to the help of the disabled ones, broke through the fence, reached the slit trench, seemed to hesitate and then slowly veered south as if to continue parallel to the trench. The tank at the head of the middle column crossed over the canal and the road, entered the garden - flattening the trees in its path - and made straight for the twin Deganyas." It was then that it was hit by two molotov-bottles, both thrown simultaneously from distances of twenty and ten yards respectively. One was thrown by Yigal, the other by Uzi a few yards away. As soon as the third tank began to burn while the first one milled around helplessly with its chain gone - the other six tanks veered round and trundled back towards Samakh. Two more of them were put out of action while turning. The attack was over, and they were never seen again.

"Now the Syrians know that Deganya is an impregnable fortress," everybody was proud and happy. Esther wrote in her diary:

> "I'm prepared to believe that our pioneers, who put up a firm resistance with their counter attacks, will help to recapture other settlements. One thing is certain: War is the maddest

thing men could ever have invented. It is all vile, brutal and absurd! What I saw today was incredibly evil and foolish, not to mention terrifying! Today I stood very close to death, and very close to the hero who threw one of the two molotov-bottles that put an end to the Syrian attack. I've the greatest respect and admiration for him.

Danny, my love, I pray that everything will be O.K. again and that we get married soon! I love you beyond words!"

...

The Syrians did not attack again, although there were air raids, and work was resumed in the fields and elsewhere in the kibbutz. Naturally most of the boys and girls were now scheduled for defensive preparations.

Not until noon did Esther hear from Nira about Yigal's departure. It was so sudden. A jeep had come early that morning to take him away presumably back to his base in the South. He left a note saying he would write, that he hoped he would not be away too long, and that in the meantime they should keep brave and cheerful. The note was addressed to the twin sisters.

Esther didn't feel in the mood to talk about anything. She was sorry, and her sorrow became stronger when Danny approached her with a letter that had arrived from Kiryat Anavim. It was from Tammy. "Gad is in hospital. He was slightly injured. There's no reason for worry. Keep well. Regards to Esther."

"It sounds more like a telex than a letter," Esther said. Danny looked up, his brow furrowed, his face full of grief. Gad was an old friend. Gad and Danny were like brothers. He had married a kibbutz girl, Tammy, and had moved to Kiryat Anavim three years before. "I don't believe that for a light injury one is hospitalized nowadays when each bed and every square meter is so badly needed!" he sighed.

"All we need is courage, Danny. And an unwavering faith in God," Esther tried to comfort. That night she jotted down a fervent prayer in her diary:

> "O, God, let there be peace! Let's hear the birds sing; the lake is the fountain of love that never dries. Let it flow smooth, O God! Danny, Esther, ever! And, O, God, keep a watchful eye on our boys, and see that Yigal come back to Deganya unhurt."

During the next few days a khamsin (hazy, vapoury weather) hot wind blew over the battlefield, and the stench was such that the Deganyans were afraid of pestilence. The Arabs didn't collect their deads, but the Deganyans did, and buried them all, villagers and Syrians alike. The bodies were carried in on carts, and buried in a communal grave, air raids there was not time to dig a grave for each one. In the days that followed Deganya was not attacked in force again, but the air raids continued, destroying and damaging many houses. There was scattered fighting, but no more heavy battles, and Deganya continued to stand guard over the valley. The burned out tank remained as a reminder of the bitterness of war. Lovers were not seen in the parks or under the trees carving on the barks of the trees or making love in secret or just walking hand in hand. "Will the old days come back?" Esther kept asking, and Danny had no definite answer for her. Gideon was now in charge of the tractor, but the girls did not go out to work every day, only when the Syrians did not send over an air attack. Boys were not sent to the groves and orchards, being more useful in other fields that required heavy work. Girls over sixteen, too, were given rifles and sent to patrol the boundaries of the village like guards instead of working in the fields and vegetable plantations.

Dora's mother, Hephziba, was now the nurse replacing Hana who had been killed a few days earlier. It was good to see the motherly, efficient little woman moving quickly around the dining hall, which was turned to "first-aid and casualty station", performing minor treatments, dressing a wound or giving injections. She worked under Micha, a retired doctor. Micha had managed to escape when the Nazis began putting the Jews into camps. On his arrival to Deganya Micha would no longer practise medicine, protesting that he was too old. He preferred working outside in the fields, poultry quarter or the silo, but in those days of skirmishing before the war, when casualties were brought in from the fighting, he returned to his profession, and now he was No. 1 at the first-aid station.

A few days after Yigal's departure there was another air raid. Several houses were destroyed, specially those on the borders of the kibbutz, those that belonged to new families. Two people were also killed, a boy and a girl. The girl was Yudith, only eighteen. She and Esther had been standing side by side, each with her rifle, a few yards away from the laundry shed, when Yudith was hit by a steel splinter. She fell against Esther, splashing her with blood. The dead boy was Arye. His father, Micha, was busy with Hephziba in the "casualty station" when his son was brought in, wounded and unconscious. Arye died only a few minutes later, and the shock broke down the old man's health. A few weeks later Micha, too, was dead!

The night Yudith was killed Esther did not sleep a wink, but wept like a child all night long, trembling and sobbing with shock. She longed to be with Danny, tell him about it, feel his strong arms around her, but he was on duty and she had to face it alone. "Be brave, Esther. Take things as they come. Remember the words: ..They that sow in tears shall reap in joy.." Yigal's voice almost deafened her.

...

For the past week work had returned almost to normal. There had been less air raids, and the man and young boys

71

worked hard to remove the debris of houses destroyed in previous raids. Only a couple of days before, Danny and Gideon had had a narrow escape from death. They had been sorting the belongings of a friend who had been killed when a bomb fell just outside. They were buried under debris, but Uzi and two other boys dug them out.

Since May 20th Esther had not written a single word in her diary. The few minutes she could snatch for herself were either spent with Danny or in resting wearily on her bed. Now that the scattered fighting had ceased it was possible to catch up on outdoor work. There was a great deal to be done in the fields, orchards, plantations, groves, almost everywhere; and what more, many defences had to be strengthened against further possible attacks.

When Gideon drove the girls to the fields there was no more singing or hand-clapping. Life had become a solemn thing, and gaiety and laughter were things of the past.

It was June in Deganya. A new day. The sun shone brightly and the air was warm. The weeds frayed and edged back towards their roots, wilting in the dry, thirsty ground. Every moving thing lifted dust into the air; a walking man left a thin rising layer, a wagon lifted the dust as high as the fence tops, and an automobile boiled a cloud behind it. Once disturbed the dust took a long time to settle.

Work over, Esther hurried to take her shower as usual, then hastened to the park to meet Danny. She walked slowly, deep in thought, glad of the chance of spending a few minutes all by herself. She was acutely aware of the beauty around her as she penetrated deep into the woods. At the agreed meeting place, enclosed by leafy undergrowth, she sat down on a soft bed of pine needles. She could feel the existence of living creatures all around her: birds, insects, small secret animals going their own way unseen. There were damp, aromatic smells, and the silence, total and penetrating, was almost like a living thing. She turned round several times thinking she had heard the footsteps of someone behind her - and then from behind the uneven trunks of the great trees Danny appeared. "Hello, darling!" he flung himself down beside her kissing her quickly on the mouth. The sunshine seemed to tighten its clutch on the earth, whitewashing the pathway leading to the forest where it was splendidly cool and fresh. The blue density of the air, the corrugated, soaring columns of the trees, the damp, pungent smell and the half-sensed knowledge of life around them, filled them with delight as Esther and Danny lay close to each other. "To the one who is my ideal for all that's beautiful in the world," Danny's voice recited while his strong, sinewy hands were round her waist. "What's that, Danny!" she chuckled.

"It's the dedication for my book," he sounded serious. Danny had submitted his book which he had been writing for several good years for publication just before the war started. "I'm indebted to you, Esther, for you taught me all that's beautiful and happy in this world and this life," his words were low and heart-born. He looked her into the eyes, and added, "Esther, I've an idea. A truce seems certain nowadays. We'll go ahead and make all the necessary arrangements for our marriage. Traditional wedding, as you have always desired. O.K.? We'll put in an application for a family home. How's that?"

"Glorious, Danny! Terrific!" Their eyes met. "But," she added after a short pause. "I wish to fulfill my mother's request. She had always wanted and dreamt of a wedding celebration in a synagogue in Jerusalem. The holy city of the holy land, she would say! I was too young to understand what made her want that badly. I must fulfill my promise to her." Danny's heart was beating on her breasts as he drew her closer and kissed her. Her eyes were now flooded with tears. Recollections came thrusting in upon her, and she couldn't resist, he guessed.

Esther's parents had been among the first pioneers who had built Deganya and breathed life into it. In those days they had only one son, called Yaron, and at the age of ten, when the mother was in the sixth month of her second pregnancy, the lad died of malaria. The loss had been very great - too great for the father to bear. Two months later, he died of a heart attack, and a month later the mother gave birth to a beautiful baby whom she called Esther. That was in 1930. As the child grew up, her mother told her everything about her father, her brother Yaron whom she had never seen or known. She also told her that she, Esther, was very much like her father; the same shape of nose and mouth, the same small, round chin and long dark eyelashes. The little girl would hold her father's photograph and gaze at it for hours trying to see for herself the resemblance her mother had spoken about. When she was thirteen Esther lost her mother in 1943, She was buried in the cemetery of the kibbutz, but before her death she had asked her daughter to be a "good" girl, and to stay "good" till her wedding night. The child had been clever enough to understand what "good" meant to her mother. And then on her deathbed the mother had uttered only three words: Marriage, synagogue and Jerusalem.

"Please, don't cry! I'll make you happy!" Danny shared her feelings. Comforted, she dried her tears and flashed a smile, "I'm sorry, dear," she apologized for spoiling their precious time together.

There was good news over the radio that evening. People gathered to read the papers that had arrived with the bus. There were reports about Egyptian naval vessels being beaten off by Israeli naval forces. There was also heartening news from Ramat Rachel and rumours about the Old City getting liberated. Was the reporter raising his hopes too high or was it real?

The war had changed everything, except Friday evenings!

Saturday was always a special day, so the Friday evening meal was special, too. It was usually more elaborate than the weekly evening meal, and the tables in the dining hall were covered, unlike the rest of the week when meals were eaten off the bare wood. Every place was taken, and more chairs and benches had to be brought in to seat the incomers, because of addition of city friends, of members of the settlement who worked in the city and returned on the Sabbath, and of kibbutz youths who served in the army and had received week-end passes. There was a perceptible change in the spirit of the group at the Friday evening meal, and afterwards there was usually a lecture or a concert with the pleasant knowledge that there was no need to rise early the next day.

Danny was holding Esther's hand under the table when the twin sisters entered the hall with Gideon and Simha. The four took their seats at the same table of Danny and Esther. Nira broke the news that a letter had been received from Yigal. It bore no address, but he wrote about the Burma Road, about a wound he had got in his right arm, about the Hagana, now called the Israel Defence Army. He also wrote that he was happy at hearing good news from Deganya. "And that's not all," Nira added with a mischievous gleam in her eye, "he sends his regards to Danny and his girl-friend. Tell that girl to keep smiling, she looks much better with a smile on her face, he says!"

"Gosh! Stop it!" her twin sister sipped her coffee.

...

On Sunday Danny got a favorable reply from Dov of the housing committee. There was a common room with a kitchenette and private toilets ready for the couple. They would get the key on their wedding day.

June 30th: the last of the British troops left, and Ben Gurion cried, "Good riddance! Today ended a chapter of deceitful and false rule. If peace does not come we are ready for war..."

July 8th: ..Summer clamped down upon the settlement of Deganya with a heat so intense that there was no air to breathe. The whole kibbutz, with its fields and orchards, was stifling, and a drought settled over the already thirsty land. The so-called "khamsin" sucked all day long like an obstinate leech, and workers had to seek shade several times a day to avoid sun-stroke.

Right after work Esther rushed to take a shower. She wrapped a towel around herself and emerged dripping from the bathroom, and was still drying herself when a bunch of girls came in. Martha was panting like a dog. Esther stood soaking wet in the draught. The heat made her head spin, and she made for her room, almost staggering under a sudden wave of fatigue, and fell in a disorderly heap on her bed. The air in her room lay inert and stale. She was utterly exhausted. After a while she rose, walked over to the dressing-table and gazed into the full-length mirror. Strange, she thought dreamily, how much time you can spend studying your face, and yet still scarcely know it. She saw her nose, short and straight; her blue eyes; her mouth, the upper lip thin, almost prim, the lower one full and sensual, red with the blood of youth. The lock of hair she was combing across her high forehead was blonde, but the rest of her hair, still damp, fell in chestnut waves over her baked shoulders.

Suddenly she felt under scrutiny. She glanced into the right hand corner of the mirror and there she caught Danny's eyes upon her. She turned, her face lighting up with gladness.

"Come in, Danny," she called to him. He was standing in the doorway, tall, broad-shouldered and handsome. He didn't move, and she felt a sudden chill of fear.

"Anything wrong?" she asked curiously, her comb still on her hair. He walked slowly towards her, took her in his arms and rested his cheek against her hair. "Esther," he said gravely retaining her hands in his. "I was on patrol today."

"Patrol?"

"Menachem said that he, Yehuda and I had been assigned for patrol today, so we went. All along the shores of the lake, close to the borders. All three of us loaded on a jeep with molotov-bottles, rifles and jerry-cans of water and petrol. We left early this morning. Three o'clock. Before dawn!" His speech was broken. He sounded horrified.

"How could you? Why didn't you tell me last night?"

"I didn't know. It was sudden. Now, Esther. Listen. We discovered several mines along the coast, and on the road that forks from the main road leading to Deganya Beth, also on the road to Shaar Hagolan and the neighboring settlements. I say, I'm horrified by what I saw. Everybody is on guard. Many other armed jeeps patrolled the area, officers and military forces from Ein Gev, Tiberias, Capernahum. It seems that a day and night vigilance is being kept in this area. Matters aren't so quiet as I imagined. Fishermen at Ein Gev told us that they are being shot at every day. The Arabs will attack again."

"Will they?" Esther's face paled.

"We saw a jeep driving along the coast towards Ein Gev. It ran over a mine and blew up, killing all four patrolmen."

"God Gracious!" the comb fell from her hands and she drew closer to Danny.

"On the way back an enemy machine-gun suddenly opened fire on us. Bullets whined all around. Only by miracle we managed to come back safe."

"Danny..." there was a short pause before she continued. "Must you go again tomorrow?"

"If not the three of us, others will have to go. Menachem will surely notify me late this evening."

Esther drew a shuddering breath. "You always say God is on our side. I must keep on believing." Her breath mingled with his in the short span between their lips. She looked at him, then slowly lowered her lids. The gesture was one of sadness and surrender, the lowering of a human being's flag. In a rush of fear, tenderness and deep love she flung herself into his arms and began to cry.

"We can't take the trip to Jerusalem," his voice was low and feeble. "Every inch of Israel is a battle-field now. Can we have the ceremony in a synagogue in Tiberias?"

"Danny, O, my darling, but of course!" Esther raised her eyes to his. He had sounded like a boy asking permission from his mother to play with the other boys.

The girls were already approaching their room, back from the showers, their wooden sandals went clickety-click-click on the stone floor, raising little sharp echoes. Danny gathered her in his hands.

There was a talk that evening in the dining-hall about the disaster of the jeep that had gone over a mine. More news poured in as soon as the bus arrived at the usual hour.

Esther wrote in her diary that night:

> Danny, dear. I don't want to think of it, but as I confide in this diary and I know that neither you nor Yigal will clap eyes on it, I feel I have to make this confession: I am afraid. Again. Afraid. Fear is creeping inside me once again. I feel like a crippled soldier. I try to keep cheerful as Yigal told me to, but I smile only to conceal my fear. I'm a coward, and I don't want Yigal to know it. I'm afraid of war and its consequences. O, God, how I love you, Danny!
>
> Esther..ever!

...

"Not all news is bad. I've some good news for you. My book was accepted for publication. My dedication will appear on the flyleaf!" Danny boasted joyfully.

"Terrific!" she responded.

"How was work today in the fields?"

"We spend four hours in the fields, and after lunch we go to make more molotov-bottles under the supervision of Arie Alouf, Uzi and Katz. I'm fed up. I yearn for the good...."

Danny wasn't paying much attention to her. He was thinking of how to put what he had to say. "You see? Tomorrow Menachem, Yehuda and I will be on patrol." He stopped to see the effects of the shock on her. "I mean...."

"Patrol? Again?"

"Yes. But the day after tomorrow I'm going to have a couple of days off to take the trip to Tiberias and get married," he broke the news. "Two days off! With Saturday make three!" "Two days with Saturday make three!" she repeated after him. Leaning over her Danny became suddenly still, his gaze fixed on her throat. There are moments when a humble being, a human being, has not the power to retain moments of ecstasy, to restrain his desires. Danny felt weak as he kissed her, trembling so violently that he felt her breasts quiver like twin flowers and her whole being stir. He drew her to him and held her, panting, fainting away with the desire within him. Her body was no longer hers; so lucid had it become, full of resonances, blood, warmth and appeal, a body as sensitive as a soul, a body she was willing to give for him, so that she too had no control over her desire. She was full of joy as she listened without stirring to the deep throbbing of his heart, and she came to know him better through the regular pulsing of his blood, the twisting of his arms around her and the warmth that passed between them. They lay beside each other, breathing in unison, and the girl entrusted her entire being to him. Yes, the living have no way of expressing the truth to each other, other than through the flesh, she thought with wonder. A miracle was taking place. It was real love, the one so well known by adults, no longer a childish infatuation. She wanted to spread at his feet the infinity she held within her, the fact that she needed him. She felt his whole presence around her like a thousand arms, so that to love was to think perfection, light, truth. He murmured in her ears, and the words flowing from his mouth warmed her with their generous wine; the love he poured forth made her rejoice and forget the worries that had preoccupied her.

At last he was silent. She thought perhaps he had fallen asleep. No, his eyes were staring straight ahead. "What're you thinking of?" she asked fondling his tousled dark hair. "I think you dozed in my arms, darling."

"I was just thinking..." he went on whispering to her as he walked with her, steering her to a dark corner in the woods. They walked for a while slowly through the trees, and she showered upon him all her love and affection. A blow seemed to strike her bowels; abruptly she tightened her fingers, and all her muscles became tense. An evil fear made her shiver, and Danny raised his face to look at her. She had never seen him look so sad. His features were stern, his eyes swimming with tears. "What's wrong, Danny? You are keeping something from me."

"Everyone has his weak moments. I'm afraid to lose you. I'm so afraid. Sometimes you seem only an image, a picture disappearing into the darkness of night. I stretch my hands, and the image disappears. I call, but in vain!"

"You sound so frightening, Danny!" she hugged him like a mother. "O, please, let's go into the open. Let's get away from here." She clung to his hand, and led him towards the fading light that still glowed through the trees. The houses of Abrashka, Dov and the elder members of the kibbutz stood just within sight. The moon, a half crescent, came and went from behind scudding clouds. The earth smelt fresh and wet beneath them, a warm breeze fanned their cheeks. His hands gently caressed hers until suddenly there was light from the moon above, and a feeling of shame came upon her as she saw with her own eyes the nakedness of her thighs and breasts. She lay motionless close to him, afraid of being watched, but when it became dark again and the moon disappeared behind the clouds, she forgot her fears. The two of them moved and breathed heavily in the intoxication of the pleasures of the flesh. They felt swallowed up by secret darkness where passion was scarlet and nothing existed save arms, lips and naked flesh.

She was going to say to him "the wrong you are doing" but it seemed too severe a sentence to use, and she didn't say it. Her voice reached him from behind the mask of her hands like a fabulous sound that hopelessly betrayed, still more than pity, the anguish of renunciation, and with it the balm of sweet gratitude.

...

That night she tossed and sighed in bed. Her head was heavy with thoughts that jostled in her brain, and all sorts of dreadful contingencies and possibilities began to lurk around her, filling the darkness of the room with fears and ghosts that had no names, and forms that had no shape. They had to get married soon. There was no time to waste. She had committed her soul and body to Danny, and did not regret it, but now he moved inside her, and was in her blood. She knew she might well be in trouble, and longed for someone to confide in; a fond mother who would listen and forgive, for instance. There were many skeins she had to disentangle in that little head of hers, and sleep would not come. How natural that his seed should be growing inside her body; and yet only marriage could save them from cruel gossip - and the sooner the better! Sleep at last came, but thoughts lingered heavily. Some time before dawn the other girls in her room were awakened by a sobbing and bitter crying which seemed incessant.

"Wake up, Esther. It's only a dream!" Simha called as she slipped out of bed.

"She's having a nightmare, the poor thing!" Tiqva approached her with a glass of water. Martha started removing the quilt from Esther's perspiring body.

"O, God! What a horrible dream!" Esther murmured heavily. Her wide-open eyes were wet and looked dazedly about the room as though looking for someone who was supposed to be there. Slowly she became fully awake, and lay trying to reconstruct the dream, most of which now eluded her. She took a sip of water and her looks lingered on the photograph of Danny which stood on her dressing table just opposite her bed. For a moment terror seized her, and the dream came back to her as though it were real. The face in the photograph looked back at her, smiling. She pushed back the sheet and got out of bed, the girls watching her in silence as she walked slowly towards her dressing table, took the photograph in both hands and kissed it. She held it before her, gazing at it for a while, then turned it over and read the inscription, "Danny.. Esther. ever!" She put it back on the table, and mumbled a few words which none of the girls could understand. She behaved like a somnambulist. "I'll stay with her. Go, girls, go to sleep!" Tiqva said. "It's fun watching the stars and the milky way at this hour!"

Esther stood motionless, holding on to the window frame with both hands as she gazed up at the twinkling stars. The horror of the nightmare still haunted her, and she felt oddly unreal.

The light was put out and the girls went to their beds. Tiqva and Esther stood side by side watching out of the window. All nature was resting. Nothing could be heard save the lowing of a cow in the barn, the bellow of a restless bull or the plaintive cry of a lamb for its mother. Esther could still hear the receding thunder of a distant train whose passing had echoed in the eastern valleys of her sleep. The lone shriek of its whistle at the crossing had been like the calling of Danny's name. The sound of its ebbing down grey lanes of dawn was like music, awakening memories of things they had done together. She wanted to follow the whistle down the mystic river of the years, back to the gates of time, the beginning of herself, to trace a tangled thread of life to the sources of its origin.

"Are you all right, Esther?" Tiqva dared ask. "Whatever were you dreaming about to upset yourself so?"

"I don't want to talk about it." Esther was real again.

"It's better if you do!" Tiqva urged, sounded quietly insistent. At first Esther hesitated, but then she began to speak in an almost inaudible voice: "I was playing the piano in the big dining-hall. 'Twas late. Nobody was there. My mother's house was next to the dining-hall. She was ill and had to rest. But I had an irresistible urge to play. Suddenly the door opened and in came mother. She reproached me for disturbing her, but I went on playing with an intensity and pleasure I had never experienced before. Like kissing or making love! My fingers danced over the keys, and my heart danced with every tune they played, and all the walls seemed to shake and throb with life. The piano, strange as it was, seemed to grow bigger and bigger, so huge that the whole dining-hall was filled with it; the sort of thing one feels only in dreams. When I had finished I smiled and raised my eyes to mother. "That was for Danny! I had to play for him." Mother's hand rested on my shoulder, "You must be sick. There's no Danny here." Her face looked very old and wrinkled, like dead.

"Mother," I said, "Danny is here. He comes every night to hear me play for him. I must play for him till dawn!" I insisted.

She looked at me. I was frightened. She pleaded, "Esther, don't ever come here to play anymore. He won't come. You are only disturbing him as you disturb me. He is asleep. I am going back to bed. To sleep. He, too, has gone to sleep. He'll never come to hear you play for him. "I was so afraid, but I was sure he was there. I could see his image reflected on the polished surface of the piano, like an ordinary medallion portrait. "Mother, see!" I called, but when I raised my eyes to her, he disappeared. I was so sad, mother stooped down and kissed me, "Esther, don't cry over spilled milk. He's gone!" Her voice echoed in the room. "He's gone!" I looked around but she wasn't there, neither was he. I became terrified, ran about the room, but the doors and windows had disappeared, and I couldn't get out. I beat my hands against the walls, but neither mother nor Danny heard me.." Esther's eyes were fixed on a twinkling little star up above in the sky. She allowed herself to be led back by Tiqva to her bed.

...

She couldn't wink an eye, and went back to the window to watch the dawn planting a foot.

"Danny! Danny!" Esther called at the top of her voice as she leaned over the window-sill. The girls thought she had gone mad, or perhaps they were dreaming; but as they approached the window they saw in the distance a jeep. At the wheel was Menachem, and two other boys were loading their rifles while two elderly men were talking to them.

"Abrashka and Pessah are fixing some stuff into the back of the jeep!" Simha put in. "Yehuda and Danny are getting on." Esther was almost ready to jump out of the window, run down the lane across the garden, and out onto the winding lane that led to the gate to talk to Danny; but by the time she reached them they would be gone. Her heart ached with longing as she watched them get on the jeep. Danny was wearing his blue shirt and khaki trousers. "Danny!" she called again, and the engine was already ticking over. The jeep jerked forward, and just before it reached the gate Menachem turned his head and saw the girls at the window. He nudged Danny, and the latter began to wave his hand frantically. He blew a kiss to Esther. Her eyes blurred but she managed to blow back a kiss. "God speed! Good luck, boys!" she managed to say. There were a million things she wanted to say, but her tongue cleaved to the roof of her mouth, and the tears choked her. "Shalom!" Off drove the jeep. The two elderly men walked away. Dawn was beginning to break. The girls were already getting ready for work. Esther was the last one to leave the window. The early sunlight had a reassuring effect, and her night-time terrors took wing and flew away. Just as she was leaving her room she noticed a note pinned on the door. It read:

> "Esther, dear, we are going out early this morning. I presume we shall be back around six o'clock. The whole evening will be ours. And then, Esther, two days leave - with Saturday they make three. Dov promised a nice 'family house' for the young couple! I shall think of you all the day, till we meet again, All my love. Danny.."

She kept the note in the breast pocket of her blue shirt, and read it several times that morning. The late summer sun was scorching, but despite the heat Esther's mind was very active. When she thought of marriage she smiled to herself, but when suddenly she remembered that horrible dream she felt on the verge of crying. Afternoon was drawing on lazily. Work over, Esther ran to take her shower. Being third in line for the bathroom, when her turn came the water was only tepid. Quite O.K. for that season of the year. She had mixed feelings of sorrow and happiness. She had never been so excited before. Hadn't they met every day? Why the excitement, she couldn't tell herself. She hastened to her room. First she tidied up her things, then she ironed her Sabbath shirt for the evening, wore fresh, clean clothes. "Two days off! With Saturday they make three! What a holiday! A honeymoon!" She had a feeling of health and well-being as she walked out of the room along the curved lane of eucalyptus trees, her eyes fixed on the highway beyond the gate. Any minute the jeep would be in sight! Her excited breaths, the emotions in her breast, beat against one another like birds in a cage struggling to get free.

The road was empty, swept by the sudden summer wind, and she almost sobbed with frustration. She could not bear the thought of returning to her room and waiting for Danny there. The walls would close up on her like a prison. She took a perverse pleasure in the biting wind of evening that blew through her thin shirt as if the discomfort night hasten Danny's return. The very roadway was in need of repair, and the dead leaves that no one troubled to sweep up rustled hither and thither in the gusts of the wind. She might as well walk back to the gate where she could stand and watch for the jeep. Any minute Danny would show up, jump off and take her in his arms, swing her off her feet and embrace her lovingly. Her head sang with imaginings as with swinging step she returned to the gate. Like a swarm of birds a hundred thoughts flew about her head. Her imagination clothed the russet branches with tender green, and in her happiness the sky turned to red. The day was declining and the lowering clouds seemed to shut out the light. Back to the gate of the settlement. It was nonsense to walk and walk along the road to meet the jeep. Her feet led her towards the dining-hall, the social center where everybody was waiting for the bus. She was nibbling her finger nails - a bad habit she could not break, which became worse under stress. The words that reached her ears sounded broken and meaningless: Syrians .. attacks..war..casualties.. curfew.. borders.. border police..patrol.. She was biting her finger nails nervously. Fear was rising and a dreadful premonition clutched at her heart.

Was it getting late, or her watch might have been running fast? She walked to and fro, anxious, afraid, nervous; and waiting was like a death endured over and over again. There was the kibbutz-bus creeping down the lane in sight. When it arrived at long last the driver was questioned as to whether he had seen or heard anything about the patrol-jeep that had left early that morning. He shrugged his shoulders and his face, like all other faces, was disturbed. Esther was unable to control herself. She crept about as pale as a ghost from one place to another, her ears willing to hear but words wouldn't leave her choked throat!

It was the end of summer. The shadows of tree-trunks and plants had already lengthened, and the colors were soft and fresh. Two months before, the settlement has still been aflame at the same time in the afternoon. The days had shortened since then. Summer would be soon over!

...

A few kilometers away a patrol-jeep was driving fast on a lonely road along the coast of the Kinnereth, between Ein Gev and Deganya. "Faster, Menachem; it's getting dark!" Yehuda was saying. "We're late. We shouldn't be here at this hour!"

"That blasted mine!" Danny added with a grimace. "If we hadn't stopped to remove it we'd have been home by now!"

Just before sunset the three boys had detected a mine along the coast and had also seen footprints. It had taken them half an hour to remove it and trace the footprints. Now they were thinking how they'd boast it at home! Suddenly there was a rifle shot from the direction of the Syrian territory on the other side of the lake. "What's that?" Yehuda shouted, his finger tightened on the trigger of his rifle. "Menachem. Faster, for Heaven's sake!"

"I'm already doing over a hundred and ten!" Menachem at the wheel retorted. The jeep edged to the coastal side closer into the Israeli territory. He was wrestling with the steering wheel. Another shot was heard. On they roared along the lonely dark coastal road leading home. They were now less than a kilometer away and it was nearly dark. Another shot was heard. Closer now! "There's an Arab ambush somewhere round here, boys," Danny said, and right then he felt Yehuda's head on his shoulder. Something warm splashed his hand. It was blood. "Menachem!" he shouted supporting Yehuda as best he could - but before he could reply Menachem himself was shot in the throat and fell on the wheel. The jeep swerved violently. Danny seized the wheel and somehow steered the vehicle to a halt on the stony shore. He jumped out ready to defend himself and his friends, but had only fired two bursts of his machine gun when he himself was shot in the stomach. He fell, raised himself on his hands and knees and crawled, panting, gasping along the shore leaving a trail of blood. After only a few yards, however, his strength failed and he collapsed, his life's blood oozing away into the shingle.

Two Arabs ran hastily to the spot, carried the three corpses to the edge of the lake and flung them in, got into the jeep and roared off across the border to the Syrian territory. There was a brook of blood as the three dead boys sank slowly into the shallow water at the edge of the lake. The smell of the trampled grass filled the cool night air. A half moon glittered overhead and the moonlit, glassy lake was as peaceful and serene as ever. Soon the bloodstained water cleared and all was as before - except for the silent, huddled presence of Yehuda, Menachem and Danny.

...

At a little before midnight three command cars with Uzi, Zalman and five other boys from Deganya, together with a police command car armed with sten-guns and equipped with molotov-bottles, flash lights and mine-detectors, drove out of the kibbutz gate to begin an all-night search for the lost jeep. Motorboats and patrol boats combed the edges of the lake; but nothing was found!

Towards morning when they were driving from Tel-el-Qasr towards Deganya Uzi noticed some footprints. He stopped his car, got out and motioned to the others to follow him. The prints led along the coast towards the Syrian border. "Syrian infiltrators!" he said. "Planting mines. A cowardly way of fighting! Savages!"

"But I don't think mines or explosive charges are involved," Zalman put in. "If they were, surely we'd have found the remains of the jeep."

"There's no sign of any debris," added Dori; and just then Uzi, who had been walking along the shore looking into the lake, gave a sudden cry, "My God! Look there!"

There was an appalled silence; then one by one, the sodden, pathetic corpses were pulled from the water..

It was late after midnight. The stars were beginning to fade as a new dawn was planting a foot far beyond the horizon. The cars bearing their sad load, their shame, their most-beloved loss, drove into the settlement.

The first rays of the sun shone on the notice-board just at the entrance of the social room, the dining-hall, a black ribbon framing the board. The notice read:

> "Haverim, friends! Our sons: Danny, Yehuda and Menachem, have been found - dead!"

All the settlement was in mourning that day, and the evening papers published this:

> "Death at midnight! Recent casualty lists released by the War Department include the names of Danny, Yehuda and Menachem, killed in action. All three are from Kibbutz Deganya. They were shot dead while on patrol some distance from Tel-el-Qasr. Footprints along the coast led to the Syrian borders and traces of infiltrators were found. The jeep in which the three boys drove was spotted in Syrian territory.
>
> Readers will remember the budding writer, Danny, whose first book was published only recently.
>
> Service for the dead will be held at the kibbutz cemetery."

....

The next morning Esther awoke to find herself in bed. She could not remember how she got there. She learnt later that she had been given a sedative and put to bed by her sorrowing, sympathetic roommates. Her head felt heavy yet empty, and after a moment the sickening memory flooded in "..Danny .. was no more!" A nurse was sitting by her bed keeping watch. She was laying a hand on Esther's forehead, "Lie still. You need rest!" she was saying "I know, Hephziba," Esther uttered. "He's dead!" Her heart had to burst with anguish, or she would burst! The nurse looked at her with pity and love, but before she could speak Esther burst into tears: "Leave me alone!" she sobbed. The nurse went on patting her, talking to her, but all Esther could hear was silly, meaningless words: something about "sacrifice", "patriotism", "homeland", "martyr" "Jewish cause", "fate", etc... No, she wasn't a child anymore, to be appeased by a chocolate bar or honeyed words. "But you must try to understand!" Hephziba insisted.

"That's the trouble, I don't understand!" and she burst into another fit of crying. Esther thrust her legs out of bed and tried to stand. Lifting her feet was like trying to lift tombstones, but somehow she dragged herself to the window to lean her forehead on the cool pane. She felt dizzy, and turned crying out in panic; then, before Hephziba could reach her she crumpled to the floor.

Hephziba coaxed her to bed, and there she collapsed, a black cloud descending over her whole being. Now she could think! Fate was so cruel, she thought. Death so harsh and final! She wondered if God had shaped Danny's life from the beginning in that dark frame. She had once seen a man drowning in a river. She had been eleven years old. She remembered the police pulling him out of the water - Arab boy, he was - and the big crowd of people stood and watched. They had put a respirator on him to pump the water out, but he was dead, so they put him in an ambulance and drove away. That was the only dead person she had seen. But, Danny? Danny, shot dead!

In the afternoon when Hephziba returned with Dr. Abrams to Esther's room, they found the girl tearing at the pillow, sobbing, her face ravaged with tears. The tray with her meal remained untouched. "You must eat!" Hephziba said, looking at the doctor as though summoning his help.

"No! No!" the girl shrieked and burst into another fit of violent, hysterical sobbing.

...

August was a very hot month. Even indoors the breathless heat suffocated like a blanket, and outside the scorching sun was unbearable. It was a little before noon. The sheeted shadows cast by the sun burnt and smoked in bluish waves. Esther had been several times to the shower that morning. Now she had returned to her diary and her cell!

For the past fortnight she had not written a single word. Laxie had been a good companion. She gulped a pill, patted Laxie's head and sat at her desk. The dog watched her steps carefully.

Leafing through the pages of her diary she was amazed at how much she had written since that night!

...

The fourth day of August was Esther's first day back to work in the fields. It was strange to be human again! When she was being driven to work that morning Danny's image rose before her eyes.

She could see him waving a hand to her, calling her name, "Underneath the eucalyptus tree!" he would remind her. The words kept ringing in her ears and the image was so real. She craned her neck the better to see the image and almost waved a hand. They all existed, even that eucalytus tree, their meeting secret place, except Danny himself!

That morning she learnt from the twin sisters that Yigal had written after a brief interval. "He expresses his sorrow," Nira said and took out that piece of paper from her pocket. She read: "See that you comfort Esther. She must be taking it very badly. Esther is a highly sensitive and emotional girl.

Don't allow her to feel lonely or depressed .... I have changed bases lately, and am now stationed close to the border. We are setting a military out post. It's a very serious and hazardous mission. I may come over to see you one day, and I'll explain .... Regards ..Yigal!"

Evening, late August.. the old man in charge of the mail, Rafi, approached Esther, "You don't collect the mail anymore," he said in a low voice. Their eyes met and she could see a tear playing in the corners of the old man's eyes. "This is for you!" She took the package and tore it open. The rays of the westerly sun illuminated the lettering on the cover of the book she discovered in her hand: IN SEARCH OF LIGHT by DANNY.." She opened the book. The flyleaf read: To her who is my ideal for all that's beautiful in the world ..Esther.." She held the book in her hands, and suddenly fell into Rafi's arms sobbing ..

"Easy, girl!" the old man led her through the eucalyptus boulevard that led to the library center and the museum. Just before she went to sleep that night she wrote in her diary:

> "Danny, you will never read what I write here. Somebody else will. Some time, some day! Perhaps! It is as though the two of us walked for a while along friendly parallel paths, side by side, and then the paths diverged so that we parted from each other forever. You went your way, Danny. I'm here. Still here, on the same way. There was nothing strange about our love, yet I kept asking myself: "Will life allow such love?"
>
> Danny, I think of you, all of you! You'll have to learn to live without him, just like one learns to live with a withered arm or a blind eye! That's what Nira, Hephziba and everybody tell me ..I'll write again, Esther ...."

Laxie, however, did not help Esther to forget. The setter sat with her most of the day and lay at her bed. The dog's eyes were sad. As September advanced her health deteriorated. She had to take the nurse's advice and stay in bed. All she had to do was think and think, write and move her hand gently on

Laxie's back or stroke his head. The setter always raised his eyes to her, then dropped them. The sorrow was deep. It was then that Esther saw for the first time the light blue dots in the dog's eyes. Laxie's nose was hot and dry one late evening, and as she jumped out of bed and knelt beside him he began to struggle for breath. His thin sides heaved, and he raised his head feebly trying to lick Esther's hand. Then fell back, his faithful heart stilled at last. In the welter of the news about the war which was still in full swing many things went unnoticed. One of these was Laxie's death!

PART THREE

How long does it take to draw a full circle?

...

Fear not; for thou shalt not be ashamed; neither be thou confounded, for thou shalt not be put to shame...

Isa. 54:4

....

Sept. 22nd, '48

"Dear Esther,

You will be surprised to get this note. For the past several weeks I've been thinking of you, hoping to come over to Deganya to see you; but I see no chance at the moment. Here, in this military outpost one must detach oneself from the world. We're having a pretty hard time, mounting guard night and day, constructing a sort of a new settlement that will probably be the nucleus for a wealthy border settlement in the near future. Meanwhile we have to tolerate heat, cold, diseases on one side, and the enemy on the other. We're only a handful of young people, and every day when darkness falls we wonder who the next victim to enemy snipers will be.

As I said I've been thinking lots of you. I must ask you to take things as they are, not to hurt yourself too much. It is necessary to seek consolation in our moments of desolation, Esther. Do so. You'll find it somewhere. You cannot chart your life as a sailor charts his voyage.

I must close now. There's a jeep leaving the camp for town in a few minutes. I'll ask the officer to post this letter for me, or else it'll never reach you. There's no knowing how long it will be before another vehicle makes the journey to town. All my love and sympathy... Yigal..."

She turned the letter over in her hand. It bore no address. "You'll find it somewhere.." she re-read that sentence and folded the paper and put it in her pocket. It had taken ten days. In normal times only two- or three days, she wondered as she stretched her legs out before her while sitting on the grass propped against the trunk of a tree. The green underneath looked like a real green carpet and the trees sprang from the midst of it just to create a cool, pleasant shade. Suddenly her attention was attracted by a beautiful bird that had perched on a bough close by. She had never seen one like it before - it had white flashes on its wings, and a rosy red throat and breast - and after it had flown away she looked around and recited to herself:

A poor life this if, full of care;

We have no time to stand and stare!

Nearby the brook was a glassy mirror full of stars like a sky at night. Nature was so beautiful, yet how many people had time to find solace in that beauty?

She, for one, seemed to find it there, and in her diary:

"Danny, my beloved, there is an awful din going on in my head. Right now I feel two Esthers struggling inside me; the one, mournful and sad, looks behind at a dead past; the other, strong and young, looking forward to the rising sun, the eternal dawn. But whoever wins, Danny, she will carry the dear souvenir you have left behind.."

Myriads of stars. Millions of galaxies. The tranquility of night brought to her ears voices of people laughing, talking, shouting. She recalled a time, long ago, when she had been travelling in a train. It was spring. The landscape, swallowed up in long gulps by the window of the railway-coach, had a sombre fascination for her. The train ran fast, and the rows of trees which had been silhouetted against the sky when seen from afar, turned into a black curtain as dusk fell. Here and there houses stood out as though groping in the dark, one field swallowed up the next. The train was entering a plain, where the green of the meadows was deepening into mauve. That had been the last time she travelled in a train from Beer-Sheba in the South to Haifa in the North. She could still remember the excitement of that journey as she stood by her window watching the glittering lights of the surrounding settlements, of the houses of the elders down the alley, of the dark, starry sky above. They were like stars hanging in the air. It was like travelling in a train, except that now she was standing still while everything and the whole world just outside her cell was in constant motion. She felt Yigal's letter in the breast pocket of her shirt. "You will find it somewhere!" She wondered if he would ever come back to live in Deganya. She took out the letter, put it between the pages of her diary and hastily slipped into her bed.

In her diary she wrote this poem

THE SEASONS OF MY LIFE

I take the Winter to come
With embracing darkness,
Hiding the secrets of nature
Under the eiderdown of snow,

It is naked and lifeless
And slowly dying, but not in vain.
Just sleeping, resting
Ready to wake up again.

Pinned indoors, deafened by driving rain under my roof
Recollecting the sins and memories of a distant summer'
I am not alone, yet I am lonely, aloof,
I shall not forget this wonderful time. Never!

I stop and I wonder
And look back at my Spring
Walk with open eyes towards my Autumn
And do not fear the Winter anymore.

O, God, send me the Spring
Call for the miracles of life
Germinating – searching
To waken up my frozen heart.
And make me believe in something
I'll never know what, but feel
To climb to it in my fear'
To lose myself in this one time
And realize all this beauty of mine.

Scenes from my childhood when
With that nameless pathos in the air
That dwells with all things
And makes them so sweet and fair,
Soft mists in my hair.
A goose sailing on the serene lake
Going everywhere, going nowhere,
Time throbs with life and color
O, how I dream, how I live without fear!

I take the Summer with a smile
Treating myself to cones of ice-cream, cold drinks,
Leaving memories on the sand, and recollections to file
By, with all the pleasure the season brings.

O, send me the Autumn
With tearful grass bending to earth,
And shivering leaves

In desperate attempt to climb to
The tree that gave it life,
Standing there naked again
Ready to sleep and rest As it gives me hope, oh, yea,
On my lonely way towards my own....

AND AGAIN.....WINTER....

"Seasons don't happen to our calendar"
I say to myself many a time. "They happen to us,
Moods of our lives, sometimes rough, at others tender.."
O, God, if only we could live with seasons forever!!!

...

The October sun warmed the fields. Esther had only worked a couple of hours that morning, but she was already feeling tired. Her back ached and there was a bitter taste in her mouth..

Deganya had not changed much in spite of the war, she thought. Those secret places, the walks, the lanes, forests, gardens, parks, pastures, cornfields - they were all there. Only the people had changed. Gone were the children who had skipped ropes and rolled hoops. Gone were the long, sunny afternoons when parents would lie lazily on the soft grass that separated the swimming pool and the brook from the dining hall and the library centre, parents who used to chat and play with their children after work, children who used to feed the birds, the sea-gulls, the ducks: Now it was different. War had left its scars, and war was still in the air.

When she was young Esther used to ask countless questions about God and about where He lived, but now she knew for sure that He existed in the beauty of a rose, in the wind, in the falling leaves, in the twisted trunk of a tree, in the appealing smile of an infant, in the warm clasp of a child's hand, in the storm, in the rain, just everywhere except, maybe, in the graves. Was she wrong? Suddenly the calmness and order of her thoughts were interrupted by the barking of a nearby dog. She turned around. Not Laxie, of course! Just a street dog startled at the sight of Alon, Avi and Micha pulling along a sick horse. The animal would not move, but neighed shrilly while the three boys pulled and pushed. A cart came along and Udi got down to help. They pushed the horse, but still it would not move. Perhaps it sensed that it was on its way to be slaughtered.

Tucked under her arm Esther could feel Danny's book which she had been reading the last few days. She felt sorry for the animal and walked on. It was far from pleasant to watch a sick horse being hauled for slaughter. At the end of the road she could see her nurse coming her way. Should she tell her? Maybe that was the time! Sooner or later she had to. Why not now!

"Hi, Esther," Hephziba called with that cheering smile. "Are you all right?"

"Hephzi, I'm going to have a baby!" the words burst from Esther's mouth as she turned sharply away as if unable to bear the shame. "Darling!" Hephziba embraced her, held her face and kissed it. "Danny's child!" she said "You intend to go through with it?" Esther remained silent. "Would you consider an abortion?" Hephziba was like a mother to the young girl.

"O, no!!" Esther sobbed. "I want to have my baby. The only living reminder of Danny.." she wiped out her tears. The nurse waited patiently for the storm to subside, then looked at Esther, and said, "You'll need strength and courage, my girl. I'll help you. But you'll have to make some thinking..."

> "My dear Danny, I'm no longer afraid of the past. I've come to accept facts, though bitter and unwanted. It's only the beginning of October, yet I feel that winter is already upon us. Has spring forsaken my soul for good? Autumn is nice, but sad. I feel on a crossroad. I must make decisions. One thing for sure: Our child will share me those decisions! Esther.."

...

The girl clung to her lover and kissed him. Esther could hear her little sobbing breaths. Then, with her hand gently plucking at the base of his neck like one wishing to uproot a little tree without hurting it, she pressed his head down to hers and kissed him again. He was a young soldier. The scene was so familiar to Esther. It was like a sword stabbing into her heart. Glancing from the corners of her eye she saw them in each other's arms, too engrossed to be aware of being watched. Just outside the woods bordering the further end of the Kibbutz a military camp had been set a few days before, occupied by a handful of officers and young soldiers who busied themselves all day long with all sorts of military routine activities. Esther walked past the military tents. She couldn't help thinking of Yigal. A lonely lane stretched before her as she walked through the woods leaving behind her the dimly lighted camp and the fleeting thoughts about Yigal. The sky was clear and starry, and a waning moon cast its feeble light through the trees alongside the lane. Her feet led her to the brook where she halted at the edge and looked at her image in the water. It was dim; like a person with no identity, a person with no present nor future, just a dark past that shunned scrutiny and examination. She leaned closer, and suddenly she became aware that there was another image in the water; a dim image like her own. Her heart gave a lurch of terror and she spun around.

"Yigal!" she cried half frightened. "You startled me!"

"The grass muffled my footsteps. I came a long way to see you." She noticed his heavy boots and military uniform. "Three stripes!" she smiled. "A sergeant already! My congratulations!"

She looked at him, then moved backward. "When did you arrive?" she seated herself on the grassy bank and patting the place beside her for him to sit down too, she added, "Was it a long journey?" "I should say yes. I came with two officers.

We're on a special mission to see Uzi regarding certain military affairs."

"Have you seen the twin sisters already?"

"O, yes. Said hello to everybody. They're having a great time at the club. I had to see you, Esther."

"You know that Martha and Uri are getting married, don't you?"

"O, yes, Nira told me!"

"Martha doesn't let chances escape her," Esther said.

"What do you imply?" Yigal drew closer to her as if to catch the idea.

"She believes that men are like street-cars. One goes and another comes! She had at least a dozen of boy-friends!"

"You're telling me? How can I forget those years I spent here among you. I've come to know each one of you.." His eyes were fixed now on Esther. She couldn't avoid his penetrating looks.

"I was going to thank you for your letter, Yigal. Very nice of you!" she said.

"Esther, I've been thinking of you since Danny's passing-away. I've always been lonely. You can see that I'm always on the roam."

"You need someone to bring your heart home!" Esther put in.

"Do you remember the Bar Mitzva celebration of Oz. Dori's son. Remember?"

"O, but that was ages ago! What makes you think of it now?"

"That was about five years ago. Do you still remember the musical piece you played on the piano in the dining hall?"

"You drive me crazy, how come you remember this?"

"Well, the other night I thought of it. Out there in the wilderness in the south I was on duty, you know on guard at the gate of the outpost, and I thought of all that. The music came fresh to my ears as if it was only yesterday!" Yigal was trying to make her understand an inner feeling he had been too shy to disclose.

"I liked that part you played on the piano. It was Tchaikovsky, I believe!"

Esther chuckled, "You are a genius!"

"It had a million of meanings: broken hearts, faith trampled on, hurt pride, lost happiness, love unrequited, and all that's dear and sweet to a man, mercilessly taken from him!" he was speaking in such pathos that it almost touched Esther anew.

"Your memory doesn't fail you, Yigal."

"I was thinking of myself, but most of all of Danny. My past rose before my eyes, and all at once I felt I really missed my parents even though I had lost them years before. One can't forget, Esther."

She nodded, her eyes wet. She was going to say something, but the lump was too big in her throat.

"Sometimes one tries to forget, but it's always like shutting a door and locking it on a house on fire in hope of forgetting that the house is burning!"

At last there was one person who agreed with her. Everyone else said that she had to forget, not realizing the impossibility. There was a long silence, during which they felt so united in their sorrow that nothing could separate them; but then Esther remembered that she shouldn't be seen alone with Yigal. She hated the sort of gossip that went on in the kibbutz once a girl was seen in company with a boy. There were those who would jump to conclusions without second thoughts.

"When are you going back?" she succeeded to change the subject.

"Tomorrow. Afternoon. Five hours by jeep; that's driving fast.

"A long way, eh?

"Very!" he jumped to his feet, stood close to her, "Esther," as his eyes met hers his face changed and he leaned closer,

"Esther, Esther!" Now he was too coward to speak up, the words wouldn't leave his mouth.

Esther took a step backward, "It's about time to go. The girls must be waiting for you in the club."

He looked at her entreatingly, but all his valor and bravery, his manhood and strength were unable to make him say his say.

"Let's go, Yigal!" she made him understand her intentions quite clearly. He raised an arm as though to put it around her shoulder, then lowered it and whispered, "You don't understand, Esther." O, yes, she did. Her eyes could tell that she did, yet she pretended ignorance, "Give me your hand, let me lead you back to reality!" she walked him back to the kibbutz, and to her quarter. When they approached her room she looked at him and pitied him. "Go to the club. You have an evening to enjoy with the girls and everybody there," she urged him.

"I'd rather spend my time with you. I must see you tomorrow before I return to the base," he said broken-heartedly.

"Very well," she flashed a sweet smile, sweeter than anything Yigal could think of there and then, and before entering her room she said, "Good-night!"

"Good-night!" his lips shaped the words.

...

Strange how thoughts come rushing by like a flock of sheep when you are all by yourself. Slowly Esther began to undress in the dark. She slipped into her pyjamas and got into bed, but sleep wouldn't come. She lay there thinking, turning over many thoughts and pictures in her mind. The image of the loving couple she had seen earlier that evening rose before her eyes, and now she could see the girl holding up her face to be kissed, eager for her lover's caresses. Then her thoughts drifted to a more practical situation: the girl in her nudity, demure face, bound-up hair, lying in bed with her deep-swelling mounds of soft flesh; then he too was naked and his mouth touched hers at last. He was squeezing her in his arms, and their breaths intermingled. He was growing strong and lustful, his desire finding at last its secret source and secret destination, his infinite desire aching in the tight caress of her throbbing body, her warm breath beating upon his half-shut lids, and then her slippery body writhing in his arms. Esther had experienced that before, and the very thought of it made her blush as she turned and tossed moaning in her bed. With an effort she turned her thoughts to Yigal. Would he come back to Deganya? Did he really love her? Was he trying to be polite to her? The diary was such a good friend, the only one she could confide in...

The quiet beauty of the morning stirred within her a new feeling, a lust for life, as she drew a deep breath. Suddenly her attention was drawn to a figure coming down the lane towards her room. She stood at the window and leaned to check who it was.

His military beret in one hand and a red rose in the other Yigal made it quickly to the tree just below her window. "Good morning, angel!" he propped himself against the tree, resting one foot on the ground and the other on a large stone.

"Good morning," her glance lingered speculatively on his uniform. In the clear light of morning his eyes, with their long lashes, were of a more crystalline grey than the sea. He gave her a long, lingering glance. He looked at his watch, then back at her and said, "We have a couple of hours to sum up a few things."

"What things!" she was embarrassed. "Where's everybody? Uzi? Alon?"

He changed feet, the other foot now resting on the stone. "Let's go for a walk. They're all in the camp." Yigal was smelling the rose in his hand. "A lovely morning, isn't it?"

"All right, I'm coming!" She got out of her room and hastened towards him. Unaware of the big stone that lay in her way, she stumbled and almost fell. Instantly Yigal's hand went out to help her regain her balance. Esther's hand trembled slightly at the contact, but she didn't withdraw it. If ever a palm could feel remote, his did. He was staring at her, and as his gaze travelled over her, a deep sense of shame enveloped her. Could he have guessed? Had Hephziba disclosed her secret? Could anybody tell she was pregnant? Yigal led her along a narrow raised path between shimmering fields, and she followed meekly. "I think I'm scheduled to work in the library today. Eva is expecting me to give her a hand…" She kept on following him. "Where're we going?" She felt she had to ask after all.

"To see the lilacs," he replied. "They're in bloom now."

"What? At this time of year?" she was astonished to find herself walking hand in hand with him through the park. O, she had to see the lilacs, to breathe their piercing, sweet scent. It seemed to her that whatever ugly illusions existed outside the place, there must be a God after all, and that He must be good and beautiful. They were approaching a large pond with water-lilies growing all round the edge. The dark water streamed in it like juice in a water-melon, where a segment had been cut out. There were several boys busily working by the pond, which was one of the several fish ponds. They walked past the water, through some trees, until they came to a wide stream which blazed in the sun, hurting the eyes. It shimmered, bending and unbending like sheet metal. They sat down together beside the stream and Yigal felt free to talk about himself, his unhappy childhood, the great escape from the Nazis, his youth, his mother, his studies that were cut short, the career that he had chosen for himself, and most of all, his long-cherished dream to proceed in his studies and take up medicine as a life-long career. But only when the war was over and neither the army nor Deganya needed his services. Esther listened attentively, her eyes on the shining water following him in her mind from year to year, from one picture to another. "But that's a dream, and it'll take years before I take off these military boots and this khaki uniform and sit down to concentrate on my studies..." he was saying with a sigh "Have you ever been in love?" she found the courage to ask. He was staring at her, and when her eyes met his and she read his thoughts she added, "I mean, have you ever had a girl-friend?" "O, just friendship! It was short-lived because the Palmach undertook several off-the-record missions, and I had to be away most of the time. I didn't see her again. She went her way, and I chose mine." Esther's eyes were searching his. "And that was the end of it..." he added to her relief. They remained silent for a while, their eyes met, and seeing his ardent glance she felt a sudden surge of blood to her cheeks. Fear crept inside her, but her terror was quickly dissipated when he said, "Strange how suddenly out of the blue a face rises before your eyes. At first when you recognize it you stand and look, you ponder - and then it dawns upon you quite suddenly, and without your being aware of it, that you're in love with that very face and that you cannot carry along without it.." Esther remained silent, her throat totally constricted by the strength of the emotion he was arousing in her. The implication was clear as clear can be.

"Esther?" he said.

"Yes?" she averted her head.

"You avoid my looks. I owe you an explanation, Esther."

"I realize how you feel, but...."

"Look at me please, for only when persons look each other in the eye a human feeling passes between them....Like electricity.." his voice was low but quite audible. She lowered her eyes. She was now looking at her watch..

"Esther, you're going to tell Eva that you didn't feel like staying indoors specially on such a beautiful morning..."

When they were together, Yigal took every opportunity to show her his courage and fearlessness. He remembered the words of Willianm Blake in The Auguries of Innocence, which he had studied at school, and now recited them in her ears:

To see a world in a grain of sand,

And a Heaven in a wild flower,
Hold infinity in the palm of your hand,
And eternity in an hour!

She was silent. He took her hands and said, "You're not listening to me. You're miles away... I need your love, Esther. More than ever before. I have been lonesome all those years; that's why I chose this life. I'm a friend, not an enemy, Esther." he broke off, then went on passionately, "I've reasons to call myself a friend. Esther, I'm weak inside. You're strong, you're brave, stronger than I... Esther..." suddenly his words reminded her of that heroic action of his in the battle for Deganya, when he had thrown that molotov-bottle on the Syrian tank, the bomb which paralysed the Syrian army and brought an end to the battle. "Esther..." his eyes were wet. She looked into them and saw the bravery of the Palmachnik who knew no fear. She could see herself sticking to him fearfully asking for defense and shelter. "Esther.." her name kept ringing in her ears, while the picture of the hero wouldn't leave her mind's eye.. He drew closer to her, and closer, and like a vanquished party, surrendered himself with the words, "Esther, I feel like a slave! Esther, I love you!"

The words fell on her ears like a bolt from the blue. It had happened so suddenly, like a short circuit between two live wires. She drew back trembling with shock, her breast rising and falling visibly with emotion. His eyes were wet. She felt embarrassed.

"I must go now. I'm afraid..."

"Afraid of what! Don't go!" he asked beseechingly.

"I don't want to be seen here."

He retained her hand, but she slipped out. "I must go!" she insisted.

Yigal looked at his watch. "I must go back. We are leaving now!"

"I'm sorry," Esther apologized.

"I shall love you as long as I live. You'll understand one day!" he looked again at his watch, and with a brief wave of his hand went off. "Good-bye! You'll come back one day, I know that!"

"Good-bye!" Esther called. At the bend of the road she wanted to turn her head, but controlled herself and walked on.

"You'll come back one day. I know that.." The words rang in her ears long after he had gone...

...

"Dear Danny... Now I feel stronger than before. I have made up my mind to tell Yigal simply, plainly and bluntly that though he had stirred the blood of youth within me, he in no way was able to make me love him. I'm still young, Danny. Yigal is a handsome fellow. I like him; but love him? How can I?

I've an idea: I'm going to tell him that I'm pregnant. Who would want to be involved in such an affair, or get involved with a pregnant woman? Yigal is young and has a million hopes and ambitions."

...

An engine revved, then roared away. It disappeared beyond the hills that enveloped Deganya until it could be seen no more. When would he come back? She wondered. It had always been like this with Yigal. He had always appeared suddenly and in the same manner disappeared. "You'll come back one day. I know you will!" His words deafened her, and now she wished that he would!

The yellowing afternoon light bathed the road and the fields and the houses with a wash of gold. The corn-stalks too were golden. Esther spent the rest of the day curled up on the bed, thoughts spinning round in her head and pictures filing by in her memory. There were two Esthers within her, and she felt torn between a past strongly rooted within her that refused to recede and scorned burial, and a promising future, a mysterious world beyond the veil! Lying on her side, she thought of Yigal's horrible story, the horror of the escape and the gruesome experience which had not warped his personality.

...

News poured in. The war in the south was in full swing, and in the late afternoon of October 15th the Israeli Air Force attacked heavily Egyptian airfields and bases. They succeeded in establishing and maintaining air supremacy. On the 17th, the Egyptians, in their effort to drive back the Israelis, put in many counter-attacks all along the line. It was then that Esther began to hear much about Lt. Alon, the officer who had been in Yigal's company. Yigal had been fighting under Alon's command, she guessed. On the night of the 19th-20th there was a strong attack, and she lay awake all night. Everybody was taking great interest in the news.

Things were going fast, faster than one could grasp. There were again much talk and long discussions in the settlement. Another war was breaking out in the north. Clerks counting eggs, cooks at work in the kitchen, boys in schools, girls in the fields, young boys and girls on tractors and workers sorting out vegetables in the sheds stopped whatever they were doing and hurried silently to the dining-hall to take shelter and to listen to the news about Kaukji and his unorganized army. On October 22nd Kaukji moved out against the Israeli settlement of Manara, close to the Lebanese frontier in the Huleh Valley. In view of its nuisance value the Israeli high command decided that Kaukji's army in the Upper Galilee had to be eliminated. Speed was essential, and at dusk on October 28th the Israeli Air Force heavily bombed most of the objectives. In this operation the Druse threw in their lot with the Israelis and together they marched on the villages. They created havoc with their vigorous night assaults and by midnight on October 30th they had occupied all the villages and were in command of the cross-roads.

Kaukji and his staff fled northward. On October 31st Operation Hiram drew to a close. All the Galilee had been cleared and Kaukji had been driven out, with it the Arab Liberation Army had been broken up.

"The Israeli armies, heavily out-numbered, astonished the world by their feats of arms, and began doggedly pushing the invaders off Israeli soil," the papers wrote.

Esther had always felt proud of her identity, of the boys who played those "heroic feats" as she would call them. She had known one, Danny. Now she knew another, and she felt so proud: Yigal! She was undressing for bed when suddenly she heard an unidentified noise; perhaps more unexpected that unidentified.

"Hello!"

"Yigal! What on earth are you doing here!?"

"Being a soldier in my position is being always on the roam. We've been doing hundreds of kilometers lately."

"What're you doing in my room?"

"Aren't you happy to see me? I know," he seemed to apologize for intrusion. "I know it seems wrong of me. Your door was wide open. Anyone could have come in.

"But..." she felt embarrassed. He must have seen her undressing!

"Don't misunderstand me, Esther. All I could see was your framed profile motionless against the dark night like an ebony cameo." She was irritated, but he went on, "It was then that I knew there could be beauty in black, beauty...." He stopped for a while, "Esther, I know that when I say your name I remind you of Danny. Esther, you have to understand that Danny is dead, dead and mute as a stone."

"Yigal, go away, please. Leave me alone."

"You must admit it, Esther. We loved him beyond words, but he's dead now. The greatest respect we can pay is remember him, but anyway he belongs to the family of the dead," Yigal persisted gently. She was half-hypnotized by his words, and he began to lead her gently out of the room towards a nearby bench just outside the narrow avenue. "Esther, I must make myself clear. I feel that I have to tell you a few things before it's too late."

"Too late?"

"We'll be leaving again soon and it may take long before we meet again. You've to listen to me, Esther."

She sat beside him on the bench. There was a feeble moonlight. "Danny wouldn't want you to go on grieving, to shut yourself away from life, from those who love you." There was a pause. Esther was speechless. She made no attempt to stop him, however, as he went on. "I'm in love with you. I watched you in your room as in a dream. I saw a fabulous creature rising slowly before my eyes. You were undressing, and I really thought it was a vision." Yigal's thoughts were concentrated on her neck, then the long back, the stately buttocks, the smooth fleshed thighs, the tapering calves; and above all the Esther that he was in love with. "I'll make you happy, Esther. You'll be my wife." He took a deep breath and moved towards her. The lift of his long jaw, the imperious turn of his shoulders were clear and unmistakeable. In his leanness, with his tanned bony face, he was not wholly unlike Danny. His thick, wavy hair, his luminous dark eyes, his height, his energetic gestures, the very handsomeness, all that gave him a touch of extravagance. "You have to begin a new chapter in your life, it may be better for you and your..." his words were so low and sweet.

She looked up at him. "Your....?" she asked. Had he meant to say: "Your child?" How would she know that he knew! His lips parted as she gazed at him irresistibly.

"This's how I want you to look at me; not with lowered eyes," he murmured laying his palm against her cheek. "There is warmth in your looks, humanity, understanding..." he paused, his eyes searching her face. "The heart is a muscle, Esther," he was saying. "It loosens and stretches with exercise. You must learn to love. Again. You can't seal your mind and heart forever. The change in your life will not be sudden. It will take time." His whispers were appeasing, and his breath was warm. "It will heal. Time is a great healer. The airplane burns and crashes. The pilot walks away from the crash and takes another plane into the air. Right?" She nodded, without uttering a single word. "That's life. See?" he was saying. "It depends on such a hair-like thread of coincidences such as the one that took away Danny.."

There were tears in her eyes. He took her face in his hands. "You, little torturer! Will you allow me to love you? I've never loved or wanted a girl so. Esther, you need love. You're willing to love. Sooner or later your passion will force itself up out of the soil you have built around yourself like a tree. Your heart is empty, yearning. You're young and beautiful. Love goes on from age to age, death was and forever will be, life is forever the same. You can't change the laws of nature. I can still remember the night of May fifteenth." Yigal's voice remained piercing and strong. "I kept a watchful eye on you. You didn't even know that I was there. Maybe you did, but overlooked. I saw you as you danced the hora, and I saw you when you sneaked away into the woods. I was jealous, but Danny was your boyfriend and you loved him, and I had no role to play at all." His voice was trembling. "Now, God so willed it, your heart can't go on living with memories. There's a gap that has to be filled. This is why gaps are made. Surely you realize that!"

Esther could no longer supress her emotions. Her breath came in a little sob as he drew her closer to him, and she felt suddenly defenseless, quite paralyzed against him and without any desire to defend herself. She fought off the temptation to surrender to his arms and warm, trembling lips. He swiftly pressed his mouth to hers in a long kiss of unrestrained passion. He almost crushed her close until only her toes touched the floor, covered her face with kisses while she leaned helplessly against him, astonished, unprotesting and more than a little stirred. A shudder went over her whole body, and suddenly she burst out crying again.

"Please, don't cry, Esther. I love you, more than ever before. I don't mean to hurt you," he groaned between the kisses.

"I'm weak. I'm a woman.. I admit my weakness..." she sobbed. Slowly he mastered his passion and released her. Deprived of his supporting arms she swayed and passed a trembling hand across her face. She eyed him with fear and shame, and said, "Yigal, I'm pregnant. Danny's child, and I'm determined that it shall live to see the light of day.." she sobbed.

For a moment there was utter silence. It was one of the longest and most difficult moments of Esther's life. Slowly she raised her eyes to his face to see the effect in him.

"It's no news to me, Esther. I've guessed it. I love you just the same. Your child will be my child. It will get all the love a father can give," his arms tightened around her, and with a warm kiss he proposed to her, "Will you marry me, Esther?" She raised her eyes to his imploringly, and weak with relief she snuggled in his arms. Her eyes spoke more than words could tell.

...

Yigal's departure that night was so sudden and saddening. His heavy military boots crunching on the gravel path made such a noise that she couldn't help wanting him to stay. She listened until the noise had died away.

Brilliant sunlight was coming in a slanting shaft through her window. It took her a few moments to remember what had happened the night before. She lay blinking in the strong light.

Yigal? Who was he? Why had he come into her life? Was he a stranger, a lover, a spectator, a ghost? What right had he to take her away from Danny? She lay tensely awake in her bed gathering pieces of a puzzle in her head and solving them. She could see herself sitting down beside him on the bench, crying, damping the front of his battledress with her tears.

"Will you marry me, Esther?" Would she? His voice seemed to haunt her room. It was like an aural hallucination.

...

November had a sign of its own. Big clouds sailed across the sky. High, heavy clouds, rain-heads. The men in the fields looked up at them and held out wet fingers up to test the wind. Rain would not be welcome there and then, but the clouds only dropped a little spattering and hurried on. The sky cleared, the sun came out again and a gentle wind sprang up to dry the corn.

Everything was quiet on the northern front, but what worried Esther was the southern front. Yigal had been serving there, and she had not heard from him since his departure late that night in October 31st. She had been searching the mail more often lately but not a word from him. She felt she could tell him about her dream of the night before. In the dream she had seen the end of the war. Israel was licking its wounds. But in Deganya she had been all by herself, looking for friends, but there was none. She folded her two shirts with her other socks and her best Sabbath dress, weeping as she packed them all in the little blue cloth her mother used to tie around her hair when she worked. The whole kibbutz looked to her like a large cemetery which she was going to leave once and for all. She had a feeling that it was she who had caused all that disorder and havoc. She had killed them all, burnt all their houses down, and blown all those buildings to the ground; and now she was going away like a coward, a sinner. In the dream she was a little girl of ten, with her pack on her shoulders, walking away, weeping for her father whom she seemed to remember so well. He looked so much like Danny: the same chin, the same mouth. The image of her father clung to her mind as she wept on bitterly. She began to run until she reached her aunt's home. What would her aunt say? Would she offer refuge for a sinner. She was breathless, and when she stopped to look at the lake and the curving sky above it, she heard the waves slapping against the shore and the wind howled in the dark night. She knocked at her aunt's door, but there was nobody. She knocked frantically until her knuckles hurt. Suddenly she saw Danny rising from the waves calling her name. His voice was a strange roar. It came from the depth of the sea. She was going to tell him about the sin she had committed, but he suddenly disappeared. The waves were riding higher and higher, knee-high, and they were engulfing her. They tore her dress. She fell on the shore. She dropped the pack. The waves and the wild wind carried it away. Suddenly a voice that was coming out of the sea called her name. A foaming wave covered her and when it receded the voice was heard no more. She struggled against the waves that pushed her back fiercely to the shore. "Don't take another step or the waves will toss you on the reef," the voice warned. It was Danny's. "I'll come back soon, don't move!" She called back, "I'm naked. I'm ashamed! I'm pregnant, Danny!" "Wait for me I'll come back. We'll go together again," Danny's voice was clear though the waves were high, raising a wall of foam. The wall became so high she could see him no more, hear him no more. What a dream! She had to speak to Yigal about it. The thought almost drove her crazy. Suddenly the whistle of a distant train cut through her reverie, banishing all memories of the nightmare. November 8th .. The radios blurted/out the news that Seweidan, the eastern bastion of Faluja, was surrounded. It was a great success for the Israelis, but there was no way of knowing whether it meant the end of the war.

..

"Dear Esther,

I've become used to thinking of you as my invisible angel. All the charm of my friendship with you is based on my love to you, so infinitely dear to my soul. You are the only person who can make me happy, after all I had gone through. I'll not give up the right to take care of you and your child. I kiss your hand with all the warmth my heart contains, beseeching you to realize that no one has greater sympathy for you, no one feels himself more truly part of your being. I hope you will express your feelings towards me the next time I come to see you. How unbearable it is when one offers love and it is silently received! Scold me even in a friendly way, but do not remain silent. How hard and bitter life is sometimes? And what a price one pays for a moment of joy! From all my heart I press your hand, Esther. Yigal!"

...

Walking through the dusk Esther thought how beautiful was the orange grove. The moon cast a slender line of silver among the trees, a long line of light that fell on the trees and thin branches. The delicious, penetrating scents of the season filled the air, and among the dark foliage of the orange trees were thousands of fireflies whose tiny flames looked like the seeds of stars. Esther had mixed feelings of confusion and doubt. She wished she could make up her mind. There was another letter in the mail. From the publisher. It read:

"Dear Danny,

We have much pleasure in informing you that our editorial staff have reported favorably upon your work. OUR DREAMLAND is an absorbing work set down with skill and feeling. There's simplicity, truth and above all profound compassion in this deeply moving tale.

Written in a lucid, straightforward style, the story is entirely engrossing. The characters, specially Esther, the heroine, possess an enviable warmth and vitality.

A fine achievement, your second book "OUR DREAMLAND" merits wide readership. You'll hear again from us. If you've any special requests regarding the jacket design please let us know... Publisher.."

"They are publishing his second book.." Esther told Eva. She was putting some books on the shelf.

"No, Esther, you should make a list of these books first!" Eva who was in charge of the library knew each and every one of the three thousand books she housed therein.

"Suppose he should come. Should I let him approach me?"

"Well, of course!" Eva regarded her with surprise. "Yigal loves you and if you have a feeling towards him you should show it." Eva sat at her desk and took the list of books in her hand to show Esther how it should be done. "You see? The show must go one. This is the stable Law of Nature. It is nourished by what we know and understand as love."

"Don't we sometimes confuse love with pity? Does one lead to the other?" Esther was glad she had Eva to talk to.

"Pity begets love?"

"And the other way round," Esther nodded.

"It sounds strange: to love those you pity!"

"Not really! After all, love has many faces."

"Yes, but real love is the one that.."

"Fills a gap," Esther interrupted. "Is that what you mean?" She took the list from Eva's hand and went over it, ticking one book after another. Eva meantime looked at the pile of books on the other desks. "We have plenty to do for the whole week," she said. Then looking at Esther, she added, "You must not be too introspective. Time is a great healer. We love our boys. We pay them tribute. Our deads make history. We love them, remember them. That's all we can do. We can't bring them back to life. Our hearts must be left open to those who need love and affection. Living hearts crave for love, dead ones claim and demand remembrance and respect. The dead belong to history, and history can only be read over and over again. The living want action and experience!" Eva's words fell on Esther's ears like those of the preacher on those in search of prayer and redemption. "I understand ..." Esther had always hated to be given advices, but that was different. Yigal's military boots crushed along the gravel in her ears, his face was boyish and innocent, his arms strong and manly around her, his kisses warm and friendly. If only she knew where he had been down there in the south. Back home she would resort to her dearest friend of all, the one in whom she could confide. Her diary.

> "Dear Danny... Do you remember the low wall that shelters the chrysanthemums at the end of the garden? Years ago we used to walk along the top of it. I can't make up my mind about Yigal. I think it is not just pity. Much more than that. Please forgive me. Don't misunderstand me. He needs my love. Esther."

The child was stirring inside her, and she laid the palm of her hand gently on her abdomen to feel it. "I'll call him Dani-el if 'tis a boy, and Dani-ella if 'tis a girl." A slow tear trickled down her cheek.

...

The wind of December grew stronger as the days stretched on. It whisked under stones, carried up straws and old leaves; the air and the sky darkened, and rain began to fall heavily.

For three days it rained, lashing the leafless trees which tossed their branches wildly in the gusty wind. Esther leaned her hot forehead against the window enjoying the cold contact of the glass, for she had contracted a feverish chill and had been confined to her room for several days.

There was good news. In Jerusalem most of the railway line was now in Jewish hands. Making good use of this newly-won territory the Jews constructed an alternative route called the Road of Valor, which ran from the coast to Jerusalem, but further south than the original Burma Road division that had been constructed merely as a by-pass and was in dangerous proximity to Arab-held Latrun. The Road of Valor was formally opened in December. In the Social Room, the Library, or the dining-hall of the Kibbutz all ears were glued to the receiving sets. Esther heard the news over radio. The wind howled and beat against the window panes. Was Yigal among those boys who had moved in and taken possession of that deserted post. Yigal had been just anywhere!

"A soldier in my position has no home, he's always on the roam!" he would say. He could be just anywhere. While thus playing with the thought, Esther heard a knock at her door. "Come in," she answered instantly.

Nira and Nurith stood at the door. "It scares me to think of it," Nira put in.

"Of what?" Esther asked.

"Of Yigal, and the war over there in the south! I doubt if he's still alive."

"Yigal is a man of courage and faith," Nurith said pulling her skirt down over her knees with a neat, precise gesture.

"Neither courage nor faith have anything to do with it. Death is a cruel reaper!" Nira's eyes were almost wet with tears. It was unlike Nira to be so irritable. Esther gazed through the window and said, "It stopped raining."

Choppy clouds scudded across the sky revealing little by little a shining moon. "When did you hear last from Yigal," Esther asked.

"Long time ago." Nira said.

"Don't get excited! I heard from him a few weeks ago." She fished a crumpled envelope from her drawer and showed it to the twin sisters.

"What does he write?"

"Sure you want to read a personal letter?"

"You know how we like you, Esther. Please." Nira was curious as a child.

"Here you are!!" she took out the letter and handed it over to Nira.

> "Dear Esther,
>
>> "Never a lip is curved with pain
>>
>> That cannot be kissed into smiles again."
>>
> I quote from Harte's "The Lost Galleon".
>
> I am O.K. Please don't misjudge me. I love you beyond words. It is frightening to live here where I am, to walk around, to fight. It is frightening for a tree to stand straight in the wind; yet man is stronger than a tree, man is like a forest that stands the wind and the rain. I want everybody in the kibbutz to know that I mean love, that I wish to marry you, and your child will be ours. Our home will be in Deganya. If you requite my love, this is the only triumph I promise myself on earth.
>
>> Pray for me and for Israel. I love you, I ache for you. I am afraid of nothing, Esther. I love you. Yigal.

The girls hugged Esther, and embraced her with tears of joy and affection. Esther watched them. "Should I give up to him?" she asked for advice, her eyes brimmed with tears.

"He loves you, I swear!" Nira could not contain herself.

"He does, I bet!" Nurith was happy. Yet Esther felt that present happiness could not eradicate past sorrow, or would it?

...

January, 5th, 1949 .. The dawn came silver to the window of her room. Esther smelt the cool morning wind blowing through the curtains, bringing in the odor of grass and roots and damp earth. Birds made much noise, sparrows chirped and quarreled among themselves, a blue jay's squawk of false excitement, sharp warning of a cock quail on guard and the answering whisper of his hen somewhere near the tall grass. A wintry sun had crept into the room to warm itself within its walls. An idea came to Esther's head. She jumped to her feet, dressed hastily and was off. On the open road a few yards away from the library hall she fell into slower step with another walker.

"Good morning, Hephziba," she greeted her nurse.

"Good morning, dear. Where are you going? You're exempted from work, aren't you?"

"I wish to visit the cemetery. I'll water the flowers!" she said.

"I thought you were there last month. You must not make a habit of it, Esther," Hephziba put a hand on her shoulder.

"I feel like going there. I've some reading to do, some writing. I'll make me a few sandwiches and be with myself!"

"You shouldn't walk long hours, Esther."

"I thought the doctor advised me to do a lot of walking."

"You shouldn't overdo things, Esther."

"It's always a relief to drop a tear on the soil that gave me birth. You call this overdoing? 'Bye!"

"You're in good company. Yourself!" Hephziba laughed. "Bye!"

The climb to the cemetery was long. Up and up she went along paths and lanes overgrown with damp grass. At the top of the hill she paused for breath, gazing at the graves laid out one beside the other. The utter peace and serenity of the place were overaving. She stood gazing with solemn-eyed memory at the weather-rusted stones, then raised her head and looked around - and gradually the winter landscape faded. The sun was beautiful. Half shutting her eyes, she felt her body drenched in sunshine. She listened to the murmur of cornfields swaying in the wind, and the music of the breeze playing among the reeds around the distant lake. She shut her eyes entirely, there were words that she wanted to remember: Danny..Esther..ever .. She drew in a deep breath, smelling the fishy odor of the lake. She had an irresistible desire to plunge into the water and feel the cool wash of it across her floating limbs. But that, too, belonged to the past!

The afternoon wore on, and the sun was almost at the end of its journey. Around her the air moved with a lazy, drowsy warmth. There was the last plaintive evening song of robins, and broken sounds from far away, a voice in the wind, the barking of a dog, the tinkle of a cow bell. There was in the air the fragrance of intoxicating odors; the resinous smell of the pine and the eucalyptus, scents of grass and bushes, of oleander and fir. That was the past rushing in her memory.

The wind was sweeping and weeping around the graves. She raised her eyes to the sky and found innumberable pictures and images filling her world and filing before her eyes, far beyond the distant horizon. The winter sun sunk lower washing the fields and the distant roof-tops with a warm yellow light, poking inquisitive fingers round corners and picking out details clearly like aperfectly exposed photograph. The sea rubbed itself like an amourous cat against the rocks. The whole past was rising before her eyes. Skeletons looked at a harsh and wicked world, then turned their backs and disappeared like vapour. There were so many of them: Gordon, Ephraim, Mordechai, Oded, Menashe, Loar, Porath, Ben Canaan, Hanna, Gideon, Shmulik, Yehuda...and Danny...just one more! They were all standing in a row, the Family of the Dead, watching silently! Sunset drove down the sky like a ship in flames. When the light was gone from the bronze clouds in the west, Esther set off slowly for Deganya, the settlement. As she walked she thought of Yigal, wondering where he had been, if he was living or dead!

Her feet led her back to the center of life, yet her lips phrased a sentence for Danny, "O, even if all those waters of the lake turned into the waters of Lethe and I were given the chance to drink from them, I would never forget you, Danny!"

It was getting late, and crows scattered the first drops of dew as they settled on the heavy branches of the trees, their cawing echoing like cracking wood. Dogs came running across the road out of the clearing where building was going on, and where lights shone in the gathering dusk. Soon the first stars appeared, not as serene jewels hung on the domed surface of the sky but as fierce origins of light profoundly embedded in it, their rays piercing its blackness like needles of crystal.

Back at home, there was too much noise. Joy! Chattering, laughter, everybody was elated over the news. What news? Had she missed any news? Everybody was talking about a new chapter opening in the history of Israel. The end of war! The war has come to a halt, an end. This time it was final! The first thing that came to her mind was Yigal! Was he alive! Would he come back to Deganya? Would he really marry her? Her belly was swollen now, and she looked so "funny". How would she face him?

...

"You shouldn't walk around the library with all these books," Eva said. "You sit down here and take it easy, Esther."

"Dr. Abrams says I have to move around. It helps when time comes for delivery."

"You've been doing a lot of walking lately."

"How do you know?"

"I am just making a guess."

"That's perfectly true. I went yesterday to the cemetery."

Eva regarded the girl with astonishment. "You want to tell me that you walked all the way up to the cemetery?"

"A..ha..." Esther went on sticking some labels on the books that lay in a heap on her desk "Death is natural, Eva."

"Quite right."

"Reading the inscriptions on those stones is like reading a book of history. You read and it reads to you like a book."

"Men are born, Esther, to die gloriously..."

Esther stood to her feet, walked over to the shelves and took out a book. She turned the pages of the Phaedon greedily, "You should read how Socrates pursues the theme of the spirit's detachment from the flesh."

"Socrates!" said Eva. "I read that book. Socrates believes that a man, while living, should struggle continually to separate soul from body, to live as nearly as he can in a state of death.." Appalled by her new understanding Esther felt nevertheless an odd excitement, as of one who discovers a fresh truth. There was truth in what Socrates had to say. She read on, then suddenly she felt pain in her abdomen.

"What month is it?" Eva asked

"Fifth already. I can already experience the feeling of life inside me," she laid the book on the desk, and put a palm over her abdomen. "Quickening, doctor Abrams calls it!" she said. Those feelings were like a gentle fluttering or tapping inside the abdomen, and when they occurred she held her breath, feeling a miraculous awareness of the living creature that was part of herself.

"I'll take the book home to read more of it!" she said.

That night Esther read until the book fell from her hands and her eyelids were heavy with sleep. All night in her sleep she was pressing up a long slope. All night long in the grey and red figuration of the dream she was trying to reach the crest of a hill - but she woke up before she had attained it. She seemed to curl up entirely in herself like a sick bird that gathers its feathers around it to protect itself.

...

On the seventh of January, 1949, just as the Israeli troops were completing their preparations for mounting the attack on Rafah, Egypt asked for an armistice, which was granted immediately. The fighting ceased almost at once, thus bringing to an end the Arab-Israeli war. Cease-fire! For days the good tidings had been blared forth over loud hailers. On the great day, as word of the cease-fire sped through the kibbutz, a strange thing happened; all the workers stopped and hurried silently to the dining-hall, where they stood in expectant groups, waiting for the midday news broadcast It was pouring with rain, rain that brought good news along with it. In the welter of the news so many events went unnoticed; but who cared? There was a lot of thinking to be done!

...

Rain rattled against the panes and the blue-grey light of the stormy sky fell across the page of the newspaper in Esther's hand in her room. Soldiers were returning home! There were stories about citizens in Jerusalem staggering out of the city, in those horrible days in the battle over Jerusalem and the siege, with their clothes stripped from them, and the skin hanging in shreds from their burnt limbs. There were other more gruesome tales that made the flesh crawl. Soldiers, nurses, workers, and others told so many stories about the war that Esther preferred to think of peace. "Let's turn a page and start a fresh beginning," she would say. But when a government lorry came to Deganya with orders to remove the tank that had been halted at its gate she objected and there was an outcry against this in the whole kibbutz, and finally the trophy was left where it stood.

...

Days drifted by. Time is a great healer, she reminded herself when she saw how even those who had grieved over lost ones were now smiling again. As for her, she was unable to forget; she could only make room in her heart for someone she had been anxious to see: Yigal. So many soldiers had been coming back into the kibbutz or leaving it to Tiberias and distant places, even the number of passengers using the kibbutz bus had increased to such an extent that there was hardly an unoccupied seat and sometimes there was no room for those passengers who preferred standing to waiting for the next bus. Esther had a feeling that Yigal would show up one day provided he had been alive. She looked at herself, fat and inflated, and thought of the first encounter with him. Her thoughts were suddenly cut by the honking of a jeep that had squealed to a halt just close to her. "Esther," the soldier at the wheel called. She blinked, hardly believing her eyes for the young soldier was no other than Yigal himself.

"Good Heavens! You shocked me! It is you?"

"Weren't you expecting me?" he asked.

"Which wind blew you off to us this time?" she asked sarcastically.

"Wind from the far South," he clasped her hands, took them into his and whispered to her ears, "Esther, you do believe me that I missed you, don't you?"

"Are you going to...?"

"I've come back to Deganya. Everybody is returning home? Have I no home, Esther?"

She raised her eyes to his face. There was a scar right on the left cheek just below the eye. "How did you get that?"

"Just a slight wound." He studied her face curiously as if he had never clapped eyes on such a beauty before. He kissed her gently, and she did not resist. "The beginning of love is a many-splendored experience. Love, Esther, is like a tremor in the voice, a glance of the eye, a touch of the hand..."

"Are you going to stay overnight?"

"Uzi and Alon want me to live at Deganya. They have some plans for me."

"What plans?"

"Let's not discuss it now. Shall we sit here at the foot of this tree?" He led her to a nearby stump. "The sun is warm and lovely. I've dreamt about batting the breeze and basking in the sun; and now I have you as my favorite companion."

Just across the path that bordered the last row of trees stood the gnarled ancient olive tree where Esther used to meet Danny after work. "Lovely isn't it?" she pointed at the tree. "How old is it?"

"Probably centuries old!" Yigal snuggled close to her.

"Danny told me one day that it must be about three hundred years old."

"I know some ancient olive trees in the western Galilee that are almost completely hollow - yet there's still enough life in them for the branches to put out leaves in the spring. It makes you feel quite humble: to look at trees that have been in existence for hundreds of years."

His fingers were now playing with her hair, touching her neck. Esther lowered her eyes as though guessing what he was going to say. "I've always wanted to tell you how much I love you, now more than ever before; and it has suddenly dawned upon me that I can't possibly live without you. I've always wanted to bring joy and happiness to your eyes, your very being, to protect you and care about you and for you. In my daydreams back at the base in the south I was your champion against a thousand evils. Sex almost never entered into my thoughts about you. You were, you are, and always will be pure and queenly in my eyes. You live in my mind constantly, a misty white figure of a dream. Will you agree to marry me?" his eyes were imploringly gazing at her.

She remained silent while her eyes watched his face closely.

"I'll not take "no" for an answer, Esther!" his breath was warm on her cheek.

Dark clouds suddenly began rolling towards them, riding a cool wind. It was much colder now, and from the overcast sky a few chilly drops fell. Suddenly it began to rain, and the wind came at the couple with a sudden whoop and a buffet that made them scramble for the shelter of the trees. It was raining very hard, slantwise. Esther looked at the road where raindrops were breaking in little gray stars. Since her infancy she had loved those little leaping stars. It was getting colder than expected. Yigal drew Esther close to him, burying his face in her hair. He writhed in helpless torment, longing for her. Between blushes of clumsiness and innocence, and echoes, too, perhaps just perceptible in her breathing, of secret, involuntary sighs, yet gravely, like someone very experienced, Esther felt the longing for love and the fear from it. Yigal's heart beat faster, and Esther could feel all the thirst and the hunger that had ravaged him. It was the anguish of a life bilked and thwarted; a river that could not run, lightning that could not strike, sun that could not rise, earth that could not be born, dynamite that could not burst, wind that could not blow; a wild horse that could not gallop; a living heart that could not beat freely. She could feel all that in his whole being from head to toes as he leaned over her and kissed her passionately. She didn't resist him, remained close as though consulting her own mind. Then, as if she were pushing away a part of her life which had become too precious to be carried carelessly, she forced her hands against his chest and slowly pushed him away. She was sobbing, but the tears that fell on her cheeks were his, and they weren't just rain drops, for she could feel their warmth.

"I'm sorry, Yigal. I can't. You don't understand! You never will," she said entreatingly even though she understood his agony. Her voice was thick with unuttered sobs. He took her two hands, drew her close to him again and supported her rigid, awkward body with his own. His hands tightened about her, and his face was lost in her hair kissing her over and over again as he whispered, "Esther, I do understand. That's what's drawing me towards you. I know how you feel about me. I read your minds. I know the judgment you're giving yourself. I want to help you overcome, to help you think. I know.."

Yigal was right. He knew. He did. She longed to submit to him, to throw in her lot with his. She yearned for love, for she, too, was blood and flesh, and she knew him as a sensitive man, honest in love, in everything and capable of deep affection; yes, and above all, she endeared him and was beginning to love him..

If only she could tell him; if only he knew how much she hated to be left without him, for love and protection!

...

If it wasn't for her diary, Esther would have gone mad! There was no pal in the whole kibbutz who knew as much as her diary did. Secrets and confessions, shameless and confidential personal confessions, found their way on the pages of that diary begun on May 14th, 1948...

Stretched out on her back with closed eyes, but sleepless and fully awake, Esther could see pairs of eyes watching her, also those distant eyes of Danny's; but closest to her were Yigal's brown eyes that shone in the dark. Her roommates were deep in their sleep, while her thoughts ran wild, and she could feel his arms around her, strong but tender; his lips full and red with life, his chest broad and comfortable, his body throbbing with life pressing against her.

She was a woman, and as the soil needed water, so her flesh ached for human flesh to warm and be warmed by it. Yigal could give her all she had been longing for! Her mind was set! He could fill all the gaps in her body and soul, if only she would allow him to come near....

...

How shameless and indecent of her to think of all this?

When you're alone in the dark, fighting to fall asleep, you allow yourself too much liberty to let your thoughts run wild! It's always the world of after-dark that brings forth all the sins of man!

In broad daylight one wouldn't dare let one's thoughts run like a wild animal, uncontrolled! Especially, Esther!

No, she won't tell anybody, not even Yigal himself; but her diary should know everything; anyway, nobody knew where she used to hide her diary, and there was no chance on earth anybody would read in its pages...

PART FOUR

...

Care! Your circle must be round!
Your steps, taken carefully; your words, drop milk and honey
like the land you live upon!
Home! How sweet it can be, if only....

...

"Well, Yigal, you must be surprised why I called you to my office!"

"No, Uzi. Not the least! You've always said you had plans for me."

Uzi remained silent. Yigal's smile faded slowly as he watched his senior pondering on how to coin his thoughts for the young man.

"Peace seems to have come all of a sudden, almost unexpectedly!" Uzi took out a cigarette, lighted it and puffed the smoke, which began curling over his head. Another silence followed, which Yigal preferred to break.

"If only I could proceed in my studies. My mother had always wanted me to be a doctor. Sounds funny? Am sure it does; but in those days a doctor had been the most respectable man in the neighborhood. His was the greatest contribution to mankind. Mother," Yigal pondered, "has always urged me to study medicine!"

"Yigal!" Uzi's words cut through the young man's thoughts like a sharp knife. "Too early for that," he took in a deep breath and puffed the smoke. "There's a lot of work to be done here. Also there."

Yigal got the idea. They had founded an outpost, a sort of military-civilian base far in the South. The outpost had been pitilessly shelled. Now Uzi was offering him a mission.

"Every single soul is badly needed there." He watched the smoke curl above their heads. True, there had been so much to be done.

"You know, Uzi," he was beginning to surrender to his senior's plans. "When the war is over and you begin to lick your wounds, suddenly you find yourself lost, not knowing where to begin. I really don't know what..."

"Yes, you do, Yigal.." Uzi interrupted him. "You are going to stay right here. You're a welcome member. All your life you have been like a rolling stone, gathering no moss."

"And now?" Yigal seemed happy to read Uzi's mind.

"Now you are attached to the soil! Deganya needs you badly. The Land, the settlement, and moreover...." Uzi took in another breath, crashed his cigarette butt in the ashtray that lay on his desk, and added, "Haven't you thought of getting married? Of being attached to the flesh as well?"

"So far I didn't have the luxury of such rosy dreams. I get you, Uzi. You mean that in order to feel part of the place I must be attached physically and spiritually to the flesh and the soil!"

"I knew you'd get the idea!" Uzi put it. "We'll have to explain to Allon down there in the South that the furlough he had granted you will be extended, and that you have made up your mind to agree to the secretariat's proposal to accept you as a permanent member of the kibbutz, entitled to all privileges, including a "family house" etc..etc..."

Yigal was jubilant with delight. His heart jumped with joy. Would Esther welcome the idea?

"In time Deganya will have better plans for you, and you will..."

"Such as?" Yigal asked curiously.

"Have you heard of Tel-El-Qasr? Not far from here, eh?"

"Well?" Uzi's words whetted Yigal's curiosity.

"This Arab-forsaken village should turn Jewish, a daughter settlement of Deganya!"

"And what can I....?"

"Yigal! One step at a time." Uzi stood to his feet. "Good day, my friend. Welcome to Deganya! Go right ahead to the secretariat and get your things to make all the arrangements for settling here. Tomorrow an express letter will be delivered to Allon."

...

"I'm beginning to believe, Yigal, that time is really a great healer. You get strength and wisdom from the birds of the air. Somehow after a while it begins to blur the harsh outlines of the background against which you must live."

"I haven't heard you speaking like this before!"

Esther snuggled to him, cradling his head in her lap, as they sat at the foot of a huge fir tree. "What do you think?"

"I think you are just right. The earth is not shrouded in darkness forever. It has been mercifully ordained by the stable Law of Nature that the wound must heal, the ache must grow less poignant, the pain must disappear: and this, Esther, happens so slowly and insidiously that we do not realize it.

"If only it could happen soon. I'm afraid, Yigal, that as time passes the pain and ache will return."

"Time passes, Esther, but it cannot loiter. It's up to you. You cannot order Time to stand still until you have made up your mind. You must put up with everything. There will be more to-morrows, and there will naturally be more yesterdays. The show must go on. Remember? You cannot linger to a certain "yesterday". It'll have to make room for other yesterdays to come. Get me?"

"I'll try, Yigal!" she lifted up her lips to be kissed.

"We are the product of Time, Esther. Our minds and hearts are shaped with the invisible hand of Time. We cannot blame ourselves for that. We were not born like it, nor did we create ourselves that way. Time worked hard on us, Esther. Like a sculptor on his stone. Time has operated on us, like a plastic surgeon on a crooked nose; and here we are, ourselves - our real selves!" He planted another kiss on her lips as she nodded in acquiescence.

"Nor you can blame others for what Time has made of them, "he went on, remembering his parents, his childhood, his experience.

"They did not perish. They lived through horrible circumstances. They endured great shocks, they had narrow escape from death or lunacy, which is another sort of death; yet they..." the thought almost choked him. He tried to banish away those horrible memories, but he had to make Esther understand.

"I get you, Yigal!" she saved him the trouble of working hard on his unwanted memories.

"This scar," she said as though to change the subject, passing a finger over the scar just below his eye.

"I remember, Esther," he started again, "I remember the first time I left Deganya to join the Palmaoh a story that comes to my mind every now and then. There were five of us, young boys: Zvi, Barak, Ben-Ami, a red-headed chap called Doodoo and myself. Our unit was called the "guerrila unit", and most of the officers who had been in charge of the operations were old-timers in their mid-twenties. You could never tell what danger lay in stores at any hour of the day or the night. The troops were no uniforms, nor was there any rank below the officers. Boys and girls were treated the same." Yigal's eyes roved up gazing into the leafless branches of the tree as he was remembering. "We were trained to be as hard as nails. One night Barak, Doodoo and myself were sound asleep in our tent. It was a trouble spot. We had known that it was a "trouble" post. Suddenly a voice called, "Doodoo, come over, quickly!" We threw off our blankets, grabbed our rifles and hastened outside. There was a small crowd gathering a few yards away, and they all became silent when they saw Barak approaching. He pushed through and stared at the ground. It was blood-spattered, and a trail of blood led off into the hills. "Rivka!" Doodoo, who was our officer then, called. Rivka was one of the best and bravest girls in that unit, a real Palmachnik. Doodoo had been in love with her. "Rivka!" he called again and wept. Two days later her body was dumped near the camp. Her ears, nose, and hands had been amputated, her eyes had been gouged out, she had been raped countless times by Arab infiltrators. It was horrible! I myself wept bitterly. Everyone, including Doodoo, had to accept that tragedy in the same way we had learnt to accept all tragedies. Nothing could be allowed to interfere with our aim to build the homeland, to fight till the last breath!" Esther had tears in her eyes as she moved her warm palm gently over his forehead, then his temples, ears, cheeks and back to the scar. She pressed with her forefingers on it. "Does it hurt?"

"Not any more."

"Was it a bad wound?"

"A rifle shot that missed my eye. It cut deep into the flesh here, but it healed. All wounds must heal sooner or later. They leave scars."

"Scars," she repeated after him thoughtfully.

"One must have an iron heart, but an elastic muscle."

...

"Yigal You will take this letter by yourself. Allon has troubles down there. You'll deliver it by hand. He must see you before you return to Deganya for good," Uzi handed him the sealed envelope.

"After all, he's the commander in charge down there!"

Yigal drove back to the South, and all the way he thought of the two most important things that attracted him to Deganya: In his thoughts he summed them up as "love for the flesh, Esther; and love for the soil, his new permanent home, Deganya!" He could even see himself strolling hand in hand in Deganya with the newborn child. Everybody knew it was Danny's. So what? They would have a child of their own, and they will be one family.

He covered long miles, and when he reached his base the sun was already beginning to set.

"No, Yigal. Not so soon. I cannot do without you. Everybody will go back home one day. But, it your case, it may take another month or two. See what we have got here?" Allon pointed at the havoc, the debris, the houses that had to be re-built, the bridges that had to be re-constructed.

"A month or two?" Yigal looked aghast.

"You know the post inside out. You're not a new hand here."

The officer put his pipe in his mouth and puffed at it, while Yigal stared. "You shock me!" he murmured.

Lt. Allon stood up, and brushed down the lapel of his battle-dress. He stood taller than Yigal, but he was slender, with deep-set eyes peering from beneath dark eye brows. He had sunken cheeks, but his full lips had a ready smile. His dark hair grew well down on his forehead, and he spoke with the grace of a man who had been both a soldier and a scholar. Yigal knew it was no use arguing with the "boss". Allon had a special affection for Yigal, and to him he spoke freely, his orders and commands sounded like friendly requests which he knew beforehand he would get. The commander was the boss and there was no arguing. "Have you committed yourself?" he put it briefly.

Yigal stared at him obediently. Allon noticed that sad look that was playing round the corners of the young soldier's eyes. "I mean, attached?"

"Sort of.." Yigal managed to say.

"A girl?" Allon put an arm over his shoulder, and led the young man to the communal dining-hall.

The soldiers were in high spirits that evening. Yigal sipped his coffee silently and looked gloomy. A good-looking, well-built girl in tight shorts strode to the table, dealt out some cups and saucers and began pouring more coffee. Slamming the pot down for second cups, she went off to fetch some sugar, returning with the bowl, and a broad smile on her face. "Hi, Dina!" the soldiers greeted her.

"Hello, everybody!" she hailed. Turning her head to Yigal who had been absorbed in his evening paper, she said, "You're not in the mood today, Yigal," she said.

"I'm quitting, Dina. Back to Deganya!" he said earnestly.

"Sure?" she poured coffee in his empty cup. "When?"

"In a couple of months."

"Back home, eh?"

"The war's over, isn't it?"

"More interesting there? Tilling the land, watering the flowers, tending the vegetable gardens, driving a tractor down to the fields, feeding the chicken..."

"Sundry, odd jobs!" he said.

"And you're going to leave this post in chaos? What happens to those who have no home, and want to make a fresh start here, if everybody just packs and leaves?" she asked innocently.

"That's why it'll take a couple of months before I pack and leave. I'll give a hand here!"

"Jolly good, boy!" Dina moved on to the next table.

Yigal watched the stocky girl as she moved efficiently among the tables, serving coffee. For a moment he felt himself like a traitor. He had got used to the place, to that sort of life, among such friends, a good bunch of people he would badly miss; but then he was torn between Deganya and the military post in the south.

"The spirit has gone, Yigal," Udi, a soldier next to him, said. Udi had no parents, no home of his own, nowhere to go, and had preferred to remain there at the new outpost among the new friends he had made in the Palmach. His words stabbed Yigal like a knife. He was betraying his friends, his beliefs, his mottos, his seniors; and asking them to understand and forgive.

"No, Udi!" Yigal retorted vehemently. "The spirit still exists!"

"Then there's something else that's calling you back to Deganya!" Yigal remembered an old saying he had heard from an Arab, "There are three things you cannot hide: love, smoke and a man riding on a camel!" Could everybody tell? Did his looks speak louder than words? Could be!

...

"Dear Danny, Feb. 17th, 1949...

I have to forget. I pray, for I know that prayer is power. I pray to whatever God there is that I may forget and look ahead to a bright future. I pray, for by praying one learns. I pray and ask the goddess of memory, Mnemosyne, to set me free! I read the Bible. Love is great! Danny, I love Yigal! I love him. My heart yearns for love, and I catch myself waiting for Yigal to come back home, to Deganya. He agrees with me that you deserve recognition, remembrance and respect, but neither pity nor love, for you're gone forever, and the dead need no pity and no love. The living live by these; not the dead! Danny, you get me, don't you? Esther.."

...

February 24th.. Armistice between Israel and Egypt signed at Rhodes. It came into force instantly. Heavy rain was falling in Deganya, and the rattle of the raindrops on the window panes of Esther's room gave her more inspiration to write. Sometime in the afternoon she sat at the desk going over some letters. Yigal's. She read them, and before night fell she opened the window to see that it had already stopped raining. The clouds were scudding across the wintry sky, pale blue now, and pricked with the first stars. The fields glittered after the rain, and the sun sunk in the western sky in a blaze of red and gold.

...

"It's only nine-thirty," the young man said consulting his watch. "We've arrived early."

"That's all right, Har-El. We've only half an hour to wait. The gentlemen will be here at about ten," said Uzi removing his beret and making himself comfortable in his chair.

"You know? It is only a two-hour drive from Jerusalem. That's why I made the appointment here at Haifa." Uzi added, watching the young waitress moving from table to table.

The ginger-head waitress in her late thirties approached them, and politely asked for their order. "Two coffees please," Uzi was fishing a cigarette from his pocket. Har-El lighted a cigarette for himself and offered one to his companion. He was astonished to see so many people. A kibbutz-member all his life, he was not used to city coffee houses. The people around him looked happy and relaxed, but he thought that he himself would never get used to living in a busy, noisy city life Haifa. He looked across the bay and drew a breath of the fresh sea breeze.

"I never go out of the kibbutz. I think a kibbutz-member should work out in the city from time to time," Har-El said.

"In order not to feel a complete stranger when he happens to be in a city coffee-house," Uzi read his mind. The sight from the Carmel was breathtaking; the whole hillside was alive with green trees and half-hidden brownstone houses and apartment buildings, with a twisting road leading from Har Ha-Carmel into the Arab Section by the waterfront.

"Fascinating!" Har-El remarked. "It must be breathtaking at night, that hillside over there alive with twinkling lights!" he went on dreaming. "Very romantic, I bet!"

"Oh," scoffed Uzi. "Very romantic! You can hear the small orchestra playing light music, while lovers gaze at each other and touch wine glasses!"

"Look at him! A dedicated soldier drooling over love and lovers!" laughed Har-El.

The two old friends from Deganya were bachelors. The years of war, the Jewish Brigade, the British Mandate, and then the Arab-Israeli war and the establishing of the State of Israel had claimed the best years of their lives. Love and marriage had been out of the question in those days; but now, just entering their forties, they still looked quite young and energetic. Nevertheless, marriage was still not a thing to be considered. First things come first, and there were other matters that called for priority. Having devoted so many years to the Hagana, the secret underground movement, to the Palmach and to the soil of Deganya, they were considered dedicated soldiers and kibbutz-members, closely attached and committed to the service of their home kibbutz, and to the State and its welfare. Uzi craned his neck to look at a group who had just entered the restaurant. "Here they come!" he stood up to his feet, pushed the chair behind him and waved a hand to two gentlemen at the entrance. They saw him and waved back as they began to thread their way through the crowd towards the table. Uzi pulled two chairs from the adjoining table, and made a sign to the waitress.

"Shalom!" They exchanged greetings. The lean, tall man introduced his companion. "This is Mr. Schwartz, my aide," he said. "This is Uzi and Har-El, both from Deganya."

"Mr. Schwartz," the lean, tall man turned to the aide, a short stocky fellow. "These two are very well known to the Jewish Agency, as well as to the heads of the Hagana."

Schwartz nodded without smiling. The waitress approached the table.

"Dr. Elazar, what'd you like to drink?" Uzi asked the tall man.

"Two orange juice, please. All right, Mr. Schwartz?"

"O, yes, of course," replied the stocky fellow. "Elazar, we've a long trip ahead of us. We'd better make a move!"

"A jeep is waiting for us outside, Uzi," Dr. Elazar explained. They gulped their orange juice hastily, and the four began to leave. Har-El was talking to Dr. Elazar about land reclamation, soil and the life of a kibbutz-member, while Uzi walked over to the counter to settle the bill. He joined the three at the threshold of the restaurant, and as they stepped into the street a jeep squealed to a halt. The young driver leaped out and opened the door for them.

"Let's go straight to the spot!" Dr. Elazar said.

"Tel-el-Kasr!" Uzi gave his order to the driver. "You drive past Deganya!"

With deft turns of the wheel the young driver was soon speeding along the ancient road that led to the Kinnereth Lake and Deganya.

"So this is the base from which the Syrians were launching their fires!?" Dr. Elazar looked around him.

"One of the bases," Har-El corrected him.

"And this is where the boys will found the new kibbutz?" Dr. Elazar asked curiously.

"Right you are," Uzi said. "We have about a hundred young boys and girls, pupils of high schools in Jerusalem, Tel Aviv and Haifa; members of the scouts movement. They've formed a group for agricultural training with a view to settlement on the land. Most of them are to be trained in Deganya." Uzi went on explaining his points to his seniors.

"I see!" Dr. Elazar nodded his head thoughtfully. Mr. Schwartz joined him. They were now driving past the Kinnereth. The water was clear like blue glass, and the surrounding mountains that were reflected on the clear surface of the lake made a fantastic sight. The wintry sun shone over the buildings and the serene lake.

"What's it like, this Tel-el...?"

"Tel-el-Kasr." Uzi came to Schwartz's rescue. "Well, it is a long, narrow "tell", a hill east of the Arab village of Tsemach, and close to the meeting place of the Israel-Jordan-Syrian frontiers." The Jewish Agency men's faces were vacant as Uzi went on. "We shall divide this group of youngsters into two. A small group to occupy the hill immediately, and a larger one to remain in Deganya for further farm training." Uzi sounded plain and serious. It was so easy for him to put such a big project in one short sentence that the two men from the Jewish Agency felt amazed. Now they were coming to a desolate "tell", where signs were to be seen everywhere of the Syrian occupation and the bloody fighting, emplacements, communication trenches and demolished fortifications. "That's it!" Uzi looked at his guests. "You can halt here," he said to the driver. The jeep came to a stop. The four men got off, and stood on the mound and looked all around them. The view was marvelous. Far to the north was Mount Hermon, and below the "tell" was the Lake; to the west, the Jordan Valley settlements; to the east, the Syrian mountains, and south east, the Jordan and the Yarmuk rivers. At the foothills of the Syrian mountains lay the Syrian village of Tawfik with its well-cultivated fields. North of there, and just close to the Lake, lived several families of the Arab village of Samrah. On the "tell" itself there was a watermelon field with an Arab watchman. The four looked at him, but did not go near him or speak to him.

"Well," said Dr. Elazar. "And what do you plan for the boys?"

"Well, a Jewish settlement of course!" Uzi's reply was short, but pithy. The silence and the looks on the Agency's men began to worry Uzi and Har-El.

"Well, of course it will be hard in the beginning. Very hard!" Har-El regarded his guests. "We hope they will be able to settle in a few months' time."

"And when they do, it'll be a festive day for them and for the people of the Jordan valley. We shall help them put up the first structures: wooden huts, I mean." Uzi explained.

"But it will naturally take a great effort to create, to found, to open and start a farming settlement in here!" he was half-talking to himself.

Uzi and Har-El tried their best to impress the men from the Jewish Agency. "You know? To prepare the land and develop first branches of production, to find the necessary funds for their food, living, and what not; these present difficulties!"

"The Agency will provide the first equipment. We will send them tractors," Dr. Elazar said. "There will be shortage of funds. No financial aid. Your boys will have to go on outside work at older settlements to earn something."

"But that's a long way," Har-el said.

"I'm afraid you've no alternative," Mr. Schwartz replied. Then after a short pause, he added, "As soon as you gather your groups together, you can notify us to send them the necessary equipment and tractors."

Dr. Elazar cast another look at the beautiful view that lay before his eyes, saying as he reluctantly got into the jeep, "It is very beautiful up here!"

...

Dr. Elazar and Mr. Schwartz, guests of Uzi and Har-El at Deganya, saw the Syrian tank, that war trophy at the gate next to the ditches and near the garden. They took a short walk through the parks and visited the cemetery, the nursery, Beit Gordon museum and other attractions of the kibbutz. When they visited the dairy, they were amazed by the high production of eggs, fruit and vegetables.

"Tel-el-Kasr, too, will have a dairy farm. Right?" Schwartz asked. "And a poultry quarter, and..."

"It goes without saying," Uzi replied. "It'll be named Tel Katzir. When they first set up their dairy, they'll produce perhaps one pail of milk a day." Uzi laughed and the others laughed at his joke.

"Everyday their tractor will drive down to the Tnuva collecting station here at Deganya, drawing behind it a wagon and on it one churn of milk," Har-el went on with the joke. They all chuckled.

"And what will the drivers of the other kibbutzim, with their loaded trucks, think when they see that solitary pail?" Schwartz asked, with a smile of irony on his face.

"They will welcome it!" Uzi's reply was sharp retort.

...

That evening Uzi and Har-El held a meeting with the secretary of the kibbutz, Rafi, and two other elders, Baratz and Yiftah. The founding of the new kibbutz at Tel Katzir was discussed, and the topic now was the water problem.

"Of course, in the first months there will be no water in the settlement," Uzi was saying. "They will have to bring it up in tanks from the old government quarantine station in Tsemach."

"What about hot water?" enquired Yiftah.

"They'll have to go to one or other of the settlements in the area for hot water, for showers, until they can put in their own pipes and pumps," Har-El replied.

"Telephonic communication?" Baratz asked.

"There won't be any for some time," somebody said.

Baratz moved uneasily in his chair, then laid down his trump card: a question that may well have no solution. "The danger of malaria! Haven't you thought of this?"

There was a brief silence. Uzi grinned, "Tell me, fellow, did you think of the danger of malaria when you first came to settle at Um Junni some four decades ago?" he queried. Um-Junni was the name of the Arab village upon which Kibbutz Deganya was founded.

"Do you think the spirit has changed? Or died? Our boys will have to put up with the situation. They will have to fight for survival as you and I did, as your forefathers did when they first came to the swamp of Um Junni." Uzi was brilliant.

Baratz nodded silently. Many years of suffering were now running past his eyes like a fast moving reel of film. Baratz had been twenty-four when he had joined the Zionist Youth Movement in Russia. In 1906 he and some of his friends had gone by train to Odessa, and there they had embarked on a tiny ship to Palestine. The journey to Jaffa had taken ten days. Jaffa then had been a little Arab town with flat topped, cream-washed houses like boxes, minarets poking above the roofs, dusty palm trees, crowds of dark, loose-robed people in the streets. He had had several hard years before settling down to farming; then one summer day in 1911, Baratz and his girl friend, Bracha, together with ten other men and women, had gone to live in the Arab village of Um Junni. They had built a wooden dining-room, and brought some clay huts and rickety wooden cabins from the Arab villagers. Living at Um Junni had been hard. In summer it had been very hot. The place had buzzed with mosquitoes, and the air lay heavy and close between the hills. The flat valley had been like a hotplate in summer, while in winter when the rains came the land became a lake of swampy mud for months on end. The settlers had overcome all difficulties. Six men doing the plowing, two acting as watchmen, one as secretary-accountant and two women to do the house-keeping. A few months later Baratz and Bracha announced their engagement. A year later they chose the site for their permanent buildings. They had to fight malaria, learn to toil the land, to plant, by trial and error. By the time World War One broke out there were forty or fifty in the small kibbutz, and the numbers had steadily increased.

Baratz was sitting comfortably in his chair as he faced the two leaders from the younger generation, Uzi and Har-El. His eyes met the secretary's, and he said, "Very well, lads, go ahead! You certainly know what you're doing. Deganya will offer help and know-how to give you a boost. If the Jewish Agency men agreed to send the equipment and the tractors, we have no right to stand in your way. Choose your team, your men, and go on with the work until it is finished. Call the boys together, Uzi.. Today!" Baratz was enthusiastic. Uzi's face flashed a smile of triumph. It worked! The two of them departed from the kibbutz elders late that evening satisfied and happy.

...

Discussing procedure late that night Uzi and Har-El set their minds on a leader for the young boys and girls who were going to found the new kibbutz of Tel Katzir.

"He'll be responsible for the group we are going to train here. Allon will have to release him right-away. I've already drafted Allon on what's going on here." Uzi spoke as he puffed at his cigarette.

The next morning an envelope addressed to Lt. Allon, Commander, Southern Front, left the secretary's desk by express mail.

...

It was early in March. The Kibbutz bus zigzagged its way back to Deganya. A lot of passengers, most of them visitors who had friends and relatives in the kibbutz, alighted. Among them was a familiar face, a tall young man, in civilian clothes this time. In one hand he carried a military knapsack, in the other a small suitcase which contained, besides clothing and toilet personal items, an old photograph showing him standing with a rifle among other boys and girls his age. "Palmach,

1948," was written on the photograph in ink. The handsome young man walked straight to the office of the secretary of the settlement. He looked around as he made his way to the office. His arrival had been sudden and unexpected, so nobody had been waiting for him. He pushed the door open and looked in.

"Shalom, Yigal, come in!" Rafi greeted him warmly. "Welcome back to Deganya!" He offered him a chair. "Make yourself comfortable. Uzi will be here in a few minutes."

They chatted for a few minutes about the situation down there in the South. "Allon isn't so happy to part from me. I had to quit in the middle of the job. Others will have to carry on!" Yigal seemed happy to be back home. He wanted to see Esther, but before that he had to see Uzi. After all, Uzi had called him back!

Uzi entered the office, greeted Yigal warmly, took his suitcase and went out with him to the living quarters of the senior released soldiers. They settled in his room, put his things, and got straight to the point.

"Yigal, I'm aware of the hardships you'll face, but it is a job, a mission which Deganya regards with utmost seriousness," Uzi began... and throughout the evening he went on to explain the whole story of the founding of a new kibbutz at Tel-el-Kasr.

"You'll head the group we are training here. You will be their instructor, and you will choose your aides and assistants from the group. In due course, when they have completed their training at Deganya, they will join the other members in the settlement. Then, we hope and believe, the settlement will begin to take shape. They will plant vines, work the fields surrounding the "tell", establish a poultry run and cattle sheds. Later, we shall help them replace their wooden huts with stone houses on a different side, further north on the hill." Uzi sounded confident that all would go well as in stories.

"What is the size of the allocated area?" Yigal asked.

"Two thousand five hundred dunams. The area on which the settlement will be built is seven hundred dunams, that leaves you one thousand eight hundred dunams for agriculture."

"I see!" Yigal looked at his senior and at the smoke that was curling above his head. "And when the settlement is properly organized.. what then?"

"Then, of course, you will be free to choose your future home: Deganya or Tel Katzir. You will be welcome in either place."

The first thing he was going to do after Uzi had left him was to see Esther.

Winter over - the days were lengthening and growing warmer. No longer cold.

...

Uzi was the first one to hear Yigal's news. He helped him put an application to the secretariat for a "family house", shook his hands, congratulated him and promised fulfilling of commitments on the side of the kibbutz.

"When are you getting married?" Uzi asked warmly.

"As soon as she delivers the baby."

"And the child?"

"We'll call him Dani-el if 'tis a boy, and Dani-ella if 'tis a girl."

"Is she O.K.?"

"Just fine!" Yigal was jubilant with delight.

"I mean ... ehr..how did she take it?"

"Well, she has no objection. We may choose to remain here at Deganya. She loves the place beyond words."

"I used to be her tutor once. When she was a little girl. Danny's, too." Uzi pressed Yigal's hands warmly and heartily. Yigal's eyes blurred. Uzi's, too. One of them had tears. Or maybe, both!

...

It was a clear, sunny morning. Esther had decided to go out for a while. Yigal would be occupied all the morning with the youngsters, a bunch of forty-six boys and girls. She would see him at noon break for dinner. She took her diary and set out to the park, stopping by the huge tree where she used to wait for Danny after work. She gazed up into its leafless branches, marveling at the thought that it had sprung from a tiny seed, and how such a thing could split rocks and soar skywards for a hundred feet. She thought of how the tree could hoard its power and calmly increase it year by year, not like animals who burn themselves up with their living. Trees have a blessed power to repair injuries, and grow over what they cannot thrust aside, she thought. Raising her eyes to the sky, she felt as though a life was burgeoning within her. Across the lawn she could see a group of several boys and girls clustering around their tutor. The girls wore blue shirts and khaki shorts. Some of them wore an Arabian kaffiya that covered the crown of the head and ran all around the neck and throat. They looked so happy, young and careless. She recognized Yigal among them. She sat on a bench almost entirely hidden between two large trees, watching the group as they moved slowly from one place to another, listening to their instructor. She could hear Yigal's voice over the air. He was saying, "You see this trench here? You see how the trench-works run past a few straggly trees?" She admired his youth, his....his .. everything .. just everything .. his being .. It wasn't a bad choice, after all. He would be a fine father for the expected child, she thought.

"One of the trenches was dug close to the root system of this huge tree, and the roots are laid bare. You can see how the trench reveals layers of solid stone under the top soil. Sandwiched between the rock there are thin layers of earth, some only a few inches thick. This tree here is stunted from trying to grow in such ground, but the roots are fighting a stubborn fight. See how they run over and under and about the rock in thin veins, thickening wherever they find a little life-giving soil between the rock strata. How the tree fights to live? How it tries to dig its roots into rock. This, friends, is the story of the Jews who have come to build a homeland..."

Esther consulted her watch. She took a last look at the group, hating to disturb them or to be seen by Yigal, and walked along the solitary lane that led to the library. Eva had been expecting her to give a hand.

Since Yigal's return Eva had become an intimate friend of Esther's, and during most of their free time at the library they talked about Esther's plans after delivery and about Tel Katzir and Yigal of course. Danny was never mentioned.

....

Life returned to normal in Deganya. The settlers found a new satisfaction in their work, new pleasure in their recreation. The youngsters worked in groups together all day in the fields or in the kibbutz industries, and in the evening they met again for discussion and talks, lectures and committee meetings or casual entertainments. Esther's relations with Yigal became common knowledge. There had been gossip at first, but now it was looked upon as quite normal, natural and approved of. They were seen together.

It was raining. The storm had raged all night. The thunder crashed so close that Esther jumped out of bed, terror-stricken, to make sure that the shutters had been securely closed. Outside the downpour went on. The rain lashed the glass and the wind redoubled in strength and howled at the dark vault of the sky. She wondered if it would clear. Everybody had already gone to work. Esther remained at the window wishing it would stop raining so that she could walk down to the library, the nursery or the dining-hall where she could give a hand. She wondered where Yigal could have been right then. Perhaps giving a lecture in one of his classes. For the first time she felt a pang of jealousy as she thought of the young, beautiful girls in his class. When the weather was fine, she could see them walking around with their long, slim bare legs, clustering around their tutor, Yigal, laughing, telling jokes, listening and being alive. It was not an extraordinary thing for a young girl to fall in love with her tutor, who happens to be young, handsome, gay, courageous and manly as Yigal.

The afternoon wore on, and the setting sun flooded with rosy color the rooftops and the fields. Esther had spent all her day in bed, reading or writing; and only some time before noon it cleared, but then it was wet and cold outside. Now Esther was looking forward to meeting Yigal at the usual hour, four-thirty, after work, at the usual place, the large fir tree at the entrance of the park.

...

When they entered the hall hand in hand, Esther and Yigal attracted several pairs of eyes, but soon the members and the youngsters got used to see them together. Esther's pregnancy had not made her look any older. Her youth, high spirits, rosy cheeks, innocent smile and pleasant talk made her so popular, so friendly, so altogether amiable that many a girl had envied her, calling her "the goddess of youth and beauty" or "the ideal for all that was innocent and pure".

There were white cloths on the wooden tables in the dining room, and the smell of freshly baked Shabbat bread filled the hall. The dinner was delicious: stuffed fish, chicken soup with noodles and a fat roast with potato pudding. After the meal all the chairs and tables were pushed back, and the hall rang with the singing of nearly two hundred youngsters; some of them Yigal's pupils, some belonged to other sections, and some were guests from other settlements who had been getting their training at Deganya, the "mother" settlement. Salim, a newcomer from Iraq, was beating with his deft fingertips and the heels of his hand a rhythm to a reed flute playing an ancient Hebrew melody; Hana, a newcomer from Poland, where she had been called Chalina, was presenting a Polish country dance; some oriental girls and boys danced in slow, swaying sensuous gyrations and with each new song and dance the party quickened. Suddenly some youngsters joined in one cry: "We want Dalia! We want Dalia!" A pretty young girl stepped into the ring formed by the youngsters, and a cheer went up. An accordion played a Hungarian folk tune, and while everyone clapped in unison, Dalia whirled around the edge of the ring pulling out partners for a wild Czardash. One by one she danced her partners down, her hair flying as she spun. Faster and faster played the accordion, faster and faster clapped the on-lookers, until Dalia herself stopped, laughing and exhausted.

Now twenty boys and girls began forming a ring in the centre, and a hora was started. The ring grew larger and larger, until everyone was up and a second ring formed outside the first. The circle moved in one direction, then stopped as the dancers made a sudden leap and changed directions. The watchers stood close to the walls to make room for the dancers. Yigal and Esther held their hands together. They watched the singing and dancing which had been going for two hours, but the fun was still fast and furious.

A beautiful young girl, who had been dancing one swift hora after another, drew closer to Yigal. Her cheeks were rosy with excitement and her eyes bright with enjoyment. She smiled at Esther as she approached them saying, "You don't mind, do you?" and held out her hands to Yigal asking him to join the circle of dancers. Yigal cast a glance at Esther and reluctantly went off, seeing Esther forcing herself to smile.

Tamar stood almost to his full height, and the first whirl of a dance made them look a perfect pair for the dance. Yigal's tall, handsome frame moved with masculine grace through the peasant steps, while Tamar's slim body spun and twirled in a lively pirouette, her petticoat flying out parallel to the floor. Esther's eyes followed them eagerly. The other watchers clapped hands in rhythm.

...

It was hard for her to get some sleep that night. The throbbing inside her abdomen, the thoughts about Yigal and his pupils, the girls in his company, and most of all, the coming spring and summer, kept filling her head. In due course, she thought, the boys would put on hats, long-sleeved shirts, shoes and socks to protect their ankles, and the girls would shed some clothing. They would wear sleeveless blouses, shorts, no stockings or shoes and after a few days of sunshine they would become bronzed goddesses, rounded and beautiful. They would be so alluring. And Yigal would naturally fall in love with one of them: Tamar maybe! Tamar was a beautiful girl. Her smiles are so tempting and alluring no man could resist! How silly of her to let such thoughts drive away sleep from her eyes!

...

Most of all she liked work at the nursery, not because Eva had no more work to be done at the library but simply because it was really pleasant to work with the children of the settlement, to devote to their care several hours a day and share their little, innocent world. "It's comforting to cuddle them, sing to them, tell them stories and play with them. Theirs was the true human voice of innocence, and in their company she could feel the warmth which was shared and communicated from one to another.

For instance, there was Noga, a seven year-old girl, who had been born in Aushwitz concentration camp and whose parents were dead. Esther felt that she could give her warmth and love that she had been denied in her childhood, and in return Esther felt comfortable and satisfied. There was Ilan, a little Italian boy with no known family. Aliya Beth people had found him crippled in his right arm as a result of beatings; and now she could sit and talk and chat with the little boy to laughter. How pleasant! O, those little creatures, those little human beings that rendered broken hearts like Esther's perfect and full of love and affection. In that world of children, the children of the kibbutz, Esther felt she had discovered her own happiness and peace of mind, her perfection and self-searching. And that little Perry, the Pierre of French nationality, who had been an eye-witness to the death of his parents and his little sister. Perry was found at the Bergen-Belsen concentration camp by British troops. And now he was there, at Deganya, an Israeli child, happy and being cared for and looked after. Dina, too, a little girl of twelve, of Dutch nationality, who had also been found at Aushwitz. She, too, had no known family. Esther looked at all those boys and girls. Each one of them had a story. She knew how to make them happy. She made each child a paper airplane with his or her name on it: Saul, Yona, Ilana, Shmuel, Perry, Ophir, Danny, and many many others, who needed her love and care. She, too, she discovered, needed their laughs and smiles. They gave her comfort. For, it was only when working with the children that she realized how much one with a troubled and difficult childhood suffered. It was there and then that she, for the first time, heard the true story about Martha; now married. Esther had never liked Martha, that cheeky and low-minded girl who had always teased her. Many a time Esther had wanted to leave her room just because of that girl! Now that she heard the story from an old woman at the kibbutz, she forgave her for all her faults. "You will not breathe a word of it to anybody, Esther," Masha had told her one day. "Martha is happily married now. But, she too, had a sad childhood. Maybe this accounts for her crooked mind. Her father was blind, and her mother rather unbalanced. Hysterical.

Both had been smuggled from Russia many years ago, though it is not known if they were real Jews or not. Within a year two things happened to Martha: she found papers in her mother's desk which revealed that she was the illegitimate daughter of a housemaid. Her true mother had put her in an orphanage when she was three years old, and she had been adopted by the people she thought were her parents on medical advice to compensate them for the death of their own son. Later, her adoptive parents died, and she set to work to trace her true family. Martha found her grandmother first, in one of the dirty alleys of Nazareth, herself the illegitimate daughter of an illegitimate woman; there had not been marriage in the family for generations. The grandmother was not interested in little Martha, and when later she found her mother in an Arab kfar near Zikhron, this last door was slammed in her face with a peculiarly horrible twist, for she learnt that her mother had put her away when she was three because she was pregnant again. The mother had preferred the unborn child to the child of three, and had in fact brought up the second child herself. At the age of fourteen Martha arrived with some youngsters to live and work at the kibbutz here. That was the only solution to her problem. She had been brought up here and taught to forget her past life, but as you can see, Esther, it has had a lasting effect on her." Masha had tears in her eyes when she finished telling Martha's story, one of the secrets she had been sworn not to tell. When Esther heard the story she pitied the girl so much that she longed to go to her and tell her how sorry she was. What was the point, however, in dragging up past evils? Far better to let her live her own present happiness, and forget! One child who had attracted Esther's attention in particular, was little Danny. What coincidence! His name was Danny; only thirteen. Danny had been found at Dachau, and smuggled to Palestine by the Aliya Beth people. The boy suffered a great deal, having nightmares nearly every night and waking screaming about packing suitcases and smelling smoke.

Esther asked Sarah, an old member who had been in charge of the Aliya Children what the dream of packing a suitcase meant.

"Suitcases," Sarah began, "were always packed the night before the inmates were transferred to the gas chambers."

"And smelling smoke?" Esther was curious as a child.

"That's the smell of burning flesh from the crematorium."

Esther shuddered, knowing that little Danny had been an eye-witness of the death of his mother. His father had been taken away to another camp. His sister was eighteen when she committed suicide because she had been forced into prostitution with German soldiers. It was only by a miracle that Danny, whose German name was Heinz, had survived, and kept alive by his own indomitable spirit. A flood of memories surged through the lad's tortured brain day and night. The barbed wire was torn down, the chambers and the ovens were gone, but the memories would never leave little Danny. The frightful smell seemed always to hover about him, and he relived his experience every night. Esther was very interested in the little boy's story, and Sarah was only happy to see Esther as an efficient and a great help at the children quarter. Esther had expressed her intention to proceed in her work with the children right after she had given birth to her child. She said that was the joy of living, to be with children, to love them, to shower on them all your love, care and assistance. The more she heard about them, the more she loved them, and little Danny was no exception.

It was in the summer of 1945 when people of the Aliya Beth met little Heinz at Dachau, and he was smuggled to Palestine with hundreds of others. Here they were sent to several settlements, various kibbutzim and moshavim,(communal settlements|) and Deganya had taken some of the children. Deganya had blossomed since then, and with it the children grew and blossomed, too. During all those years, little Danny had never forgotten his father. "He was taken away,

I remember," he had told Sarah many times. "They did not kill him as they killed my mother. They did not drag away his body, as they dragged away my sister." Sarah went on telling Esther about the boy.

"He thinks that his father is still alive. He wants to see him. He keeps telling me that he must find him," Sara felt puzzled.

"And what is your reaction?"

"I keep telling him that if we find him, we will let him know at once. You see, it rekindles hope within him." Sarah put in.

"Hope! Just hope," Esther murmured.

"Well, at least hope if he refuses to accept the idea to forget him." Sara was right. She had no alternative. She knew well how to handle those boys and girls. She understood their bruised minds; indeed there were few others who knew how to talk to them, how to handle those youngsters who had been denied the love of parents. Esther had a lot to learn from Sarah. She began to adapt her ways to win their affection and trust. She proved herself a good candidate for the job.

What was it that made her love to work with them? Was it Yigal's broken childhood? Was it Danny's name that wouldn't leave her memory?

Every time she thought of Yigal it was with love and compassion, with pity and respect. He had won her heart, and she longed for the day when he and she and her child would be a happy family. She kept telling herself that she didn't love him out of pity. She was sure she loved him and wanted him and ached for him. Would the new life with him make her forget Danny or her diary? That she didn't know. All she knew was she yearned for happiness, which she had been denied, too. Just when she was beginning to have a taste of it, death had snatched it harshly from her. Only the day before she had read Emerson's words: "Happiness, is a perfume you cannot pour on others without getting a few drops on yourself!" Then, that was the reason why she wanted to make those children happy, why she wanted to make Yigal happy! How selfish of her? She knew the miracle would work on her as well! It was her own happiness she was in search for! Now she could read her mind!

The next morning Esther was called to the "secretariat" central administration office. She was asked to take a seat, and the speaker, an energetic woman, whom everybody called "Sarah, the mother of the children", said, "Esther, I've sent for you to ask you if you will go on a motherly mission." Sarah took in a breath, and watched Esther's curious face as she continued.

"I know how fond you are of little Danny. He told me that he likes you and trusts you." There was another pause, and the curiosity was whetted beyond words. "Esther, Danny's father has been found." The woman wiped a tear from her eyes.

"Found?" Esther couldn't help breaking into tears.

"Yes. Unfortunately he is a very sick man. He is hospitalized, and cannot travel." Sara gathered herself together.

"Does Danny know?"

"Yes, Esther. He does, and naturally he wants to see him."

"And..." Esther moved uneasily on her chair.

"Will you take the trip to Haifa Hospital with him?"

"But, of course!" Esther cried at the top of her voice.

"There is Akiva with his private car waiting for you just outside. Esther, go get the boy, and off to Haifa hospital."

...

Haifa Hospital:

The doctor sat beside the boy and explained to him that his father had to remain under treatment and close supervision for some time.

"How long?" the intelligent boy asked.

"That I can't tell you. He is suffering from arthritis and heart failure."

"Arth...."

"Arthritis. It is an inflammation of the joints. You understand, Danny, your father was tortured by the Gestapo. They made him work very hard, they beat him, and he was exposed to damp and cold in winter. You have to understand that fatigue, injury, emotional strain are also contributory causes to his condition."

"Will he ever get well?"

The doctor's eyes met Esther's. "We have every hope that he will. Meanwhile he is under medical treatment, and must stay here for the time being. "Then he turned to Haya, the nurse who had been standing next to Esther, and said, "Haya, take Danny to see his father, please."

"This way," the nurse led them along a polished corridor. She paused outside a door, then before entering, said, "You wait outside. I'll see if he is awake."

They stood by the door. Danny raised his eyes to Esther. He smiled, then looked at his kibbutz clothes and said, "Father does not know what a kibbutz is. He'll ask where I got this shirt from. He doesn't know what life in a kibbutz is like. I'll take him back to Deganya when he is well. He was a carpenter once. He will work with Arye at the carpentry," Danny was saying when suddenly the door opened, and the nurse beckoned them. Esther took Danny's hand and led him into the room.

The old man was lying in the bed. He turned his head on the pillow, and the moment he saw the little boy he stretched out his thin arms. "Heinz! Heinz! My son." He wept. "I have been searching for you all those years.." Tears of joy were spilling down his sunken cheeks. Danny ran forward and fell on his knees beside the bed. "Daddy, Oh, Daddy!" he cried, and they wept together while the two women watched and struggled to keep back sympathetic tears.

"Heinz, my son," the old man muttered over and over again.

"Daddy, is it true that you are very sick? You will get well?"

"Yes, my son, and soon we shall be together again..." his voice was weak and low.

"Heinz," the nurse began. The lad interrupted her, "My name is Danny. Only father can call me Heinz." Then he turned to his dad and said, "Do you like the name Danny?"

"Yes, my son," the old man was wiping away his tears.

"Daddy, this is Esther from Deganya. This is a communal settlement. It is lovelier than any home in the world, Daddy. You will come to live with me there. Won't you?"

"We shall be glad to have you among us, friend Goldstein," Esther said politely.

The old man mumbled his thanks, and kissed his son over and over.

"I'm sorry, fellows, but the visiting time is over." a young nurse approached them. "The doctors will be here soon."

"Shalom!" Esther said as she took away Danny slowly and gently. It was hard for the boy to release himself from his father's kisses, but Esther promised Goldstein that Danny would come again to see him.

"Will you get well soon, daddy?" the boy asked in the corridor.

"Yes, Danny, of course he will!" she replied though her heart smote her, remembering how ill the old man looked.

"I'm so happy, Esther," the little boy held her hand. She smiled down at him. It made one joyful to see other people full of joy, she thought to herself. Maybe that was the secret of living. If only she could make her last sentence come true!

...

"Now then, fellows, the activities here comprise the intensive cultivation of fruit, such as bananas, oranges and grapes; also vegetable growing, dairy farming, poultry and carp breeding, olive plantations and the production of cereals."

Yigal's voice was calm and the class listened attentively. He found no difficulty introducing Deganya to those young people. "As you see the village is set amid gardens, eucalyptus trees, groves and orchards. You have seen the cultural institute, concert and lecture halls, reading rooms, library, etc.. We must bear in mind the difficulties lying ahead of us if we wish to see Tel Katzir one day a well-organized settlement. The training you are getting here will give you reason to refer, any time in the future, to this your alma mater for help, instruction and assistance. The school of agriculture of Deganya is dedicated for all the community farms of the Jordan valley area.." A short pause followed. Rivka raised a finger, "Yigal, you promised to tell us about the tank."

"Yes, you did!" the class chorused. Yigal turned to the map on the wall. "In May 1948 the inhabitants of Deganya were called upon to withstand the combined onslaughts of the Syrian, Iraqi and Jordan forces. Their gallant resistance saved the neighboring settlements from destruction. This Renault tank is a trophy of the war...." Yigal's story held the youngsters attentive and silent. They went out in the open and inspected the tank as it stood there. In the afternoon the class had another lesson in the open, whereas they joined their tutor to the Beit Gordon Natural History Museum. Then the group moved up the hill to the cemetery. Yigal's eyes fell on Danny's grave. He read the name, and passed on, halting a little further along the path. "Here in this cemetery," he said, "besides the graves of the Deganyans and the leaders of Zionism who wished to be buried in Deganya there are many graves of soldiers who fell in the war." The group moved from one grave to another solemnly, silently as though trying not to disturb their peaceful world. Walking on, they came to a nicely tended grave, surrounded by low flowering bushes. The inscription read, "A Servitor of Man and Nature. "Here under the eucalyptus trees lies A.S, Gordon. This inscription is a quotation from one of his best-known works." Yigal led his young people to the outside court. They came to an old man who was pruning bushes in readiness for the spring.

"Good day," Yigal greeted the old man.

"Good day, fellas!" he answered.

"This is Ben Dor, who looks after the cemetery. Then he turned to the old man. "How long have you been doing this, Ben Dor?"

"Seventeen years now!" he replied. "Respect the living and the dead as well," he addressed the young people.

On their way towards the lane that led to the library Yigal was heard saying, "The whole of this area was formerly marshland and infested with malaria-carrying mosquitoes..." And as he went on talking and walking the class followed his steps.

"Class dismissed," he announced. "You will go now to the library to look through books or just while away the time. We shall meet here again in half an hour." Yigal smiled at his young people and walked away.

He had taken a few steps away when suddenly he became aware of his being followed. He stopped and turned just to see Tamar walking fast to catch up with him.

"Aren't you going to the library, Tamar?" he asked. She looked at him with her wide, beautiful eyes, "Yigal, I must talk to you!" her voice was low and deep. He regarded her as though he had never seen her before. A seventeen year old girl, slim, broad-shouldered, sun-tanned, her heavy hair cut short, a tough, almost masculine type of girl, a "flower of the cactus": prickly on the outside but sweet on the inside. There was about her lovely face something that was unmistakably Russian, her upper lip was thin but her cheeks were full with high cheekbones. Her chin was square and stubborn, and when she smiled her teeth were unusually big and white. Her strong and confident manners astonished Yigal.

"What about?" he asked, already apprehensive.

Tamar was looking deep into his eyes. He had always feared such an encounter with Tamar. She had had a fancy for him, he knew that. "Yigal, I've only known you for three weeks. You must be only four or five years older than I. Yigal, I've been trying to press such thoughts, but I can't do that anymore."

There was love in the young girl's eyes, he could bet. He remained silent, and only wished the storm would pass soon.

"Yigal, are you really going to marry a pregnant woman?"

His lips tightened with anger. "How dare you? This is none of your business," he was outrageous at the little girl.

"I'm not a little girl, Yigal. I know what I say. At least I know what I feel?"

"And what is it that you feel? Give me an advice?"

"No, Yigal," her voice was low and arousing pity. "I feel, Yigal, I feel that I love you...."

...

Esther's anxiety mounted as she looked through the window at the winding path below. A cold wind was fanning her face and black clouds rolled across the sky. It was only a few minutes past four in the afternoon but already almost dark. She had been expecting Yigal for some time. He had asked her not to go out if the weather was bad and she had spent all the afternoon in her room, reading and writing. The minutes raced by like the clouds that travelled so fast across the sky. She turned from the window and looked at herself in the mirror. A knocking at the door put an abrupt end to her self-searching.

"Esther!" A masculine voice called, and it was Yigal's.

"Come in!"

The door opened. He sat at the edge of the iron bed, took her hand and kissed it.

"You're late," she said, turning her palm to caress his cheek.

"Five minutes late!"

"I had a discussion with Uzi. The guy is setting his sights too high over the new kibbutz at Tel Katzir," Yigal made himself comfortable on her bed.

"He knows he has on whom to rely!"

"But I can't work miracles. There is so much to do!"

"How can I help you, Yigal?" Esther had always proposed her assistance, but his reply was always the same.

"As soon as the baby is born you will be a great help to me, you will work with me." He took a closer look at her face. It looked clouded and uncertain. "Anything wrong, darling?"

"Sometimes I feel lonely!"

"But not when you're with me, Esther."

"Take no notice. I'm just being silly. You know, Yigal, I was thinking the other day that there are still some parts about your past that I do not know."

"What, for instance?" he drew closer to her.

"Come on, I know, I shouldn't keep pestering you, it only shows.."

"That you are interested in me;" he completed her unfinished sentence, took her hands and said, "Let's go out. It stopped raining. Put on your jacket. Aren't you hungry? I'm starving." And he led her out to the dining hall.

The air was cool and fresh outside. It was a packed hall and the noise made it impossible for Esther and Yigal to hear themselves. The first five rows of tables had been occupied by the youngsters, the future founders of Tel Katzir. There was a little hush when Yigal led Esther into the hall to the nearest unoccupied seats. Several pairs of eyes followed them as they walked in, not excluding Tamar's.

He was telling her something and she was smiling when suddenly he paused, his attention flickering momentarily from Esther's face to that of someone at the next table. Following his eyes she saw that Tamar was gazing at him, and for a moment, she had a feeling that they exchanged a meaning glance. He turned to her instantly. She was looking at her plate, chewing food that had suddenly become like sawdust in her mouth. She looked at him, then back at her plate. Yigal said nothing. He was absorbed in his food.

"Is she a brilliant pupil?"

"Who?"

"Tamar, of course. She is beautiful, isn't she?"

"Well, I should say she is," Yigal was playing with his spoon nervously. "She's a hard worker."

Esther cast another glance at Tamar, who stood to her feet and talked to another girl. They were leaving the dining-hall. Esther gulped her cup of coffee hastily. "Are you finished? It's too noisy inside here."

"Let's go," Yigal rose. She rose slowly, pushing the chair behind her. Yigal hastened to take it out of her way, and they made their way out of the hall.

There was an almost clear sky. Still a few clouds, but the stars and the moon were visible. Yigal took her hand and pressed it gently to his lips. He was silent. He only wondered if she, too, was thinking of Tamar. Apparently she was jealous, and telling her about Tamar would only make her more jealous and furious. They walked hand in hand. He wished he could think of something to say to break that silence. It was her silence that worried him most; it was like a thousand knives that stabbed his back and front.

"Esther," he began, not knowing if he would be able to continue. His courage failed him. No, it was better not to talk about Tamar.

"Yes, Yigal," she, too, wished he could break the silence. And his reticence implied something that reminded her of the story of the thief that had been caught red-handed. No, she wouldn't ask him about Tamar. If the girl didn't mean anything to him, she would only hurt his feelings. She was thoughtful, but he was saying something about the future, celebrations of Shavuoth, the feast of nature. "We'll drive to the Sea of Galilee, go into the Genossar Valley and see the brown hills of Syria looming on the far side."

"When?" she woke up from her reverie.

"I mean right after Shavuoth, after you have given birth to our little child!" Yigal planted a kiss on her lips. "I shall go with you to the ruins of Capernahum, to the Mount of Beatitudes, then to Migdal, and beneath the Horns of Hittim into the fields of wild flowers that look like a red carpet."

"You sound as if you're reading from a book," she pressed her hand into his and walked on.

"Then back to Tiberias and Kiryat Shmuel, the Jordan River, the sea. And we shall swim there. What do you say, Esther?"

"Sounds real fun!"

"We shall dive into the water, swim, then climb on a nearby raft, breathless and laughing."

"I can feel the waters against my naked body: cool and refreshing!"

"I'm looking forward, Esther. These waters will wash away all your bad dreams and childish thoughts. We'll look ahead to a bright future.."

"Go on, Yigal. You sound so romantic..."

"It will be late in the afternoon, and in the evening after dinner I shall take you to a concert at the Ein Gev kibbutz. We shall cross the still waters of the lake and land at the docks of the Ein Gev settlement, near the basin formed by the Yarmuk river. Right on the border between Ein Gev and the Syrian hills stands the small mountain, Susita. We shall walk to the edge of the lake where the outdoor auditorium stands. I will then spread a blanket on the grass at the edge of the auditorium, and the two of us will lie and look up into the sky and watch the enormous Lag Ba Omer moon grow smaller and higher to make room for the billion stars up there." Esther was amused by his talk, and she hated to interrupt him. "Go on, Yigal," she urged.

"It will be a dream, the moment of perfection. And when the concert's over, I'll take your hand and lead you away from the crowd along a path down to the lake. The scent of the pine trees will fill the air, and the Sea of Galilee will look like a polished mirror.... And we will make love...." He drew her face to his.

"Yigal," her breath was warm against his cheeks. "A soldier! Yes. But a poet! You sound so much like Danny!"

"The sea will stir and lap against the shores. I'll make you happy, now and forever!" She leaned against him as he kissed her.

"Please, kiss me again!" her palms and fingers pressed hard on his back, she held him fast; then suddenly Danny's image came to her. Yigal, aware of her sudden withdrawal, pulled her back to him and kissed her over and over again.

"I am overwhelmed by recollections," she murmured between the kisses. "I'm afraid, Yigal."

"Afraid of what?" he led her to a lonely bench.

"So many memories come to me. Right now, as I hold you in my arms, I can remember a rainy day back in '44 or '45. Danny and I had gone for a walk. In the rain! Sounds silly, doesn't it?"

"Young people do all kinds of things. Some of them - silly," Yigal replied. "Go on, Esther."

"The rain had brought out the lovely smells in the gardens, and we felt marvelous, we felt like running and romping about like kids. You guess what we did? We played hide-and-seek. It was fun! I was young and innocent!"

"You are still young and beautiful. Esther, you're innocent and pure. A hundred per cent soul. That's what you are," Yigal held her close to him and urged her to keep on talking. "Speak up. Unless you speak up you won't release yourself from a dead past!"

"Danny caught me and before I could twist free he swept me from my feet cradling me against his chest. We were so wet and we laughed our hearts out in the rain.." she sobbed. "I don't know if I shall ever be happy again, carefree and merry!"

"You're young. The future is still ahead of us. You will be with me all your years. I'll make you happy, Esther. You don't know what the future has in stores for us!"

"That's what's worrying me most," she said.

"I can't tell you what's behind the veil. Nobody can. Why worry about the future? Live for today, the morrow will take care of itself," his words were soothing but not convincing.

Esther's sobs lessened and then ceased, and she listened like a soothed child, nestling against him as he went on talking. "Our baby will be a lovely child. Just imagine: such a frail, little creature! Bright red when 'tis born, and in a few days it will be a lovely little fair skinned boy, or girl, with thick hair like mine, lovely long lashes and dimpled little fists. As the months go by it will smile and start to play. Oh, it'll have little temper tantrums, too, when it can't get its way."

Yigal laughed, and she laughed with him. "When I was a child I was like that."

"How do you remember?" she asked like a child herself.

"I've a good memory." He laughed at his own joke. "He or she will be brilliant. Walking by ten months, running everywhere, into everything, And at the age of one year...."

"I don't believe you remember all this," she interrupted him.

"Of course I don't! You're being amused. You're laughing, That is what matters now."

...

"I keep having horrible dreams," Esther said to Masha as they were tidying up the children's room at the nursery.

"Put those toys in the corner up there!" Masha was putting some picture books on the shelves. "Again? Esther, your dreams are beginning to drive me crazy. Why don't you see Dr. Yoram about them? You know, he is a psychoanalyst."

"You want me to drive him crazy, too?" Esther put in. Then after a short pause, gathered her thoughts and added. "This time he was clad in a white shirt and shorts, smiling boyishly as he had always done when he wanted to ask a favor of me. Danny never asked favors of anybody. But his demands sounded so innocent and polite. He said, Esther, I ask you to do this for my sake. Do what, I asked. Write a book, he replied. I suddenly burst out laughing. I'm no writer, I said. A book? What sort of a book you want me to write, I asked. He looked me deep into the eyes. His looks were fierce. "A book to contain everything about us," he said in the dream. "What things?" I asked.

"All the joys and pains, all the excitements and disappointments, all the good and evil, tears of joy and tears of sorrow, smiles and frowns, all and everything we have had in common," he said. He drew me closer to him, becoming stern and then angry, so that I almost got frightened. He stood over me, angrily repeating his request. He sounded sour and looked ugly. "A book!" he shouted at me. "You can't offer me anything anymore. Just this one small request: A book!" he shouted frantically. "My soul has been searching for you everywhere, and now that I have found you I won't let you off, I won't set you free unless you write this book for me. You took away my child. You will never marry another man. We shall be married soon, Esther. I'm here to take you away with me." He sounded frightening, and his laughter and his sound had a nightmare quality. It echoed and echoed in my head. He caught me by the arm, held me tightly and kissed me." Esther was sobbing while Masha listened with rapt attention, the books in one hand and the duster in the other.

"Believe me, Masha, I had never loathed his kisses. I hated him, and I wanted to break away from his clutch. I trembled with revulsion, and he went on kissing me. There was blood on his lips, and he said, "Now you're in my arms. You'll not run away. Sweet are the kisses of death," he said, and his lips dropped blood on my face. I cried, "You're hurting me, please let me go." "No, not anymore," he insisted and tightened his grip and clutch on me. I was writhing in pain, but he wouldn't let me go. "This time, Esther..Danny..ever! I promise. I want to drink to our union ... reunion, Esther..." Reunion...Reunion... the words rang in my ears and I woke up in a cold sweat of terror." Masha remained silent. She was terror-stricken herself. Esther dropped a book on the floor. Masha knelt down to pick it up. The title read: "We shall meet again in the World to come, By Reymond Flair.." Esther's eyes were glued on the dark block letters on the jacket of the book. She moved a hand over her throat as if it ached, as if she had just escaped strangulation. "What a dreadful dream!" she murmured.

"You better see Dr. Yoram. He might have an advice for you. Maybe it is the effect of stress and strain on your thoughts."

"You know, Masha, I've not written a single word for over a month. I'm just fearful of touching..." she stopped.

"Touching what? Written to whom?" Masha enquired with open-mouthed admiration and amazement at the girl's words.

"O, I forgot I hadn't told you about my diary. I keep a diary, you see? And .. from time to time I write.."

"Write what?"

"Skip it.. Nonsense, Masha; forget about it. I mean I write whatever comes my mind, whatever comes to my head."

"About Danny?"

"Everything!"

"You shouldn't concentrate on that diary of yours." Masha's advice sounded friendly to Esther. "Yet, I'd suggest you talk to Dr. Yoram about your dreams."

Esther dropped another book. "I'll pick it up," Masha hastened to kneel to the floor. She looked at the title.

"A Rendezvous with Dracula" the title read. She put it on the pile of books by her side and said, "The girls have been bringing over books from the library to read in their spare time. These are no books for children. I better take them back to the library. You see? They forget to return the books to the librarian, so they remain here, but I won't allow such books in the children's room anymore."

...

The sky was pale with dawn. Yigal looked at his class. In the second row, third from left, stood Tamar. He avoided her looks and went on saying, "This morning I'll begin with a brief lesson on ornamental trees, most of them evergreens that grow in this area. We shall then proceed to the site of the well."

"When are you going to tell about the Acre jail?" Rina asked.

"The morning is still young. We've plenty of time. Now to the lesson.." he paced up towards a huge eucalyptus tree.

"For a start you all know the eucalyptus; an important tree which grows in many places in Israel. This genus includes three hundred species of evergreen, leathery-leaved trees native to Australia. The oils yielded by different species vary a great deal in their scent and other properties, and are chiefly used in pharmacy and perfumery. About thirty species produce oils suitable for medical purposes, and various species produce timber. Here in Deganya the trees of eucalyptus were planted to help dry the swamps." He inspected the class again and picked the shy, timid boy in the left hand row, "Now, Udi, you tell us about the fir." Udi pointed to the picture of a pyramid-shaped tree on the blackboard and explained. Yigal's eyes roamed to Tamar. He heard the boy saying ... "...Needless grow around the branch, with twisted stalks that seem to grow in rows on opposite sides, dark green above, light green below."

"Now, will Sami tell us about the pine?" Yigal's eyes roved on the class in the open, as Sami began to talk.

"Considered the oldest of all, pines have trunks up to two hundred feet high, round and pyramid shaped with thin and scaly bark, needles in clusters of two to five cones, one to eighteen inches long.."

"Good. Very good," Yigal consulted his watch and said, "Before we proceed on to the well, will anyone give me names of other trees we have learnt about lately?"

"The carob," Ella shouted at the last row. "An evergreen tree, of the Mediterranean region, bearing red racemose flowers."

"The oleander," that was Tamar.

"Yes, go ahead, tell us about the oleander," Yigal said. Tamar stood to her feet. Her fingers tapped nervously on her desk as she spoke, "This is a poisonous tree, an evergreen apocynaceous shrub, with fragrant flowers shading from white to red."

"Will you be able to recognize it if you come across it out of doors?"

"Yes." Tamar's beauty was matchless. She knew it, Yigal knew it, the class knew it.

"O.K. Now we move on towards the well. Be careful not to disturb the other classes outside."

In the fields they were met by Bar-El, a farmer who was in charge of the vegetable fields. A thin, small man, Bar-El was a Russian Jew who thirty years before had come to Deganya to plough the land. Bar-El spoke to the class with a happy smile on his face, "The vegetable is, or should be, an integral part of home economy. Land preparation is important." Yigal took a few minutes off to light a cigarette as the old man went on speaking, "... It should be dug two spits deep," he was saying. "That is double-digging, in winter, and for this the plot..." Bar-El's deep voice went on explaining what soil cultivation meant.

Afterwards, Yigal led the group southward. Suddenly he discovered that Tamar had been standing next to him. He was going to tell them now about the Acre jail. "Well, friends, be seated, all of you, the Acre jail story you read in books should be remembered, and here is a personal experience."

He stood tall and handsome, walked freely among the classmates as a hero among the "extras" in a film.

"Acre was an all-Arab city," he began. "The jail was the toughest stronghold they had in Palestine. Several Jews had been thrown into prison by the British - their end was to be the rope! There were some Palmach soldiers who could not bear the thought, and they decided to make a raid and break into the jail." The class listened with rapt attention as Yigal took a breath from his cigarette, and continued, "It was a dangerous thing to undertake, and needed careful planning. It worked, however. Hundreds of Palmachnicks got into the jail, and began smashing open the cell doors and freeing the prisoners. The escapers, Arabs and Jews alike, were soon running in every direction through Acre. With a magnetic mine we ripped the doors of the death cells from their hinges. Some of the Palmach soldiers took prisoners with them when they ran away. I drove away with two of them in a truck. The truck raced up the coast road, it had been spotted by the British, and was being followed by a motor force. The driver turned off the road into some fields in order to get past the British unit, and suddenly there was a hail of bullets. The whine of bullets was all around us. Two soldiers with sub-machine guns were hot on our tail. I fired through the back window. One of them dropped, the second opened up with a deadly burst of fire, and one of the prisoners was hit in the stomach.

We drove on, and the other prisoner suddenly cried out, "I've been hit!" Blood was pouring from a wound in his right arm, and he pressed his hand there to stop the bleeding. Meanwhile I ripped my own shirt and bandaged the other prisoner's wound." Couples of eyes were watching Yigal as he spoke, as he moved among the class. "Suddenly I felt blood dripping on my face, and the prisoner told me that I had been hit, too. I didn't believe him, but he insisted that I'd had a narrow escape from death." Yigal stopped for a moment, his thoughts racing back to that dreadful moment. He took in a deep breath and went on. "As we headed for the nearest Jewish settlement for first aid, the prisoner who had been hit in the stomach died. There was nothing I could do for him. When they washed away the blood from the other prisoner and myself, they found that we had both been hit by the same bullet, fortunately for us, not seriously." He moved a finger over the scar on his forehead, "That's when I got this..."

Class was dismissed and there was a break of fifteen minutes. After the break Yigal took his class down the path southward. He pointed at the path, "Here is a forked path. You walk through the rows, say ten in each row, and within half an hour we meet at the other side of the forest. Meanwhile, you will observe the trees, study their growth, and if you've any questions, remember to ask when we meet .. in half an hour." Yigal divided his group into four smaller ones, and when they had gone their separate ways and disappeared among the trees, he cast a glance at his shoulder for he had had a feeling that he had not been left alone. At his shoulder stood Tamar, her hair shining like gold on a lily in the warm wintry sun. She was gently caressing the bough of a tree that made a canopy over their heads through which the rays of the sun shone. Her eyes were fixed on Yigal as she said, "I'll be in your group. Do you mind?"

Embarrassed, he plucked a small branch, took the tip in his mouth and said, "No." and led her into the grove.

"You're walking too fast. Can't keep pace with you," she said after a moment of silence.

"If you're tired you can sit down and rest. Then you double your steps to catch up with the others," Yigal's reply was cold and cruel. She glanced at him distressed.

"You hurt me, Yigal. I can't tell you what I feel. You'll regard me with..." and she broke out sobbing.

"Tamar, control yourself. What is it?"

"Yigal, I've been thinking of you all the nights, all the days. I love you, Yigal!" she broke sobbing again. Her cheeks became red with shame and fear; shame of the confession, and fear of the truth that was in Yigal's mouth. He was going to say that he didn't give a damn for her, that he didn't care, that she should behave herself, but he said nothing and preferred to remain silent. She drew closer to him, her breasts almost touching his chest. "Let's go, Tamar...." he whispered.

The dense forest enveloped them and there was no living soul in sight. She looked around her, uttered a little sob and flung herself into his arms. "I can't stop thinking about you," she buried her face against his shoulders..

"Tamar," he gently stroked her beautiful hair. "You're still young. I like you, as I would like my little sister, six years my junior. You must understand that I cannot love you. It is forbidden love. I love Esther, and I'm going to marry her."

Tamar flung up her head to protest, but he was the first to speak again, "You must be sensible. It takes two to make a love affair complete. You can't keep on loving without being loved in return." He was now studying her face. The shock was too strong to be born. "You'll grow up, and maybe here or at Tel Katzir you'll find someone to make you happy."

Tears welled up to her eyes, but Yigal continued hitting while the iron rod was still hot, "Out of the blue sky you will meet your true lover. You see in me a hero, and your love is based on esteem and identification. You must not confuse between this and real love." He took her hand gently and led her through the forest. His voice came to her ears as she choked back her tears, "We can remain good friends." He looked about him. He hoped he had not lost his way. He had to find a short cut to catch up with the other groups.

"And I promise I'll not breathe a word of all this to anybody, even to Esther herself.." he said.

Tamar sidled close to him, put her hands into his. The feel of his warm palm against her own made her heart pound.

Suddenly, overcome with passion, she clutched his forearm, threw her arms around his neck and kissed him. He released himself gently but firmly, and pushed her away, fearing that someone should suddenly come upon them.

"You promise not to humiliate me before others, not to tell on me?" she asked between the kisses.

"I promise. It is our secret. O.K.?"

She felt relieved at the thought that they had a secret to share together. Whenever their eyes would meet, she would understand, he would understand; and that sufficed!

Yigal doubled his steps, and was relieved when they rejoined the rest of the groups without being noticed.

Before being dismissed the class received instructions about an excursion out to Mount Arbel to be planned, per schedule, for the next week. It was acclaimed by the class.

....

Uzi stopped his jeep and got out. "Magnificent! Isn't it?" he called, his hands still on the wheel.

"Terrific! What a beauty!" Yigal replied, still gazing with delight at the lovely panorama that spread before his eyes.

Uzi walked down to meet Yigal. They stood for a moment commanding a view of the whole panorama that lay under their feet just below the hill where they stood. "It is this land, this very tell (hill) over there that you are going to plough and live on," he pointed at a dreary non-cultivated land just next to the beautiful and green valleys and villages that surrounded it. "Not the villages overthere," he addad sarcastically.

"Aha!" Yigal replied. "The youngsters have already been taught this lesson."

"What lesson?"

"Every beginning is hard." Yigal couldn't help admiring the beautiful, breathtaking scenery that surrounded him, the green and yellow patches of land that spread before him.

"By the way, Uzi. I have promised them an excursion."

"Where? Out of the kibbutz?"

"Yes, a one day picnic." Yigal was brief. He knew he would have troubles getting the secretariat's permission for that, but he insisted on getting it.

"Yigal, the kibbutz treasury will not endorse any expenses incurred."

"Uzi, the kibbutz can and must find the means to offer these youngsters some entertainment. They're young and high-spirited, they're working hard, and I've put in them all that can be expected of kibbutz founders."

"I get you. I know you'll get what you want. I shall vote for it, Yigal. You can take my word."

Yigal remained standing, looking with eager eyes at the lovely countryside and the high mountains around. "Almost incredible! In a few months this very site will be inhabited. Gardens and trees will grow here."

"The people who achieved miracles, those who conquered the deserts and those who won battles will pass on their message to the young generation, and this in turn will follow suit." Uzi was proud of himself. "I knew I could rely on you. Commander Allon knows well enough why he had been asked to send you back to us promptly!"

It was a cold morning, and it had snowed all night in the Galilee. Now the snow had ceased, and the majestic hills were golden in the unexpected sunlight, and tipped on each rise with silver from the snow. The convulted hills twisted and turned in harmonious folds like the intricacies of music, dropping at last to the lake itself, now crystal-blue in the distance. Uzi's words fell on deaf ears, for Yigal had been too engrossed in the beauty of nature. His eyes roved all around. He was too moved to speak, "Tel Katzir will be a nice spot to visit one day, a lovely settlement. We shall all be indebted to Deganya for the aid offered." Uzi wondered if the young man had heard him. He put his hand on his shoulder, and said, "It'll take some time, Yigal!"

"I know, but I'm beginning to like the idea. Esther will love to live here!" Uzi was well aware that the younger man was being carried away in his enthusiasm.

"It is my land, and I love it as passionately as a man loves a woman, and as joyously as a child loves the dawning of a day when he is to have a special treat or a good surprise." Yigal stooped to pick up a handful of soil, crumbling it between his fingers, looking at it carefully as though examining every grain of it, then allowing it to fall again. "Hard here, soft there, but water will bring life to it."

"You know why a Sabra (born in Israel) loves the Galilee?" Uzi asked.

"It is the soil from which his people have sprung through countless generations; but I am not a sabra, Uzi," Yigal replied.

"And I love every village, every little hill, valley and dale, even the narrow paths clustering about a central wall in old Jerusalem or ancient Safed or Tiberias. You see?"

"Without this spirit we couldn't possibly conquer the desert. There's a knack is passing on this message to the young generation, in making them feel as passionately attached to the soil as to their own families." Uzi was beginning to get enthusiastic about the idea of founding settlements and turning all the hills and mountains to green villages. He was remembering an early period at Deganya his home kibbutz. "You know, Yigal, in 1934 Henrietta Szold came to visit us here. That was certainly many years ago. After that visit she said, 'My pessimism always vanishes when I spend a few hours in a kvutza, a minor communal settlement. I forget that I am a cynic. It is a life of hardship, but not of strain, and the hardship has its compensation in the form of achievement and the consciousness that both the hardship and the success are a common responsibility and a common advantage.' Yes, Yigal, this is what we have been teaching our children ever since Deganya came into being."

"And this is exactly what I taught my pupils, and with these very words I open each and every lesson. The youngsters have learnt it by heart, and it has become their motto."

Uzi's bosom swelled with pride as he realized anew that he had done well by choosing the right man for the right mission. When they drove back home, Yigal thought of the great deal of hard work that lay ahead. He thought of Esther and the new place that awaited them. He wondered whether or not he should tell her about Tamar. How could he share a secret with Tamar! Would it arouse Esther's jealousy and wrath? Would she understand? Wouldn't it be wiser not to tell Esther? But what if Tamar would play the fool and tell her? What if Tamar would blackmail him? What if she, in her young green brain, would break that secret to poor Esther? Yigal was worried and thoughtful.

...

The grim-visaged bronze bust of Sigmund Freud, the Viennese father of psychoanalysis and the great explorer of the subconscious, stares down from the bookcase in Dr. Yoram's office at the Home Clinic. It overlooks the desk of Dr. Yoram, the accredited psychiatrist, psychoanalyst and medical director from Russia.

A tall, agile man in his mid-sixties, Dr. Yoram, with a countenance that breaks easily into a smile, had come from Moscow and there he was known as Dr. Yarmelovitz. He bore little resemblance to the stereotype of the psycho-analyst overlooking his desk. Lounging cross-legged in his brown leather chair, he listened to Esther.

It was dark in his room, though it was barely afternoon, and the sun was shining brightly outside. In one corner of the room stood a desk and the doctor's armchair. The desk was relatively plain, of inlaid mahogany. On it stood a framed picture of a young boy in his late teens, obviously Dr. Yoram's late son, who had fallen in the War of Independence. A single lamp stood beside the photograph.

"Recollections are not considerate, doctor," Esther was saying. "They thrust themselves upon me."

Dr. Yoram shook a cigarette out of the pack in his hand. He caught it quickly to his mouth and lit it with a match. It was rather bent, and when he exhaled, he removed it to regard it with disgust, "You are devoting much of your time to this diary," he said after he had taken a long drag from his cigarette. "You are desperately attached to it." The smoke curled above his head, and he watched Esther recollecting.

"I can remember now another summer story," she uttered. Her third story so far. The doctor gazed into her eyes. "That was the summer when Danny was eighteen. He grew suddenly tall, like a stalk of July corn, his shoulders broadened, and there was hair on his chest, his beard had to be shaved. Often in the afternoons when we had finished the work we would go barefooted, dressed in blue shorts and shirts, down the road and across the fields to the banks of the Kinnereth. We would run and plunge with our clothes on into the lake. In that summer day a few years age we found a favorite place to be together, on the lake, where it veered away from the road. There at the foot of a big tree we used to sit and write our names in the sand. Sometimes we would just sit and read, or swim in the deep, quiet pool beneath the oak tree whose gnarled roots reached down into the water and fixed themselves in the bank like a giant hand clutched in the coil of a snake. Lying in the shade we could see up and down the water for half a mile each way." Esther heaved a deep sigh, her eyes narrowed and she looked like a medium under the spell of hypnosis. Dr. Yoram looked her straight in the eye, his gaze was unwinking. "Go on, Esther, let me hear what is on your mind." He crushed his cigarette into the ashtray. Esther was sitting at the other side of the desk, drooping an arm over the back of her chair. She looked young and beautiful, her golden hair was a little fly-away, her blue eyes big and moist with earnestness. The filmy stuff she was wearing was deceptive; it suggested that a close enough scrutiny might get through, which was not the case, but the round of her breast was brought into prominence by her posture. Dr. Yoram glanced at her, then at his watch, adjusted it on his wrist, and urged, "Go on, Esther."

"That summer Danny often brought a book of poetry to read to me. Like the lake itself, the book was a place of life. We were drunk in the sunlight of the Lake. Once we discovered an old boat that had foundered in the lake. In secret we repaired it; and one day in late June early in the morning, we floated it, and he rowed up the long arm of water where it turned back sharply upon itself. The boat cut into the water-lilies at the edge of the lake with a dry rustle, and the air was moist and heavy with the rank scent of the widening river and the flowers. Danny dug into the water with slow oars as we floated on the breast of the slow-flooding lake. I sat beside him with my feet together, my hands on the sides of the boat. His eyes glowed with a curious light in the brightness of the lake air. I reached up often to push a wisp of hair off my forehead, and sometimes I trailed my hand in the water of the lake." There was a short pause, Esther's dreamy eyes wandered as if she was in a different world. Dr, Yoram wondered at the accuracy of her expressions and description, at the importance of each and every little detail to her. He had just located a pack of cigarettes in the pocket of his jacket. He took it out and began to open the pack. Esther was not looking at him. Her thoughts wandered far and beyond. "Your life is..." he was suddenly interrupted. She went on with her story without listening to him. "The boat grounded many times on mudbars, and Danny had to get out and push it free," she went on. Dr. Yoram stripped the cellophane from the pack, pinched open a corner, lifted one cigarette out and put it in his mouth, slipped the white-gold lighter out of his shirt pocket, thumbed the flame on and lit the cigarette, exhaled, replaced the lighter in his shirt pocket, tossed the pack on the desk, and threw the cellophane in the wastebasket under the desk. "I hope you realize..." again he was interrupted.

"I had never seen so many birds, turtles and frogs in all my life before. The bushes, waterweed, willows and swamp-oaks were so dense in places that they nearly choked the little tributaries flowing into the lake. Suddenly we realized that the boat was leaking. It leaked more and more, and finally in the hot blaze of mid-afternoon, it sank, fortunately in shallow waters. We swam and walked toward the shore, finally flopping exhausted on the beach, almost too tired to walk home. That day it was sweltering hot, but with a cool breeze to keep our spirits high. We stretched out on the grass at the water's edge and listened to the shrill music of frogs. The lake burned green in sunlight, and we lay on our backs. Shutting our eyes, we could feel heat and light raining like hot arrows on our fluttering lids, drying our wet clothes. The frogs croaked hoarsely in the reeds. It was then and only then that I made a vow to be with Danny all my life. His hands moved gently on my half-naked body and I...."

Dr, Yoram smoked one cigarette after the other, squashing the butt of the previous one mercilessly in the ashtray, and looked through the smoke that curled above his head. He was beginning to see how serious Esther's case was. How could he make her forget? When would he begin any treatment? After delivery? Where? He had to consult his colleagues at Beer Yaakov Neuropathic Hospital; that was hundreds of miles away. The woman had been strongly attached to a past she couldn't forget.

"...and I felt no other man could ever enter my life."

Dr. Yoram did not want to cut off the film of thoughts in her head. He was trying to obtain clues to her subconscious complexes, he wished to explore her unconscious mind where the sources of mental illness or any psychological disorder are imbedded. "Are you through, Esther?" he asked.

"I remember my schooldays, a fourth-grader yelling and shouting with my classmates as we tore happily out of doors into the sunshine for morning recess. As the warm weather came, breaking the harsh grip of winter we became impatient of school discipline. Unfettered by winter clothing, we would rush out of class to throw ourselves more violently than ever into a great variety of children's games ...."

Esther went on talking. Dr. Yoram was thinking how far that woman had gone into the past. She had delved too deep into the years. She was retiring to her childhood, doubtlessly she had been going too far and too deep, to childhood games. Why was she trying to find refuge there? His thoughts wandered but his ears kept listening attentively. "I used to love skipping, and riding each other pick-a-back. How reluctant we were to go back into the classroom at the end of the recess!" Esther was musing. Nothing bothered her thoughts to run free. She walked slowly to the window, stood there and looked out of it. Dr. Yoram walked over and stood behind her. A part of the courtyard that was a continuation of the garden was seen, with the lawn sloping down to the stream where ducks and swans were swimming. She pointed at the water and said, "This stream never runs dry even in hot and dry summer days. This's what Danny told me one day." Silence followed. Dr. Yoram took Esther's hand and led her back to his desk. She sat down.

"Esther, I must have a few words with you. I've listened to most of your dreams and recollections, your free thinking and uncontrolled reminiscences. "True, dream-analysis is always useful for a psychiatrist for suggesting topics for investigation and for throwing light of unconscious factors. No dream is unimportant. If sometimes it appears to be so, it is only because we do not understand it. The dream, Esther, is the royal road leading into the unconscious, the signpost which shows the way to the life conflict." He took another puff from his cigarette, and added, "Every dream is a confession, a resurrection of the suppressed, an outcrop of hidden truth. Hebbel says that every writer writes his autobiography, and his self-portrait is more skillful when he is unaware that he is painting his own portrait. So is the case with dreams. Well, then you do understand that you're torn between a past full of sweet memories and a present full of happy promises. While the past refuses to recede and scorns burial, the future struggles to raise its head and dominate your life, and the present is a by-pass you hate to walk through, a bridge you are unwilling to cross, an unwanted child that wants and craves to live!" The psychiatrist's voice was calm and full of rhythmic vibrations that fell pacifically on her ears like ointment on a wound. I know, Esther, you came to see because you have implicit faith in me, because you know that I want to help you, you know that I am not a headmaster who will severely castigate you because you have played truant from school." Dr. Yoram's became louder, but then it returned to its pacific tone, "I need your co-operation, Esther. You need me, too. This dovetailing of needs will lead you to the right choice: the past or the future! Man is like a tree, Esther. The olive tree resembles man in the way it is all twisted and knotted back on itself, as though racked by some evil secret. So is man. We are all twisted and knotted back on ourselves, Esther. The point," he added while Esther gazed deep into his eyes and watched them as they winked or talked to her. "The point is how deep these twists and knots go within us, and how far they disturb our lives by their presence." A moment of silence followed, during which Dr. Yoram saw how Esther was digesting his philosophy. It wasn't beyond her apprehension or grasp, for Esther had always been an intelligent girl, and he knew that. "There is a bit of insanity in everyone. Under normal pressure and normal circumstances, this bit of insanity is harmless and ineffective; it may even show itself in strange, grotesque dreams; but under the hard pressure and the unsuitable environment that may come its way, this little bit of insanity may...." He stopped to lit another cigarette, drew in a breath, but remained silent. He chose to leave the sentence unfinished.

"It may," Esther said dreamily.

"What I mean," he was restless in his armchair. "Esther, there's no loss that cannot be recouped. This is nature's way, nature's law of compensation. One shouldn't become morose and slip into melancholy. The borderline that separates the sane from the insane is...." Again he checked his words, and chose to remain silent to see the effect on his patient's reaction. The afternoon was sifting sunlight through the tall trees that stood outside the window of Dr. Yoram's room. The houses and the lawn were gilded with lighter gold. "I recommend fresh air, and a fresh beginning, Esther..."

She stood to her feet, almost ready to thank him for his advice and leave, but he stopped her gently, "Esther, Yigal loves you. You know it. We all do. He is one of our finest and best boys. He will make a perfect husband.." Dr. Yoram had a pitiful look in the corners of his eyes. "You are so beautiful!"

Esther was conscious of her beauty but not obsessed by it. She treated it quite objectively and indifferently, as she might a handsome possession. She did not rely upon it, nor did she use it. Many thoughts came tumbling in her head the moment she walked out. "Almighty God, give us the serenity to accept that which cannot be changed, the courage to change that which can be changed, and the wisdom to know the difference between them," the psychiatrist recited as he escorted her to the door. Bright sunshine bathed the tree-lined path. The first buds were poking from the carefully tended soil. The air was warm blended with scents of flowers, and the tree-hidden houses of beautiful Deganya looked beautiful and tempting. She loved to take walks, long walks. Would she ever live somewhere else, Tel Katzir? No. She would remain in Deganya, her home. She bade the doctor "good day" and walked briskly. It was good to breathe the invigorating air.

"Take a lesson from the birds of the air," he called after her. "They have no home, no good or bad memories!"

She flashed a smile, and walked on the path leading to the centre of the village.

Before she went to sleep that night, she had opened her diary at a fresh page, taken the pen and written:

"Danny, I know that Death is a blind reaper; that it is all the same to him who falls first and who falls later. But those who escape his scythe at first imagine that death has deliberately by-passed them. We'll all die one day. Please leave me in peace, and let me love Yigal the way I'd like to, the way I should. Esther.."

....

Strange, how the weather changes. In the morning it had been almost clear except for a few wispy clouds, and now it was almost cold as a winter evening. After supper Esther and Yigal stood for a couple of minutes at the entrance of the hall wondering where to go. It was raining, and they could not take their usual short walk to the groves.

"Let's go to my room. I'll put my coat over your head," he said. They hurried through the rain, pausing at the door of his room to exchange a kiss. Then he put on the light, brushing the rain from her skirt and settling her in a comfortable chair with tender concern. "Yigal," she began. "Remember the day the Syrians attacked us?"

"Aha," he made himself comfortable close to her.

"There was a strange look in your eyes when you held me so close to you."

"I was wondering when to throw that explosive at the tank."

"But there was another explosive-look in your eyes," she cuddled close to his chest.

"You mean you could guess how much I love you."

"Love has one language, Yigal. It speaks loud and clear. I think I did." She moved easily in her chair, then added, "But as soon as that was over, I mean the mess of war, you disappeared without saying goodbye. Even the twin sisters wondered where you could have gone."

"I got a word from Uzi to return to my base in the south."

"Tell me about that."

"Well, now I can tell. It's no secret anymore. Negba, Kibbutz Negba. The settlement was in great danger. On May

19ᵗʰ the battle of Negba began. I was here. Then two officers came early one morning to pick me up and I had to go without saying a word. This is the life of palmach-soldier."

"Well, and how did you get to Negba?" she asked curiously.

"We couldn't go there. The village was under siege, for nearly ten weeks. Then a ceasefire followed. And only then we could go to help the settlers." Yigal shook his head as if a memory had come to his head. "It was there that I met Ben-Ami."

"O, Ben-Ami! You said he was eventually killed."

"Ben-Ami was one of the first settlers of the village. I was sharing a small room with him, just near the carpentry shed. The Egyptians rushed to the offensive and captured Hill 113, which lay about a mile west of Negba, from where they could oversee every movement in the colony. Some other palmachniks were also sent on an urgent and dangerous mission just outside the colony. Meanwhile, Negba was shelled from every angle of the encirclement. The people fought hard, with no weapons and no water. I was sent then further south, and five days after I had left Negba I heard that three of the kibbutz boys had been ambushed by Arabs and killed. One of them was Ben-Ami." Yigal reflected sadly. He went on talking about Negba, while Esther dozed in her armchair. He walked over to his desk and began occupying himself with the schedule he had prepared for the youngsters. Tuv B' Shvat, the Arbor Day, and the Day of the Heroes were close by and he had a lot of preparations to make for the pupils. He sat down at his desk and worked. Suddenly the silence was broken.

"Have you ever kept a diary, Yigal?"

"I thought you were asleep!"

"Now I'm awake. Have you?" Esther spoke in a drowsy voice.

"No. Never. I don't believe in diaries. Why are you asking?"

"I just wondered," she lowered her eyes and began to leaf through an old magazine beside her. "I sometimes become so submerged in memories that I feel as if I belong to that other world. It is an effort to come back to this one."

"I don't know what you're talking about." Yigal approached her.

"I must tell you about that August in 1945. The pool in the centre of the garden. Slight coolness of September. In the pool the water like a mirror reflecting sunrise and sunset. There were so many things Danny and I shared." Esther's eyes moved off, away from Yigal, and she was gazing at the ceiling.

"That summer afternoon Danny and I met after work as usual. I was wearing a blue shirt and blue slacks. I can still remember that shirt, an artistic one, with a low round neck and a bodice that scooped down and held the breasts, tied with a little black velvet bow. My hair was done in pigtails. As we walked and talked and laughed," she fell silent for a moment, moving a reflective finger over her lip, "we came across Uri and he said that everyone was going for a swim, and asked if we would join them. We did. It was fun. The water was cool. There were water lilies around the edge of the pool. Danny and I swam a little, and we had a water-fight. I remember that I jumped on him and tried to push him under." She smiled as she related the incident, putting so much accuracy and emphasis on each and every little detail that almost struck Yigal as strange and abnormal. The smile was coming and going around her mouth and her looks wandered away from Yigal and the walls that surrounded her. She went on in an enthusiastic low tone, "Naturally he was the stronger. I had great joy over his overpowering me. The struggle lasted quite a long time, and then he picked me up bodily out of the water and ran up onto the sands, and we took off our shoes and walked through the trees, to dry ourselves in the late warm rays of the setting sun. We were still gasping and nearly crying with laughter. After a while, when we had got our breath back, I said, Catch me if you can.. and I flung my hair back and began to run. He sprang after me. Twice he caught me, but when I struggled to escape, laughing and pushing him away, he let me go." Esther remained in a state of trance as she told her story: she was even unaware of Yigal's moving away from her, walking to the window to check the weather outside. She talked on and on and he wondered if she was real, in a dream or in a trance of self-hypnosis or something. "At last we came to a big rock at the bottom of a tree, and there we sat down with our backs against a fallen log. I was cold after a while and Danny put his jacket around my shoulders. Then when we stood up to go he kissed me. Kissed me properly, and for the first time I knew what a loving physical kiss that aroused physical desire towards someone meant .. That was just the beginning...." Suddenly she stopped, sighed deeply, and looked around as if searching for Yigal. She saw him standing there at the window. "Am I boring you with these memories?" He walked towards her, took her hands and led her to the window.

"Not the least, Esther." They stood for a brief moment staring at the stars and the crescent moon floating in the dark bowl of the sky. "I'm worried. I'm not amazed, nor bored. You shouldn't be indulging in such moods of retrospection and remember all these little details. You are held in thraldom, you see? You've become enslaved by a past you're not willing to let go. Give the future a chance to work its way, Esther." There was silence. She didn't respond. "You get me, Esther?" Another silence. He wished she could say something. Yes or no; it didn't matter. She spoke at last, "It's hard to believe that the moonlight is nothing but reflected sunlight. The universe must be so big, so vast! Man is so small!" her eyes gazed outside, while her hands remained in his. Again he felt how remote she had been from him and from the surrounding. He took her closer, and with forced cheerfulness, he said, "Tomorrow the sun will rise. Soon winter will be gone. Summer is coming again. 1949. Passover will come, a month after we shall celebrate Lag B'Omer, the hills will turn a rich green and the valleys will again be carpeted with wild flowers, and the buds on the spring roses of Galilee will burst into magnificent reds and whites and oranges. Shavuoth festival will come and we shall be happy together.." Esther looked up at him trustingly. She looked at him, then her looks wandered somewhere out of the window, far from him; and he suddenly felt that she was going to open her mouth, say something: to be more accurate, she was going to recollect and fall into another trance of retrospection. His feeling was true. "There was one celebration in the spring of 1945," she began. "I was a young girl then. I wore dark blue slacks and an embroidered peasant's blouse, and sandals on my feet." Yigal's thoughts now concentrated on Esther's welfare, and he was beginning to think if he should see Dr. Yoram or talk to another psychologist out in the city. He would have to check how far she was going with these recollections before exposing her case to the medical board. Could he convince her to see Dr. Yoram? Would she agree? Would she ever admit her being a "case"? His thoughts were long, but she went on talking ... "....Jeeps and trucks and station wagons came along, buried under flowers from the gardens. Trucks, with children in peasant's clothing, holding rakes and hoes and scythes and power tools were in the parade, and the livestock. That was how they celebrated the feast. Cows decked in ribbons and flowers, flocks of sheep and goats, even pet dogs and cats were in the procession..." Silence. Yigal didn't make a move. She stopped talking, then she turned to him, looked him deep in the eyes and said, "I wish I were worthy of your love, Yigal. I know how much you love me."

"But, you are, dear!" he kissed the tip of her nose and she leaned against him and sighed.

"Will anybody take you away from me?"

"None. What makes you think that?" He kissed her again.

Tamar's face rose before his eyes. He kissed her, quick little kisses, saying between the kisses, "None, I swear, Esther." She walked to the bed and sat for a while. "You were telling me about Tel Katzir the other day. When do you expect the first settlers to live there?" Suddenly she returned to reality, which struck Yigal as strange, too.

"Not before November," he approached his desk and began looking at the schedule, the papers, etc... "There's so much to do. Would you like to come one day with me to see the site?"

"I'd love to."

They looked at each other. Esther was conscious of a feeling of elation and love. He sensed it. His mouth was soft and warm and trembled on her own. "Life somehow compensates the afflicted," he said. "I learnt this long time ago. Back in my childhood ... My mother had always said that..."

The plaintive hooting of shunting engines was carried by the wind from a neighboring railway...

"Please, don't ever leave me alone!" She begged. She had so much wanted to tell him about her sessions with Dr. Yoram. She didn't find the courage to do so. She wondered if she should keep it from him.

....

It was March. Spring had arrived at last. The trees still trembled in the cool winds.

The day for the great excursion, an event eagerly awaited by Yigal and his class, had come. Indeed the previous night the youngsters had slept very little, anxious and enthusiastic for the outing. Now they were all assembled there in the yard outside the dining-hall. The trucks had already been made ready for the journey. Tamar raised her eyes to Yigal and smiled shyly. He smiled back at her as he went by, and her heart leaped. Her big dark eyes followed him as he walked among the boys and girls, gave instructions and talked to the drivers of the trucks.

Packed with the happy merry-makers, the trucks sped along the open road which wound up and down across the hills of Galilee, through pomegrenate and olive groves and scented pine woods. "These trees were only recently planted,"

Dori, the guide explained. "On the right we see the plain of El Ahme, where the Crusaders under Guy de Lusignan were vanquished by Saladin, and where after the defeat of Hattim in 1187 the Kingdom of Jerusalem collapsed. Now, we are passing by the Kadourie Agricultural School, founded during the British Mandate by Sir Eli Kadourie, a wealthy Hong Kong philanthropist." The trucks rattled on, and the guide's voice was heard again.

"The land was formerly covered with volcanic rock, which had to be removed piece by piece. Today, the community here is a prosperous one, mainly occupied with sheep-breeding and agriculture."

Leaving behind them Kibbut'z Lavi, the trucks reached the top of a hill, where Ginnorssar and the surrounding country spread out just before them. "In the distance," the guide told, "we can see the hills of Gilead. To the north we see the hills of Golan in Jordan. To the southeast, Mount Tabor. To the northeast are the Horns of Hittim. These are basalt hills topped with extinct volcanoes."

The extensive view of the Lake was magnificent and breathtaking.

"Over there," Dori went on, "in the distance you can see Kfar Hittim. This settlement was founded in 1936 by Bulgarian pioneers. In the valley, below the road on the left, there is another settlement, Mitzpe, founded in 1908 by Russian immigrants. And along here, near Hittim and Mitzpe, sheltered by the mountains of Galilee, lies the valley of Arbel..."

The hikers were excited at the hearing of the name Arbel. That was their destination, and it was supposed to be quite an experience to climb down this mountain. The trucks came to a halt and soon everybody alighted. They clustered close to Yigal and watched the visible valley he pointed at. "This valley is is well-known for its fertility. Its name comes from the former town of Arbel, now only a hilly ruin on which are the remains of a synagogue." He lowered his voice and added, "Let's go this way. Follow me, everybody."

Leaving the guide and the drivers inside the trucks, they began to walk away with their rucksacks on their backs. They walked the few yards to the top of the precipice overlooking the beautiful valley below. They could??? all around them the hills and mountains of the Upper Galilee, and the lake far below, which looked like a harp. On one side Tiberias was visible, on the other Ein Gev, and on the southern end of the harp, the English word for Kinnereth, stood Kibbutz Deganya, while far on the northern end Mount Susita and the Kibbutz lay almost too close to the Syrian bordor. With the aid of field glasses they could see as far as the hills beyond.

"These cave-strewn cliffs are called the grottoes of Arbel," Yigal explained. "They are referred to in the Book of the Maccabeens as the place where the insurgent Israelites took refuge during their battle against the Roman occuption. The caves are invisible from here, but as we descend the cliff we shall be able to see several of them." The juniors cast apprehensive glances at the valley below. The roofs of the huts looked tiny, which gave them an idea how high they were standing up there. It was frightful but extremely gorgeous and lovely.

"Down there, we can see the houses of an Arab tribe. When we go down we shall walk through the village and visit the well and the fountain where they take their sheep and cattle to drink." Yigal glanced down, then added in a tone of warning, "The descent is not easy. Before we go, you should remember to be very careful. It's not too dangerous - I descended several times when I was with the Palmach. The path is very narrow. If we go carefully and watch every single step we take, making sure that your foot is on sure ground, one foot at a time, no room for two feet, if you follow my instructions you will see how the path leads us safely down to the foot of the mountain." He paused for a moment, took a brief look at his youngsters. Most of the girls looked scared.

"You shouldn't look all the time down, just watch your steps and keep an eye on the road that you follow. It is a very beautiful view. You may stop every once in a while to enjoy a good look of the whole view, a creation of nature, but don't ever look too long downwards as you might get dizzy and lose balance. I repeat, watch your steps carefully, and if necessary use your left hands to support yourselves against the rugged face of the rocks." He instructed them to leave their loads behind. "The trucks will collect your things up here, and will meet us at the foot of the mountain. Let's move!"

Slowly and with infinite care they began the descent, each trying to tread in the preceding person's footsteps. Every now and then Yigal turned to see how the line was progressing. One or two of the boys were singing, but for the most part the pupils remained silent, concentrating on their rather frightening downward climb.

Yigal and those right behind him were soon inside one of the caves, waiting for the others to catch up. They stood for a few minutes to breathe the fresh mountain air and watch the frightening but breathtaking view, till all the hikers were inside the cave, then Yigal began to talk, "Herod had soldiers hoisted up to these grottoes," he said. "In cages, where armed with long poles with huge hooks on the end, they impaled and cast out the rebels, the few remaining being smoked out." There was an awed silence. Then he went on, "Now, let's go on with the descent. How about a song, girls? Still afraid?" he cheered them.

They continued down the zigzag path. One or two of the braver girls raised rather tremulous voices in a marching song, but this was suddenly interrupted by a sudden sharp cry. "Yigal!!" He turned his head. "Hold on, Tamar," Reuben shouted. Yigal made a quick movement and grabbed the frightened girl, who was standing wobbling with one foot on the narrow path, clutching frantically at the rugged wall of the rock as she tried to regain her balance. Yigal seized her fast, held her tight until both feet were safely on the path, then bade her take hold of the back of his shirt and follow him as closely as she could. Trembling with terror, Tamar forced herself to put one foot before the other until she had conquered her fear. "O, Yigal," she said weakly, panting with fear. "God, you saved my life!" "Nonsense!" he said. "You weren't in any real danger!"

"O, I was. I really was!" she kept close to him.

When they reached the foot of the cliff the hikers paused to look at the mean, filthy Arab houses, that had looked so small from above, built of mud and mud bricks. They inspected the well and the brook next to it while Tamar raised her eyes awfully to the cliff she had just descended and shuddered as she looked at the zigzag path winding like a long, long snake over its rugged face. "O, God, I swear I shall never climb or descend a mountain again in my life."

"The ascent is much more difficult," he assured her solemnly.

"You don't mean to tell me that we are going to climb up!" she cried with a little scream.

"Of course! How else shall we get to the trucks up there?" He laughed at her agonized expression, then added, "You will live the rest of your life here, while we go up to meet the trucks!" The others laughed.

"But you said that the trucks would meet us here!" she was on the verge of crying.

"I'm teasing you. Come on, let's have a look here..."

"Beautiful, isn't it?" he asked.

"Beautiful and strong, and rather terrifying!" Tamar replied fervently.

The whole mountain looked like a barren elliptical precipice, rising high in the air. It was difficult to believe that it was really a mountain; it looked more like a fortress without walls, an impression augmented by the harsh, rocky spur that rose to the rear, and by the rugged mountains towering beyond.

Lunch was taken in a green, shady spot and afterwards the youngsters walked about the village and studied several trees and shrubs. Later the party were cordially invited to a Druze village, where a wedding ceremony was being held. The village had teemed with hundreds of visitors who had come to the wedding from all the neighbouring villages, Druze, dancers wearing silk shirts and multicolored embroidered skullcaps were in the middle of a wild performance when the visitors arrived. They were lined up, each with his hands on the next man's shoulders, and keeping the line straight they continually jumped up and down, holding their bodies rigid and using only their feet as springs. In front of the line a fine Druze dancer went through wild gyrations with one knife in his teeth and another one in his hand. The dancing, chanting and merriment continued up to the hill in the centre of the village, where the bride who had been hidden all day, was taken from seclusion. The groom, dressed in a cutaway coat and top hat, mounted a horse and rode to her through a flower-strewn lane flanked with rifle-bearing Druze men.

After the ceremony had been over the guests and visitors clapped hands, Yigal and his pupils hastened to meet the trucks that had been waiting to drive them home.

"A most enjoyable day!" Tamar said to Nira, looking up at the high cliff of Arbel.

....

Spring advanced quickly, and soon it was time for the first holiday of the season, Purim. On the eve of the holiday Esther and Yigal made their vows to remain loyal to each other, and their forthcoming marriage became public knowledge. It was planned to take place as soon as the baby was born - an event expected about the middle of April.

Yigal made it clear to her that he had been looking forward for two important dates in his life, with eager anticipation: The one was the delivery of her baby and his consequent marriage to her; the second - some time later in November - the return of all the trainees from Jerusalem and Haifa, the termination of the semester of the trained juniors and celebrations at the new settlement at Tel Katzir.

"I'm looking forward to being with you all the time, to stooping in the fields, getting on the tractor and driving for miles through the sunny hills and the cool valleys. Hand in hand we shall share the hardships and the joys of making your plans come true, Yigal!" That was Esther's first true confession of love..

...

"You said you are expecting a lot of guests for Purim," she put the vase of flowers on the shelf.

"Well, if everybody comes, they make quite a lot!" Yigal put on his jacket. "Come on, let's go!" he looked at his watch. "Too early for the bus, but we can take a walk."

"Coming!" Esther made her bed quickly and joined him out on the open road.

"Some friends from the south are coming over to visit us. Haven't I told you about Rivka and Ilan, Ronny and that Persian fellow, Adjami?"

"I'd love to meet them." She looked at her swollen belly, then at him. "Won't they be shocked to find me like this?"

"They know. I love you, Esther," he drew her to him and kissed her.

"You remember what I told you about my friend from Baghdad, Sammy?"

"This way, Yigal. Let's go this way." She took his hands and led him into the woods. "I love the trees here." Then she added, "Well, what were you saying about Sammy?"

"O, that was in April last. We were between Safed and Acre. Sammy was a skilled scout, a brave fighter," he recollected.

"There were also Yosi and Yael. They fought alongside all the other boys."

"Are they coming today, too?" Esther became curious as a child. Yigal nodded positively, and continued with his story, "Sammy was clever in getting across the first two roads leading to the city we had been trying to capture. There was a British scouting truck moving along the main road, its searchlight flashing right across the fields and we had to drop flat on our faces until it had gone by. At dusk on the afternoon of Tuesday, April 13th, we were given the order to creep through the countryside at midnight, crawl on our bellies for about three miles and try to sneak into the town through Arab patrols."

"Terrible, I presume!" Esther exclaimed.

"If the episode developed into a pitched battle we were to return fire but keep moving forward. The unit, I say, was led by Sammy." Yigal recollected, after a moment added, "He was tall and slim, small black beard. A real guy! He was accompanied by a girl of about eighteen; thin, dark eyes and a clear skin. I never knew her name. Working silently we moved single file down the steep banks of the wadi (ravine). Suddenly a shot was heard and Yosi fell wounded. We were in a tricky position, in the bottom of the gully working our way cautiously southward towards the Jewish section. If anything went wrong we'd be trapped, with the enemy holding all the high positions. We moved on down the wadi, and then - Wow! Another shot was heard..." Yigal led Esther between two gigantic trees, and out on a lonely lane.

She opened her eyes wide with fear as though she had been experiencing that moment of horror. Yigal's hand tightened on hers. "But we made it. We made it!" There was a brief smile of relief on her face as she followed his story with attention and curiosity.

"As dawn broke that Wednesday morning we were already in the town and the settlers were swarming out to meet us, shouting and cheering at our arrival." Yigal moved forward. He stopped for a moment, took a better look into Esther's curious eyes that kept asking, "Then?"

"Then on April 16th things changed quickly. The British left the town and the bullets began to whine. They splattered into the mud walls of the Jewish houses, and in the ensuing fight Sammy was killed." He could see the sorrow in her eyes, and there were tears gathering in the corners of her eyes.

"For three days," his voice was low as he recollected, "Yosi lay in a physical and moral stupor. He was physically exhausted, and his mind couldn't cope with the tragic death of Sammy..." Yigal's eyes were fixed on the space, as though looking for something, someone; the small fragments of the whole story of his horrible experience, one of his many recollections in the Palmach, were coming back broken, fresh and clear in his mind. There was silence. "This is the price we had to pay!" he uttered.

"High and dear!" she uttered solemnly. "Danny, too, was a high price..."

Yigal was sorry to bring back a bad memory to Esther, but he had to. Anyway, he knew that Danny had never left her mind, would never, as long as she lived!

...

The bus arrived. With it many, many guests and visitors to celebrate Purim at the Kibbutz. Yigal's friends were nice, sympathetic people. Esther took to them at once. Yigal took them to the dining -hall for a drink and a meal, and made room for them.

The next day - Purim! Deganya erupted with children in delightful costumes, floats and decorations that turned the settlement into a carnival city. There were fancy dress parades and masquerades, and much laughter and joy everywhere. In the evening there was a performance of a play acted by several boys and girls, most of them from Yigal's group, and other teams, all future founders of Tel Katzir. The boys wore long robes and turbans and smoked their nargillas, while the girls danced around them as if in a Sultan's palace. Yigal and Esther sat close to the stage to watch the performance. A tall girl of sixteen, wearing home-spun robes and golden sandals, passed by. She was slender and with each step her long bare legs appeared through the slit in her skirt. Her long silky hair fell about her shoulders and her face had an extraordinary beauty with dark eyes set wide apart, a long straight nose, high cheekbones and smooth, satiny skin. She walked with conscious grace and was aware of the effect she created on the males. As she passed by she hit Yigal's head with a plastic hammer for fun, cast a glance at him and with a "hello, baby," she walked by. Esther regarded her with contempt and jealousy.

...

A few days after the feast, when all the guests had returned and Deganya returned to normal routine, Esther felt a strange pain inside her. She was unable to move her legs, and upon the instructions of the doctor she had to stay in bed until delivery time. Hephziba suggested her transference to Haifa Hospital for observation, but she begged to be allowed to remain in her own room for just a few days longer until she was quite ripe. Yigal came to see her in her room every day. Her diary was kept a secret from everyone - even from Yigal himself. Some had known that she was keeping a sort of diary, but they never knew where the thing was kept or what she was writing therein.

She made up her mind to tell Yigal about it as soon as they got married. But there were so many confessions about Danny, about him, about herself that she wished he wouldn't read.

...

Dear Danny...I shall keep on writing things as they flow in my mind without any effort; for any effort I might make to dress up this story of mine and fill it with dates and untrue events or just words unsaid or unspoken between us or by anybody, would detract the last pleasure I hope to get in telling it. I've returned to you and to the diary. Dr. Yoram wouldn't agree to that, nor Yigal, nor I myself, but it is the other Esther that's having her way now; and maybe when I become my real self again, for I feel too weak and feeble and powerless now, I shall have the courage to stop writing.

Forgive me, Danny, if you think I have been disloyal to you. Perhaps I sinned, and perhaps it will take more than repentance to purge my soul; yet in a way I feel that am not unfaithful to you. You have come to me in my dreams, and I have not remained with you, for I just ran away into wakefulness, into reality where you exist no more. What happened to me is a strange accident of fate; a result of events and surroundings outside myself.

"It's already March 26th, and for the last couple of days I've concentrated almost entirely on my diary. I don't want that; and I don't want it to end, either!

I shall not cease to visit your grave, for it has become my secret home. There is so much life there - even in its deepest, darkest corners - for in the place of death one feels overwhelmed by life. If only people could understand me!

"I shall come with my little Danny or Daniella, and Yigal, to visit you always. For them you'll mean something; for me, another. Nobody else will ever see you with the same eyes that I do. We shall bring flowers in summer, and in winter the wind bearing down on us will lash our hands and faces with cold gusts of rain as we make our way to your grave.

Vitae summa brevis.. Soon it is all over ...

Man, with all his ambitions, wishes and desires, soon passes through the gate of no return, travels on and is quickly no more!

O, Danny, I feel our child moving within me, struggling to reach the light. Truth is that sometimes I feel numb, frozen without you, like a ghost stalking in the shades of the dear departed. I'm so tired. I must sleep .... Yours, Esther"

...

"Danny, dear...There's nothing under the sun. It is already April 11th. I wonder how long will I be able to stay in bed with my pains and with this living thing inside me kicking and torturing me! How wearying it is all! I'm afraid I'm a very bad patient. Three nurses come to see me every day. They are all so good and nice. And Yigal! I wish we could be husband and wife soon! He's a hundred per cent soul! They're calling the place Harvest Hill. Yigal is so excited about the idea of our living at Harvest Hill in Tel Katzir. There's so much work waiting for us there. O, I can't think of all this.

You know, Danny, I've a feeling you'll never come back. Sometimes a strange feeling comes over me that you are far away, in a land very far from here, and that any day I might hear you call my name again. A letter from you will surely set as a lift to my drooping spirits, and dispel the gloom which envelopes me. But how can one expect to hear from the dead. Please, don't disillusion me. Let me go ahead and dream! Life is such a dream! O, God, the pains. I think I'll have to agree to go to hospital.. Yours, Esther.."

....

"April 12th...Dear Danny..

Some kind of transparent bandage over my eyes seems to show me your image everywhere. All love's rays are concentrated on a single burning spot in my heart. O, how tiring this waiting time is! Sometimes, I ask myself whom I am waiting for. At times it is Yigal, at times it is you, and sometimes it is the newborn, or just a rendezvous with you? To whom shall I give myself? You have slipped out of my arms like a shadow, Danny. My lips sought you in vain.

"Last night I could not sleep, and I got up and went out slowly into the dark garden just outside my room. I was so afraid. My anguish brought me once more to the door, that wooden door by the stone wall, and I opened it with a mad hope that you might have come back. I called, "Danny," in a low voice. There was no answer, and I went back to bed, creeping as quietly as I could. You, too, think that I am mad? Say something. Esther."

...

"Dear Danny, it is April 13th.. Spring is so lovely. The birds chirp and sing, and the air is full of sweet smells. Flowers are budding, trees are bursting into leaf. It is time of rebirth - and am still waiting for the birth of my child. This morning the doctor spoke to Hephziba about me. It seems that an operation is inevitable. I can't understand why. Yigal is so kind and concerned. He gets me my daily meals and sits with me for hours. I've faith and confidence in him and in the future he's planning for us. Though I am so tired, Danny, my soul keeps a strange childishness. I am still the little girl you had known years ago, the little girl who could not sleep until everything in her room was tidy, and her work clothes all neatly folded and ready for the next day. That's how I should like to get ready for the operation. The doctor says it can be easier than a natural delivery, but the latter is the normal one. O, how I love the beauty of nature! I've always loved the forests and the green meadows, the animals and the birds of the air, the streams of running water and waves of the lake. I hope it won't be long before... .... O, God, the pain. I must close now, Esther.."

...

That very night Esther went into labour. The pains began in the small of her back at about nine o'clock, and then progressed to her abdomen. She lay rigid for a while, terrified of what lay ahead, and then began to pant and toss in her bed as the pains became more and more frequent and intense. She put her diary away, just under her pillow, and every now and again put her hand on it to gather strength and comfort, as though it was the talisman of eternal life. She tried to pray, but her dizziness was too strong and she could not think coherently.

After some time her roommates came in. They had attended a lecture and seen a film that evening. Esther heard the sound of their voices with sick relief, and waited for them to enter. The door creaked a little and they came in noiselessly. Then the light went on and she heard their exclamations of concern amidst her own sobs and incoherent cries of pain.

Promptly Hephziba was summoned, and she sent off one of the girls to ring up the doctor while she herself talked to Esther and rubbed her back when the pain became too intense.

In a few minutes an ambulance, with Esther and Hephziba inside it, sped to Tiberias Hospital. Beside the stretcher sat Yigal, his face pale and tense with anxiety. Hephziba's was grave but calm.

...

Maternity Ward.... Operating Theatre...

"White walls..." was all Esther could murmur as she looked around. She clung to the nurse's hand in anticipation of the next wave of pain. Her face was pale, and there was a faint blue line around her mouth. Her hair hung lank with sweat and her eyes were dilated with fear and pain. Her suffering had stripped her of her beauty; soon her face contorted, and she screamed and screamed again and again. Yigal, waiting in a hall along the corridor, put his hands over his ears and groaned aloud.. Suddenly there was silence.

In the operating theatre stood a scrub nurse, tall and alert, beside a draped instrument table on which all the instruments used in the operation were arranged in the order in which the surgeon would call for them. Also on the table in neat rows and piles and tiers were packs of compresses, cups and trays and sealed containers of sutures. There was also a "circulating nurse", who stood checking her supplies of blood, plasma and intravenous solutions. Both nurses were gowned and masked, their hair done up in white cheese cloth. In the anaesthetic room the anesthetist smiled at Esther, introduced a hypodermic needle into a vein in her arm and asked her to count to ten. "..One..two...three..four..five..." By the count of eight Esther was asleep, her racked body limp and released from the torture it had undergone. The trolley on which she lay was wheeled into the operating theatre, where all was bustling with calm efficiency.

In the waiting room Hephziba was dozing on her chair, while Yigal strode endlessly to and fro, lighting one cigarette after another, his fingers already brown stained with unaccustomed nicotine.

A high instrument stand was rolled over Esther's knees. The scrub nurse stood on a footstool, from which she had a clear view of her instrument table and the whole operating area. She passed soap and antiseptic swabs to the surgeon's assistant, and he cleansed the skin on Esther's swollen abdomen. Then they covered her body completely with a large sterile sheet which had a hole in it just large enough to expose the operating field. The surgeon, masked and gowned, stepped to the table and held out his hand. The scrub nurse passed him the scalpel, and the operation began...

For some time the only sounds were the clicking of the surgical clamps and the clink of discarded instruments. From the deft fingers of the scrub nurse forceps, clamps, sponges and strands of surgical sutures flew back and forth to the surgeon's hands. The first assistant on the other side of the table helped by clamping and tying the blood vessels and exposing the organs. The other assistant held the retractors, long, curved strips of polished metal which held the incision open. Next to the surgeon on a low stool sat the anesthetist, beside Esther's head, keeping a close watch on her breathing and circulation.

From the gaping wound the baby was drawn - a boy, perfectly formed. He gasped, cried, was laid in a pre-heated cot, and the surgeon began to close the incision. Almost imperceptibly everyone relaxed. It was nearly over, when suddenly the anesthetist looked up. "Oxygen!" he said sharply. "Hurry!" A cylinder was immediately brought and his fingers worked quickly and urgently to connect it. Esther's respiration was irregular, her heart was failing. There was a flurry of activity, syringes, stimulants, but the patient did not respond.

Outside, a thin crescent moon played hide and seek among scudding shreds of cloud. The stars were fading, and beyond the hills outside a new dawn planted a foot. A new day, a new dawn. A new life pressed against the gates of Time. It was as old as the world, and yet it would be called a child. It was crying, breathing life! Lying in the cot, that was life! Meanwhile, another life was ebbing away, sinking deeper and deeper into the depths of the Unknown, into the Sea of Death. ...On the fourteenth of April, Esther kept her longed-for rendezvous with Danny. April 14, 1949, another date to remember. Danny..Esther..ever! A date Deganya could never forget...

...

PART FIVE

I sent my Soul through the Invisible
Some letter of that After-life to spell,
And by and by my Soul returned to me,
And answered, "I myself am Heaven and Hell."
..
The Moving Finger writes, and having writ
Moves on, nor all your Piety or Wit
Shall lure it back to cancel half a line,
Nor all your Tears wash out a Word of it.

Omar El-Khayyam

....

Spring in Deganya..

"For lo! The winter is past, the rain is over and gone; the flowers appear on the earth, the time of the singing of birds has come, and the voice of the turtle is heard in our land!" who wrote that? Esther couldn't remember the songs she had learnt at school ...It must have been ...never mind. Anyway, up to work! The Song of Songs, of course!

The hour has just struck four. A tractor pulling a trailer loaded with boys and girls crawls along a zigzag road that twists between green meadows and among orchards and olive groves, leaving beyond the fields of corn and maize. It had been a lovely spring day. The young workers are gay and noisy. They sing at the top of their voices as the trailer in tow behind the tractor approaches a shed to pick up more boys and girls.

They climb on the trailer, sit at the edges dangling their legs, slim smooth thighs next to masculine, muscular hairy ones. They sing and laugh. They make much noise, but the chug-chug of the tractor is even higher. The tractor stops by the dining-hall, and the youngsters get off and hasten for a quick drink of tea or lemonade and a brief sandwich of home-made marmalade. They hasten then to their rooms, get their fresh clothes and towels and make their way to the showers, thus washing away the fatigue of the day as well as the dirt of the soil and the fields. The whole evening is theirs thereafter. Some choose to relax on the lawn and the centre green, reading or chatting or just telling stories and jokes, others spend their time in the recreation hall, dancing, playing games or just leaf through books and magazines in the library. Others prefer to take a walk through the kibbutz up to the hill yonder where one can stand and watch sunset or command a view of the whole panorama that puts the beauty of the Galilee in a nut-shell. One never tires of looking at the same view day in day out, specially young lovers who know all the secret places in the park and beyond the hill like the palm of their hands.

The door of the kibbutz school opens and youngsters stream out, tumbling over one another in their haste to get out quickly. The children work four hours in the morning and study in the afternoos. Deganya is their collective home, their communal settlement. No work is too hard, no job too boring, and not enough words to describe their joy.

Three years have elapsed since the people of Deganya joined together to fight for their dear village. Now they have time to rebuild it, to watch it flourish. Nothing is forgotten, and so many lessons to learn. They are so happy with the fruits of their labour. The rights of the land should be preserved, they had been taught, and this is what they teach the new generation.

On the hill, just beneath the eucalyptus trees of the cemetery lie pioneers, thinkers, authors, writers, fighters, soldiers, toilers on the land and men of science; young and old: men, women, children. Each on his plot, each in his or her life served Israel and the Jews in general; each with all his or her wishes, ambitions, desires and dreams that have not been materialized. Among the graves, under the pungently sweet smelling eucalyptus trees lie Danny and Esther. There is a stone here in this cemetery; a stone, rising in a tranquil arc. Written on it are the words:

> Esther. (born 1929 ..Died in Childbirth, April 14, 1951. She parted in the Springtime of life with her beloved Danny, and met him here again in this place.....”

A fresh wreath of roses lies on it. A young man from Tel Katzir comes all the way to put a wreath of flowers on that grave; he comes very often. A balmy breeze blows, a bird twitters in the branches of the eucalyptus trees. The branches move gently towards each other, they lean and kiss, and then are blown apart. Such is life!

Beneath the cool shade a whole world lies at rest. Peaceful and serene. No word is spoken, no sigh, not a single breath, no groaning, no cries, no laughter ... Eternal repose!

PART SIX

Another generation – boy and girl
Danny-Esther – ever!

On a wooden bench in the beautiful garden sits Hephziba next to Pessah. He is on night duty. Before dusk he will have to go to the fields to let off the water taps and the sprinklers. Hephziba is on duty right now. She is looking after the children who are romping and playing and jumping all around. Some are gambolling on the grass under the trees. Others are sitting by the brook watching their paper boats sail on the calm surface of the water, others feed the birds, and some are bowling their hoops.

Not many years have gone by, only some years before a boy and a girl, ages 11 and 13 were squatting on one of the stepping stones in mid-stream here in this very spot. The girl was dabbling both hands dreamily in the clear running water, stirring up the water and watching the reflection of two faces ripple on its mirrored surface. She was wearing a blue shirt, both sleeves rolled up, and her wrists and the nape of her neck were glistening white. The boy looked into the water, cupped his hands and tried to scoop up something.

"What are you trying to do, Danny?" the girl asked curiously after watching him for a while.

"I am trying to scoop up your image, Esther," he replied.

"What for?"

"I want to have it for myself. I love you, Esther."

"Danny…"

"Yes?"

"We are happy together, aren't we? Like brother and sister."

"Not exactly, Esther. I love you more than a brother loves a sister. In a different way, I mean."

"What's love, Danny," the girl asked innocently.

"It's what I'm feeling right now towards you. Or maybe what I'm feeling will grow one day to mean real love.." Danny replied intelligently.

That had been eight years before. Now, here in this same spot another boy and another girl are sitting side by side on the bank of the brook, dangling their legs into the water, making ripples. They are noisy.

"I'll sink your boat." She says,

"I'll sink yours. My boat is bigger and stronger than yours," the little boy shouts back at her. Children are standing and watching paper boats sailing. They laugh, cheer and urge the boats on. Hephziba and Pessah are busy with their talk.

"How long will the fighting go on?" Hephziba asks.

"This demilitarized zone between the Israeli and Syrian border is the cause of all the trouble," Pessah puts in.

"Why? After all the border clashes between Syrian and Israeli groups and troops arising from the Israeli action in draining the Huleh swamp will come to an end one day. We shall.."

"But this is already the fourth day," Pessah interrupts.

"Well, the fighting broke out on May 3rd, and there's no sign of it ending. You see, this dispute has really been going on for a very long time."

"It all began in 1934 when the Palestine Land Development Co. acquired a concession to drain and irrigate the Huleh basin in northeast Israel. Now they have begun the implementation of the 15,000 acre drainage scheme. Syria opposes the project, claiming that it would remove a natural military obstacle."

"I'd say, Pessah, the Arabs have always opposed the scheme." Suddenly the little boy gives a loud scream and runs to Hephziba crying, "She's sinking my boat. Tell her not to.."

"Hush, Danny. Now tell me what happened." The old woman stoops to take the child on her knees, but he twists away in anguish. "She sank my boat, my little boat!" he cries.

"Never mind, Danny. I'll make you another boat. A bigger and a better one," Pessah approaches him with a smile.

"Come here, Esther," Hephziba shouts at the little girl by the brook. "Come here, tell me what happened."

The little girl walks over to the gentle elderly woman, her head bent. She kicks the ground guiltily. "Don't you believe him! I didn't sink his boat. I just turned it upside down.."

Pessah carries the little girl on his knees, strokes her hair and rocks her soothingly. "There, little one, don't cry," he passes a gentle hand over her hair. "You and Danny must never quarrel. A nice, little boy, he is. Danny, you're friends with Esther, aren't you?"

The little girl wipes her tears with the back of her hand and nods reluctantly. She steals a glance at the little boy. He looks back at her for a second, then grins showing his little white teeth.

"There. All friends again!" Pessah puts the little girl down on the grass. "Come on, Danny. Run along and play with Esther. That's a good boy!" Esther holds out her hand, Danny takes it and they run back to the brook. The elderly couple watch them, as they go hand in hand, in silence.

Hephziba chokes back a tear. Pessah looks into her eyes, wants to open his mouth and say something, but there's a tear playing round the corners of his eyes. Silence speaks louder than words. Fate is so cruel! Little Esther is daughter of Abrashka and Bracha, while Danny an orphan, his father had been killed about four years before, and his mother had died in childbirth!

....

Summer ..1953 ... It is very hot in Tiberias. A blazing sun beats down upon the molten surface of the Lake and hammers at the barren hills like a great torch seeking to set the world afire. A handsome young man walks all the way over the hills from Tel Katzir, a settlement almost three years old, to Deganya. All the way from Harvest Hill, his sleeves are rolled up to reveal a pair of sun-tanned sinewy arms. He walks slowly and thoughtfully, a bunch of papers tucked under his arm, apparently a diary. Esther's diary. Yigal had been doing this for the last three or four years since Esther's death. He wouldn't go to visit her grave without the diary tucked under his arm and a bunch of roses in the other hand. He still believes that every single line of the diary has the breath of Esther in it. Reading it, he finds the secret of life between its lines. He sees Esther on each and every page. Every time he stands by the grave, the story of Esther and Danny comes fresh to his mind, the story of Esther and Yigal comes back real as real can be as though the whole thing is being re-enacted, as if the film is being re-shown. Yes, he had known so much about Esther, but the diary, which he had the privilege and the natural right to get hold of after Esther's death, disclosed more and more facts, candidly and shamelessly. The more he read, the more he felt he had to read in order to know, and the more he knew the more he loved her even though she existed no more. His aim was to study hard, to proceed in his studies in psychology, medicine, to serve humanity, to delve into the inner cells of the human brain. He had been serving his country all those years, the soil of the land he loved so much, and now his aim was to make another dream come true, that of his father who had died in a concentration camp and that of his mother who had not been lucky enough to tread upon the Holy Land. Only through medicine and psychology he could meet Esther's soul, for her body existed no more.

The young man walks along the grassy path which leads to the cemetery of Deganya. A few people pass by. They nod and walk on. Yigal is known all over the settlement. He had done so much for both Deganya and Tel Katzir. He is respected, beloved and highly esteemed. They watch him go and stand by the graveyard. Seen today, the cemetery looks dark, lapped by the undulating surf of surrounding wheat fields. It is a good refuge from a hot day, for there is plenty of cool shade from trees planted generations ago.

From the other direction Hephziba and Pessah stroll along a quiet path, also leading to the cemetery. Others walk past. They stop at a tombstone marked with a recently carved name: Udi. Rows of graves. Rows of trees. Those who built the land, and those who were not fortunate enough to keep on building! Danny, Menachem, Yehudith, and many, many others. Old and young! But now, they are all in the same plot, the world of the dead. Esther's grave lies next to Danny's, beyond the trees, almost at the wheat field's bright edge. The old couple walk slowly, solemnly. They catch sight of the young man with the bundle of papers tucked under his arm. He comes closer, feels the papers and lays a wreath of roses on Esther's tombstone. Their eyes meet, they nod, they do not utter a single word. The wind blows cool and fresh among the trees. They understand.

"There's Yigal," Hephziba nudges her companion as they walk past. It is by no means an unfamiliar sight to see Yigal strolling there by himself, for he has been doing this since Esther's death, once or twice a week. His life stands between the flesh and the soil, between love for Esther of Deganya and love for the soil of Tel Katzir. The old couple pass quietly by. The young man remains in his place. The sun begins to go down beyond the distant hills. He looks at the far off Harvest Hill, and then sets off for home. Behind him lies Deganya, ahead-Tel Katzir. The hills of Galilee close on one side and the mountains of Syria on the other. In the distance, the snow cap of Mount Hermon.

In winter the fields are brown, in spring green with corn and barley. Now the crops are ripe; there are wild cyclamen everywhere, poppies and cornflowers and many other wild flowers. Summer is a lovely season.

The happy, noisy children are gay as ever. The grass always green. The fathers have turned the wilderness into a Garden of Eden. Gardens and parks, flowers bloom, willows and eucalyptus trees along the grassy banks of the Jordan river. Such is Deganya, a place of peace and honest soil and toil. But with the squat, ugly, sinister Syrian tank still there to remind the villagers of the horrors of war.

On Harvest Hill, between Degnaya and Tel Katzir, stands the young man, Yigal, watching the last rays of the sun as they set beyond the beautiful hills of Galilee.

....

It is with this sight and this situation that Yigal saw fate close one more chapter of his life-story. The future was still ahead ... and the year was only 1954.

Yigal turned to his lessons, worked hard to make a dream come true. Having done his job and having trained young hands to carry on, he applied to the Secretariat to allow him to take up medicine, psychology and to proceed his studies outside the kibbutz. He whispered in my ears these words.

SI JEUNESSE SAVAIT, SI VIEILLESSE POUVAIT (Ben Downing –Queen Bee of Tuscany), and when I asked what he meant. He explained; some people like to say it in English in a different way: If youth only knew, if age only could! Or: If age but could, if youth but would! The meaning is one, and the crown on the heads of the youth can only be seen by the aged who had lost it long time ago!

I agree with the Observer of 1923 that wrote: "Youth would be an ideal state if it came a little later in life!" The lustful eyes of the old can only see and admire! Yes, if youth only knew!!!! Youth is wasted on the young! I say this as I am sitting in the cage of old age, with my reflections and soliloquy. I am trudging down the roads not taken, grasping every little hour, clinging to every new day, nourishing my hungry soul and feasting my eyes on the first rays of the pacing dawn, holding fast to each ray of the fading sun at twilight time, praying to have many returns though fearing deep within my heart it may not come again, feeling the noose of time tightening around my neck, calling me back to the ashes I had come from only a few decades before!

As I trudge down the less beaten tracks I seem to enjoy every breath of fresh air more than I ever did, every shrub, plant, flower, every tree that I pass by, and moreover the setting sun in the horizon, that endless horizon, and I cling to the last rays as well as to the remains of the day lest it goes and comes no more.

It was only yesterday, or perhaps a decade ago, or more when I was younger, and I took it for granted that I had been given this life, and am living it. Today, I deem it a precious gift that I dare not let sift like sand between my fingers. I knew then about sunrise, sunset, seasons of the year, and I was too busy with all my dreams and plans for the future. I realized that nature knows how to manage, and life goes on without my intervention, while I had a different mission than taking care of nature, I had my life to live, to earn money, to raise a family and provide for them. Today, I care about little things' I am always in constant fear lest they go away from me, or rather, lest I will soon be taken away from them.

O, my God, how come? Decades ago I had so many days and nights, I wore the crown of youth on my head and didn't realize it was there, and today I cherish every moment, every precious meeting with family members, friends, I enjoy the regular views, scenery, experiences, events, and all the day-to-day activities as though they were the last gems I could hold to, and I must not let them sift away.

I watch the young, I watch them in their happy hours, in their school hours, in their free hours, they have no idea that only I, and people in my age, can see the crown they are wearing. They don't see it. They don't even know it is there.

What a shame. Youth is wasted on the young .... YOUTH ... what a magic wand! if only I could have now a day, an hour of the youth I had when I was young!

The past is always present in my life, and I look forward to the future, which is but a "to-morrow" that never comes!

Nothing stopped Yigal from carrying out his mission in life. He was a great believer in the saying: "Where there's will, there's way!" Esther's diary made him make his mark. He got all his courage, perseverance, aspiration and inspiration from those written pages which he kept secret for many years, even from his own wife, Ruth.

If it weren't for Dr. Yigal Har-Zahav who had put all his trust in me, this book would not have been written.

Looking back at Yigal the boy, Yigal the soldier, Yigal the lover, Yigal the fighter, Yigal and kibbutz-member and Dr. Yigal Har-Zahav and the wars he had been a witness to, I ask myself if this book will render him the honor and the esteem that are his.

EPILOGUE

All round circles must close to become full......

....

FULL CIRCLE:

Young Yigal's ambitions didn't stop there and then. He decided to take up medicine. The Kibbutz Secretariat allowed him to proceed his studies at the University of Jerusalem. He was going to study psychiatry for, he thought, it was the best way to penetrate your own self, your own mind, and other people's minds, thus he could keep in close contact with his beloved Esther. For the Kibbutz and for the whole world she left her child, Danny, but for Yigal Esther left her precious diary. Reading between the lines of her diary any psychiatrist could reach her soul.

At the age of 24 Yigal got married to a kibbutz girl, Tamar's close friend, Ruth. He was thirty years old when he finished his studies, switching to general medicine and surgery.

Dr. Yigal Har-Zahav returned to his kibbutz where he was much loved and respected. His first born, Yoav, was six years old then. When Yoav was fourteen, in June 1967, his mother died from a stray bullet. That was on the Six-Days War; and Dr. Yigal was left alone to take care of their only son. Esther's diary was a good solace, and kept him in good company.

Yoav Har-Zahav was only a chip of the old block, and the young adolescent, not unlike his father, loved to serve his country in his own way. He wanted to be a flight officer, and when he joined the army at the age of eighteen, Yoav began to study aeronautics.

In 1973 the Yom-Kippur war took everybody by surprise, but most of all suffered the northern settlements of Israel. Dr. Yigal Har-Zahav could never tell what the future had in stores for him.

He lost Yoav..... and the scene with which this novel opens was a regular one in which Dr. Yigal could find his only consolation. It wasn't an easy decision for Dr. Yigal to make when he took the bundle of papers, Esther's diary, from his book-shelf and handed it to me to write this book. He attached to it this letter.... EMIL, write it all! don't delete a word of it! There was a tear in his eyes that only I could construe there and then!

He handed me the Diary and a folded paper. He tried to say something, but I felt there was a lump choking him in the throat, he couldn't utter a single word. The tears that played in the corners of his eyes spoke louder than words.

Dear, dearest God,

We have talked millions of times. I talked. YOU listened. I know you listened every time I talked. This time I decided to write you a letter since the printed word weighs heavier than the spoken one, and also to keep record for future reference when I am gone. I have known YOU for over four score years, since I was four years old or maybe before, the first time I knew myself, the first time I saw myself in the mirror, naked, and realized that I exist, that I AM... And as the years passed, we talked more often. I talked. YOU listened. Whenever I was in trouble I came to YOU for help, I had wishes, dreams, demands, ambitions to realize, and YOU were my resort, my safety harbor. Moreover, in war time, and I lived in a world that knew many wars, YOU were always there with me, YOU listened to my whispers, to my unspoken words....

I have known YOU for over four score years. I guess YOU knew me long before I was born, YOU even knew my course in the life that YOU granted me, YOU charted it before I was born, for YOU are ALMIGHTY!

I was never impervious to the evil in the world, the evil that You created....the good and the bad, the angel and the devil, came into our being together, living side by side, fighting each other. I was never impervious, I said, but You were always my stronghold, and whenever I felt threatened or hurt, I just turned my face, and there You were, you stood by me, or I thought so.

I feel that we communicated all the time. YOU gave me some hints from time to time, and I knew YOU were all ears, and YOU not only heard every word I said, but YOU saw everything I did. I feel ashamed now as I remember things I did, things I shouldn't have done. I repent, O God, forgive me my sins and trespasses. There must have been quite a lot of these shameful deeds that I committed during the last four score years. I have always asked YOU not to lead me unto temptation, but I do admit there were times when I was tempted to do things I regretted later on. I am only human, O God, to err is human. All I can say now is "Please, forgive me!"

When I refer to YOU, I feel elated, full of inspiration, it is a lift higher. There's something missing in my life, something I've lost, and I try to find it while talking to YOU, but now as I am writing I am thinking of one request to which YOU will say "NO".....I have no choice, It is YOUR decision. Who am I to protest? I can only make a request. I dare not speak it, therefore, am writing it since the paper doesn't scorn, nor does it blush, or object!

YOU see, God, I got used to this world. I like it, I adore it, the way it is. I don't want to leave it. I got used to the sunrise, the sunset, the seasons of the year. I got used to the heat and the cold, to prosperity and adversity, to austerity, to hard times, to pleasant times, I got used to my other pilgrims on the Road of Life, to wars, I got used to friends and enemies as well, I am beginning to love this "action" that is going on....I got used to hazy days, to all kinds of weather, to all climates, I even got used to maladies, pains, battle fields, and am ready to be catapulted to the moon or any other planet.......but please, O God, I ask it in Thy Holy Name, don't send me away to that World of the Dead, where I will have no friends, no enemies, no people to communicate with, no human beings to talk to, no green fields, no flowers to smell, no breeze to enjoy. I will there a total stranger. Here is my home, and I am beginning to like it, and life in it in spite of all its drudgery and broken dreams. I am trying to imagine, with awe, that Other World you plan to send me to, and I feel sorry for not making the best of the four score and more years that I have been living here on earth!

I am confused, the past is always present in my life, and the future is a never-coming morrow. I wish that the word "to-morrow" will never leave me.

I am asking myself, O God, what if the present should die away, and YOU will send me forever to go to sleep? What if there should be no future day, no sunrise again in my life, who then will my engagements keep? Many a time I sat and thought and dreamed of dreams that can't come true, of happiness which I blindly sought, of moments sweet, though short and few! O, the many castles I have built in air, and the many secrets wonderful as they were, that I found, I have known my father's wisdom, my mother's care, and a world where joys and sorrows of man abound. Many a time I was sad, yet I greeted the dawn, I loved sunrise, and I loved sunset, I loved the rains, the green fields that glittered after rain, I loved everything YOU created, the roses, the rivers, the thorns and the birds of the air. There were memories that hurt, but hope still soared high. I loved this Road of Life where I have never been alone, though at times I felt lonely, and, O God, needless to remind YOU, I have promises to keep before I die!

EMIL MURAD